THE BODY AND THE BLOOD

A JOHN JORDAN MYSTERY

THE BODY AND THE BLOOD

MICHAEL LISTER

FIVE STAR
A part of Gale, Cengage Learning

GALE
CENGAGE Learning™

Detroit • New York • San Francisco • New Haven, Conn • Waterville, Maine • London

GALE
CENGAGE Learning

LIBRARY OF CONGRESS CATALOGING-IN-PUBLICATION DATA

Lister, Michael.
    The body and the blood : a John Jordan mystery / Michael Lister. — 1st ed.
        p. cm.
    ISBN-13: 978-1-59414-893-4 (hardcover)
    ISBN-10: 1-59414-893-7 (hardcover)
    1. Jordan, John (Fictitious character)—Fiction. 2. Prison chaplains—Fiction. 3. Prisoners—Crimes against—Fiction. 4. Prisons—Fiction. 5. Florida—Fiction. I. Title.
PS3562.I78213B63 2010
813'.54—dc22   2010019574

First Edition. First Printing: September 2010.
Published in 2010 in conjunction with Tekno Books and Ed Gorman.

Printed in the United States of America
1 2 3 4 5 6 7 14 13 12 11 10

For Micah and Meleah
Thanks for the best childhood a dad could ever have!
It's a Wonderful Life.

ACKNOWLEDGMENTS

Thanks to all those who've believed in and supported me and John over the years, especially, Lynn Wallace, Bette Powell, Cricket Freeman, Margaret Coel, Lou Boxer, Kim Ludlam, Carolann Johns, Jamie Smith, Rich Henshaw, Terry Lewis, Dan Nolan, Dayton Lister, Phillip Weeks, Tim Whitehead, Bruce Benedict, Michael Connelly, Pam, Micah, Meleah, Mike, and Judi Lister.

Thanks, too, this time to everyone at Tekno Books and Five Star, especially Roz Greenberg and Libby Sternberg.

CHAPTER ONE

"How much does prison change a man?"

That one stopped me—I had just been thinking about how much PCI was changing me—and if the question hadn't, the woman asking it would have.

Unlike so many of the unsophisticated and impoverished family members who braved a visit to the big house, the attractive young woman exiting Potter Correctional Institution wore designer clothes, moved with the lissomeness of a runway model, and spoke like an anchor person.

I had stopped at the gate before reentering the institution to stand in awe of the setting sun—a feeble attempt at stress relief and mindfulness—and had only glanced at her before turning my attention back to the western horizon.

It was nearly dusk in mid-October, and the sinking sun backlighting the tall slash pines and cypress trees to the west resembled a child's Halloween drawing—black craggy crayon trees on bright orange construction paper.

"Immeasurably," I said almost to myself.

I was tired and wanted to be somewhere else—anywhere enjoying the spectacular sundown in silence, my only companion an ice-cold Cherry Coke or Dr Pepper. It had been a long hard day already and I wouldn't still be here if not for the possibility of preventing a murder.

Potter Correctional Institution had the reputation for being one of Florida's most brutal prisons. Officers at the north

Florida Reception Center tell stories of inmates crying when they discover this particular hell is their destination.

"Are you the chaplain?" she asked.

The chaplain of hell, I thought, and it amused me in a slightly perverse way. *Talk about downward mobility, the parish no one wants.*

The truth was, I had never felt more fulfilled, never been happier—though what that says about my life before I came to hell I'm not sure. The happiness came from getting to spend so much time with my best friends, Anna and Merrill, and the sense of fulfillment I felt at finally finding a job that gave me opportunities to minister *and* investigate, disparate vocations not normally brought together in a single position.

"Yes. John Jordan," I said, extending my hand.

"Jordan. You related to the sheriff?"

I nodded.

Growing up in a law enforcement family, I worked as deputy in my dad's department, and had nearly completed a degree in criminology before everything changed and I dropped out mid-semester and entered seminary. I put myself through school working as a cop with the Stone Mountain Police Department. When I graduated, I traded my gun and badge in for a Bible and a clerical collar. Periods of my life were spent as an investigator, others as a minister, but returning to the Panhandle and becoming a prison chaplain was the first time I had made an attempt at doing both simultaneously. Of course, *attempt* was the operative word. The two vocations were difficult to reconcile and I rarely got it just right—or even close to right.

I really looked at the young woman for the first time.

Though not short, she wasn't as tall as her heels made her seem. She looked to be in her early to mid-thirties, her sun-streaked blond hair contrasting nicely with the tops of her darkly tanned shoulders. Her head was tilted back and she was looking up at me with green cat-like eyes.

"I'm Paula Menge," she said with an impatient edge in her voice, and I could tell she was accustomed to the full attention of whoever was fortunate enough to be in her presence.

"I'm sorry," I said. "I was distracted by the sunset."

She slunk toward me with feline fluidity, and I realized that her eyes weren't all that was cat-like about her. Her sleek, sinewy body looked to have the athleticism and agility required for pouncing. Feeling uncomfortable so close, and fearing she might curl her tail around my leg, I leaned back slightly and looked at the sunset again.

She let her gaze follow mine and we both stood there in silence and watched as construction paper orange turned to flamingo pink before becoming pastel peach in the sunset-softened sky.

"It *is* overwhelming," she said, and something about the way she said it made me think her next line had she not left it unspoken would have been, *But so am I*—a sentiment with which most men and many women would agree.

"You don't really look like a chaplain," she said. It sounded like a compliment.

"Well, I don't really try very hard," I said.

Her immediate frown was quickly replaced by a knowing smile and her eyes lit up intelligently.

I took a deep breath and waited.

Fall, what little there is in north Florida, comes late and leaves early, but over the past few days it had begun to arrive, and what I breathed in was far more than cool, crisp air. It was football games and pep rallies, a new school year and season premieres; burning leaves and bonfires, first love, freshman dances, and long kisses in heated cars on cold nights.

"I just finished visiting my brother," she said.

My mind finally finished connecting the dots, and I realized who she was.

"Justin Menge's your brother?" I asked.

She nodded. "You know him?"

I nodded. "I'm surprised I haven't seen the two of you together before," I said. "I can really see the resemblance."

"He's in protective management," she said, "so I have to visit him alone at night, but to tell you the truth this is my first visit."

"*Really?*" I said. "He's been here quite a while, hasn't he?"

She pursed and twisted her lips, then frowned. "It's a long story."

"I'll be seeing him in just a few minutes," I said. "I was just headed down to the PM unit."

"You are?" she asked, her voice filling with hesitant hope. "Could you check on him for me?"

"Didn't you just see him?"

"I know it's the first time I've seen him in four years, but he's *so* different, and I wondered if it's just because of prison or if it's something else. How much does it change them?"

"It doesn't just change *them*," I said, "it changes us all. How much depends on the person. But no one is ever quite the same."

I thought about how hardened I'd become, how I had allowed the daily assault of this place on my senses to pull me back toward the darkness, toward the man I didn't want to be again. At various times in my life, rage had taken the place of alcohol as my primary addiction, and if there were a better place than PCI to bring that about again, I wasn't aware of it.

"That's a truly disturbing thought."

"I guess it is," I said, "but more than change us, it brings out what's inside us already."

"What do you mean?"

"I've given this a lot of thought. It's as if prison's a cauldron that brings the impurities of our souls to the surface."

She smiled. "You may not look like a chaplain, but you sure sound like one."

Regardless of what I sounded like, or the title on my business card, I was just a man trying to be a better man, and though at some point I thought it would get easier, so far it hadn't.

Beyond the chain-link fence and razor wire, the institution was unusually still and quiet. The compound had the eerie feel of a small town whose inhabitants had all suddenly and mysteriously vanished. The evening meal completed, the inmates were in the dorms sitting on their bunks for the evening master roster count.

Nestled on Florida's forgotten coast between Panama City and Tallahassee, PCI is quickly becoming the largest prison in the state. It's already nearly double the size of Pottersville, and rumors persist that eventually death row will be housed here.

"He hasn't just changed," she said. "I'd've expected that. I mean he's completely different. I wouldn't've recognized him if we'd met on the street."

"How was he different? Physically? Did he talk differently? Was it his countenance? Was he harder?"

"I can't explain it, but I'm worried. Will you check on him?"

Her questions came across as demands, and I sensed that her aloofness emanated from a sense of superiority more than insecurity. As sensual as she seemed, I suspected her sexuality was more about power than pleasure, that it, like everything she possessed, was always in the service of something else—something she probably wasn't even aware of. Of course, I had known her all of ten minutes, and I had been wrong about women a time or two before.

"Sure," I said.

"Just see if you notice anything strange about him."

As the day grew dimmer, the light coming through the tinted glass of the control room seemed to intensify, and I could see the sergeant and the officer scurrying around to clear count.

"Four years is a lot of time," I said.

"I know, but I also know my brother. He's very different—and, in addition to everything else, very scared."

I raised my eyebrows. "Any idea why?"

She shrugged. "Maybe. I don't know. We ran out of time. Right now I just want you to check on him."

"Okay," I said, "but maybe he was just nervous about seeing you."

"But you'll check on him? You don't think I'm crazy?"

"Of course not."

I had received an anonymous note earlier in the day claiming that a murder would take place during the Catholic Mass in the PM unit later that night. It was why I was reentering the institution after having already put in a full day, and why I didn't think she was crazy.

We were silent for an awkward moment, neither of us knowing what else to say.

Finally, we said goodbye and she began to walk away, but after just a few steps I called after her.

"Four years is a long time," I said again. "Why so long?"

"I just couldn't see him the way things were."

"What changed?"

She gave me a tentative tight-lipped smile. "I found out he was innocent."

CHAPTER TWO

The death of the day was now complete, and as I made my solitary walk down the empty upper compound, the chapel, chow hall, and infirmary on either side of me were merely massive black shapes in the darkness. The cold wind whistling around the vacant buildings stung my eyes, and I shivered—though not from the wind alone—as if there were small slivers of ice embedded in my spine.

Count had yet to clear, which meant the whereabouts of all the inmates was uncertain. It also meant an unseen predator, shank in hand, could be stalking me right now, waiting for the right moment to leap from the darkness and pounce on me, his unsuspecting prey.

Yea though I walk through the valley of the shadow of death . . .

There was no moon, just a smattering of faint stars distorted by the clouds that shrouded them—small shards of illumination like light refracted off broken glass set against the slate night sky.

Fifty yards ahead a single flood lamp made a small pool of light in the sally port between the center gates that separated the upper and lower compounds, and I followed it like a guiding star. It was getting colder, and my earlier warm feelings about fall now seemed a season away.

Was Justin Menge innocent? Or was that just a sister's wishful thinking? The latter was far more likely, but something inside me wanted it to be the former.

Beyond the center gate, through the slight fog that had set in, the street lamps scattered throughout the lower compound looked to be a distant port town seen from the dark waters offshore.

I thought again about the ways in which I was changing, the extent to which the two sides of my convictions and calling—compassion and justice—were so often in conflict, out of balance. This happened most often when I was involved in a homicide investigation—I had yet to recover from a recent one involving a little girl named Nicole Caldwell—but it was always a struggle.

The effort it took for me to put one foot in front of the other reminded me of just how tired I was. Then I realized, *I'm not just tired. I'm weary—in every sense of the word—which is a dangerous state to be in, especially in a place like this.* It made me far more vulnerable, susceptible—not just to the environment, but to my own weaknesses and failures of faith.

Unbidden and unwelcome, thoughts of Paula Menge's sexual potential invaded my mind—she was as elegant and enigmatic as any feline I had ever encountered. I tried to banish them, though not right away, and not very hard.

People who don't really know me are often surprised that a man of the cloth is as preoccupied with sex as I am. I tell them I'm a man first, I'm *not* a Puritan, and sexuality is a big part of spirituality.

But I couldn't entertain thoughts like those for long—not even out of mostly innocent, never-to-be-acted-on curiosity. I was a married man—sort of. My ex-wife had failed to file our divorce papers and after a year apart we were attempting reconciliation. It was going well. We were different people and it just might work this time. I was committed, trying to be as faithful in my heart as I was with my body, but interactions with women like Paula Menge certainly didn't do much to help the cause.

"Where the hell are *you?*"

The voice jolted me from my thoughts.

I looked up. In the small circle of light in between the center gates, I could make out the thick-bodied figure of Tom Daniels.

Tom Daniels was the Inspector General of the Florida Department of Corrections, and I was almost as surprised to see him at our institution as I was to see him sober. Like me, he was a recovering alcoholic, but his recovery was still so recent that I hadn't gotten used to it yet.

"What?"

In his late-fifties, Daniels was an inch or so taller than my six feet, which meant I always had to look up to meet his eyes. His brown hair had the slightest of waves in it—perhaps it was more wiry than wavy—and formed a widow's peak at the top of his forehead. Though he was in remarkable shape for a man his age, he had gotten much thicker over the last few years. But he carried it well, and there was nothing about him that seemed soft.

"You havin' deep spiritual thoughts?" he asked.

"Depends how you define them. Some would say they were just the opposite."

"About my daughter?"

"But only in the most respectful ways."

In addition to being the IG, Tom Daniels was also my ex-father-in-law—or at least he would have been had Susan filed the papers.

"Things're goin' good between you two?" he asked.

I nodded.

"Think you'll be movin' back to Atlanta or can you talk her into movin' down here?"

"I'm not sure," I said. "We really haven't talked about it."

Actually, we had, but I didn't want to get into it with him.

"Well, try to get her down here," he said. "I miss her like hell."

I didn't say anything. Even though he and I had attended a few meetings together and were becoming friends for the first time in our lives, I still felt awkward and guarded around him. I was used to mean, antagonistic, drunk Tom Daniels, and finding friendly, sober Tom Daniels much more difficult to take. Not that he had been a mean drunk. He could be quite charming. His animosity seemed to have been reserved especially for me. With Sarah and Susan—his wife and daughter—the effect of his addiction hadn't been abuse, but neglect. This meant that I was trying to have a lasting relationship with a woman who grew up with an emotionally unavailable father—one she seemed to completely adore and subconsciously hate.

"What're you doin' here so late?" he asked.

"I've got to check on a service and a possible murder in PM," I said. "What're *you* doing here at all?"

He was assigned to Central Office in Tallahassee and only traveled to institutions for very specific purposes, often involving homicide.

He held up his battered brown leather satchel and nodded toward it. "Takin' depositions. Conducting interviews. I was headed out, but I left one of my notebooks in the PM unit. I'll walk down with you."

As we were buzzed through the center gate, we ducked our heads down and turned into the wind again.

"Looks like I'm gonna put Juan Martinez away for good this time," he said.

While attending outside court, and in the custody of the Leon County's Sheriff's Department, Juan Martinez escaped from the Leon County jail. Six hours later, he had been picked up at the bus station downtown. Officially, it was assumed that he had spent those six hours trying to put together some money and arrange transportation, but what he had actually done changed the Daniels family forever.

Breaking into Tom Daniels's home while he was at work and repeatedly raping his wife, violating her in ways hard to imagine one human doing to another, Juan Martinez had made Tom Daniels sober, a better husband, and given him a new mission in life. Since then he had spent the vast majority of his time searching for a way to lock up Martinez for the rest of his natural life. But it wasn't easy.

The problem had been a lack of evidence. Not only had Martinez worn a condom during the assault, but Sarah had immediately taken a shower and waited two days to tell anyone.

With no witness, no evidence, and no motivation to pursue a case of such enormous liability, the Leon County Sheriff's Department quickly concluded that Martinez had been with his family the entire time doing all he could to get as far away from Florida as soon as possible. This finding suited Tom Daniels just fine. Not only did it keep Sarah's humiliating ordeal out of the papers, but it gave him the opportunity to get Martinez himself.

All this had happened before Susan and I began our reconciliation. A lot of time had passed, but the wounds had yet to heal, and occasionally, Sarah showed just how traumatized she still was. Of course, the whole family was. Susan, who had always had a strained relationship with Sarah, tended to avoid the subject, and Tom, guilt-ridden and driven, was probably giving Martinez more attention than his wife.

"You've got to feel good about the way you've done it." Had Daniels not been sober, I doubt very much Martinez would still be alive, but the peace-seeking man beside me seemed to be searching for justice, not retribution.

He nodded. "Feels good. Beating him to death with my bare

hands would feel *better,* but . . ."

I knew how he felt. "I questioned whether you should be involved in the case at all. Glad I was wrong."

We were now in the housing area of the compound, enormous dormitories surrounding us on both sides. The dorms formed a horseshoe with sidewalks, pavilions, two small canteens, and barber shops in the center.

I looked over at Daniels as we walked against the wind. His head was down and I couldn't see his face, but even the way he walked was different. He was actually leaning into the wind, his steps intentional, his gait certain.

As far as anyone knew, Martinez hadn't intentionally chosen the IG's wife—he and Daniels hadn't had any dealings prior to the assault—his just happened to be the house he broke into, his the wife he found at home.

"How's Sarah?" I asked.

Pain filled his eyes as he glanced at me before quickly looking away. "Not good . . . but I think this'll help."

The past three months were the longest I had seen him sober. Sure, he had been without booze for a few days at a time before, trading his alcohol addiction for the adrenaline addiction of working a homicide investigation or some other all-consuming activity he could do compulsively, but this was different.

"What've you got on him?" I asked.

"A witness," he said.

"Who?"

"Justin Menge," he said.

I felt a jolt and my pulse picked up. *"Justin Menge?"*

"He's the real deal. Hell, I think he may even be an innocent man."

"His sister just told me the same thing."

He looked over at me with raised eyebrows. "Either way, he's one hell of a good witness and he's more than happy to help me put Martinez away."

"His sister said her visit with him really shook her up."

"Visit?" he asked in surprise. "When?"

"Just a few minutes ago."

"I mean *when* was the visit."

"See previous answer," I said.

"Couldn't've been. I just talked to him down in PM."

"I think she was just coming from having seen him."

"Must've been a short vis—wait," he exclaimed, shaking his head. "What the hell'm I thinkin'? It wasn't Menge, but his boyfriend, Sobel, I just saw. I'm constantly gettin' them confused. Sorry."

"Paula said Justin was acting very strange."

"Probably just nervous about testifying. Martinez has punks everywhere."

"Said he didn't even seem like the same person."

"He's not."

"Isn't Martinez in the PM unit, too?"

He nodded.

"No wonder he's scared."

"Only way Menge could get so much on him, but I've got to get him out of there now that he's agreed to testify."

"Does Martinez know?" I asked.

"Menge still breathing?"

G-Dorm was a massive two-story concrete structure that resembled a giant cement septic tank with windows. Unlike the other open bay dorms, G-Dorm was divided into quads, each with twenty-eight cells. It was designed for the inmates who presented a management problem for the institution.

Protective management was for inmates who, because of size, crime, previous job, poor adjustment, gang affiliation, or gambling debts on the compound, were not safe in open population. They were the most difficult inmates in the institution.

Many of them were pedophiles and rapists who were subject to brutality from the other inmates. Others were ex–law enforcement officers who feared retaliation for other reasons. Locking them inside their own quad saved them from having to interact with the rest of the population—and often saved their lives.

"Which service is it?"

"What?"

"Which service are you having to check on down here?" Daniels asked as we reached G-Dorm.

"Catholic. Look at this."

We stopped in front of the dorm and I handed him a flyer that had been distributed in the PM unit. He handed me his satchel and I held it while he held the flyer up toward the small light, his hands steady. As he read the flyer, he shook his head. His dark brown eyes were the clearest I'd ever seen them and his red face was the result of the cold wind, not alcohol.

Centered at the top of the page in bold were the words: THE BODY AND THE BLOOD. Beneath it, in slightly smaller letters it read: A Celebration of Murder. In the middle of the page were the words: Come Eat the Body and Drink the Blood. From Death comes Life. And then below that it listed the time and the place of the PM Catholic Mass.

"The *fuck?*" Daniels said as he read. "You gonna get rid of this guy?"

"The priest? He's just trying to get their attention. In fact, if this was all there was to it, I would've just called him, but look at this."

I handed him another piece of paper from my coat pocket. It was a flyer similar to the first. At the top it, too, read: THE BODY AND THE BLOOD. Beneath it, in smaller letters like the other flyer, it read: A Murder will take place. In the middle of the page it read: Slice the Flesh and Shed the Blood, and then listed the same date and time as the first one.

"You *did* say murder, didn't you?"

"What?"

"Earlier, you said you were coming to PM to check on a service and a possible murder," he said.

"Yeah."

"I thought I just misunderstood you."

"It may be nothing, but . . ."

"Did you notify security about this?" he asked, his tone suddenly harsh and accusatory.

"I took it to the institutional inspector when I received it."

"And?"

"Said it was probably a prank—nobody advertises murder."

"The hell they don't. Come on."

He opened the heavy metal door and rushed into G-Dorm.

I followed.

CHAPTER THREE

The front of G-dorm had three doors. The center one led to a holding room with another locked door and then to the elevated, glassed-in officer's station high in the center of the building. From it, officers could see each quad and control the locks of every door in the dorm. The other two doors led into the hallways on each side that ran between the officer's station and the two quads on that side.

Entering the hallway on the left side of the building, we ran back to the second quad and went through a second solid metal door that led to the PM unit.

A little alarm began to sound inside of me. "Why aren't either of these locked?"

Daniels shrugged. "Sure as hell should be."

The quads of G-dorm were roughly a hundred feet long and fifty feet wide, and held twenty-eight 6 × 9 foot cinder block cells. Unlike most county jails, the fronts of state correctional institution cells were not made of bars, but solid metal doors, each equipped with a locked metal food tray slot and a long narrow strip of steel-reinforced glass. The cells ran along the two longest walls—each side with seven at floor level and seven above, accessed by a set of gray metal stairs leading up to a metal grate catwalk. There were no cells along the short walls on either end.

Inside the expansive open space of the PM unit, all the cell doors closed, it was still and quiet. On the far end near the wall opposite us, Father James McFadden stood behind an altar table setting up for his service, before him a small group of folding chairs formed uneven rows.

"It's so quiet," I whispered to Daniels as we walked toward the makeshift Mass.

"Where is everybody?" he asked.

"Tonight is PM library night," I said. "Most of them are up there. A few more are in medical. The rest are probably in their cells."

Since inmates in protective management couldn't have contact with the rest of the inmate population, they went to the library at night when no other inmates were there. It was also why we had a special Catholic Mass for them in the PM unit—they couldn't come to the chapel with the open population inmates for the regular one.

As we reached the back row of folding chairs, an officer standing on the left side nodded to us, and we walked over to him.

Billy Joe Potter was an overweight white man in his mid-twenties with bad skin, a bad haircut, and a bad attitude. He was mean and slow and didn't care about anything. He didn't have to—not only was he a member of the most influential family in Potter County, but it was easier for a camel to go through the eye of a needle than for a state employee to enter the ranks of the unemployed.

Known among his relatives as the family fuck-up, Potter had worked briefly in several county jobs, including mosquito control, building inspector, and dog catcher, before being sent to prison without the possibility of parole—he could do time in brown or blue, but he was going to do time.

"You forget something?" he asked Daniels.

"Did *you* forget something? The outer door and the quad door were both unlocked."

He lifted his hands up in a helpless gesture and shrugged

nonchalantly. "Can't be helped. Only two of us."

Complacency is the number one problem among prison staff, and it gets more inmates and correctional officers killed than anything else. Employees get comfortable, forget where they are, why they're here, and when they least expect it, an entirely preventable incident occurs. The most dangerous condition in a prison is when it's been a while since anything much has happened. When security is relaxed in an area of the prison for whatever reason—ineptitude, laziness, a staff shortage—it goes unnoticed until there's an incident. It's not a problem until it is, then it's addressed, often corrected, but not until it is too late for someone.

At various times, different departments within the institution are understaffed—at least one area nearly every shift. There's not an incident every time, but nearly every incident occurs in one of these areas. You can only get away with it for so long, and then . . . tonight felt like one of those "and then" times.

"I'm over here," Potter continued. "Officer Pitts is counting the other quads. He's gotta be able to get back in the wicker after he counts."

"Wicker" is the term used for the officers' stations inside the dorms, and though everyone referred to it as such, no one had ever been able to tell me why.

"He's out of the wicker *and* the goddam door is unlocked?" Daniels yelled.

"What would *you* do?" Potter asked. "We're undermanned."

"You damn sure are. Wherever you're assigned always will be."

Standard procedure called for a sergeant and an officer in the officer station or wicker, as well as at least one officer in each quad—and with a volunteer down here to conduct a religious service, there really should have been two.

"In case you didn't know," Potter continued, "there's a shortage of correctional officers."

I looked at Daniels. "There's an even bigger shortage of *good* correctional officers."

Potter glared at me.

I tried not to quake.

"Soon as Pitts is back in the wicker," Potter said. "I'm gonna call for Catholic Mass. That okay with you?"

Daniels didn't respond.

Across the quad, an inmate walked into the dorm and Potter nodded him toward his cell, which clicked open.

"Menge," he explained. "Had a visit tonight."

I glanced over to see Justin disappear into the third cell from the entrance on the bottom just on the other side of the stairs, and felt relieved that he was safely back inside.

Daniels shook his head in confusion. "Who unlocked his cell?"

"Pitts—" he began when a yell from one of the cells stopped him. The acoustics were so bad it was impossible to know exactly where it came from. "Shut the hell up," he yelled back toward the cell. Then, looking back at Daniels, said, "Pitts must be back in the wicker."

"Must be?" Daniels asked. "*Must* be? What the hell kinda half-ass Mickey Mouse operation are y'all runnin' down here?"

"We're doin' the best we can."

"Oh, I don't doubt that."

Potter looked at him for a moment, but didn't say anything, then radioed Pitts, confirmed that the count had cleared, and advised him that he was about to call for Mass.

As Potter yelled that it was time for Mass and for those inmates wishing to attend to call out the number of their cells, I walked over to speak to Father James.

One by one, inmates called out the number of their cells. Potter radioed the cell numbers to Pitts, and they were buzzed open. Slowly, from every direction, inmates began making their way toward the folding chairs.

"I knew it wouldn't be well received when I did it," Father James said, returning the flyer to me. "But it got everyone's attention, didn't it?"

Father James was tall and thin with wispy white hair that had receded to about the halfway point on the top of his head. Age, back problems, and perhaps the enormous dogs he seemed to be perpetually walking around town, caused him to bend forward slightly and made him look stiff and brittle and far more feeble than he really was.

I nodded and frowned. "It did. But not all of it was good. Look at this."

I unfolded the second flyer—the one claiming a murder would take place during the Mass—and handed it to him. His thin, slightly deformed hand shook as he read it.

"I didn't do this one," he said, his pale blue eyes narrowing as he looked up at me.

"Any idea who did?"

"None at all. You think it's announcing an actual murder?" He looked around at the inmates moving toward him.

I shrugged. "That's what I came to find out."

He studied the flyer some more. "It's nearly identical to the one I made. Could an inmate do something like this?"

I nodded. "Not on the compound, but we have a PRIDE printing vocation program here. Lot of inmates work in it. None of the PM guys, but they could pay somebody to do it. Sneaking it down here would be the difficult part."

PRIDE Enterprises is a not-for-profit corporation that works in prisons across the state, using inmate labor to provide manufacturing and services to government agencies and the private sector. It provides the state with both revenue and savings and inmates with jobs while they're incarcerated, and gives them marketable skills when they're released.

PCI's printing program, which is operated by PRIDE, employs over a hundred inmates. They create and print books, brochures, business cards, tickets, flyers, and newsletters with the latest equipment and software. Duplicating the priest's unsophisticated flyer wouldn't have presented a challenge for them.

After a few minutes, when most of the inmates had taken their seats, things began to quiet down again, and Father James looked relieved. As the last of the inmates were seated, I walked back over and stood by Daniels.

"He know anything about it?"

I shook my head. "Says not."

Father James welcomed the men and gave his call to worship, but even after they were well into the second hymn, stragglers were still being buzzed out of their cells and joining the service.

Potter motioned for one of the slow-moving latecomers to pick it up, and I could tell he savored and often abused what little authority he had.

"Anything out of the ordinary going on?" Daniels asked.

Potter shook his head. "Quiet as church. I'm about to fall asleep. Now I remember why I used to hate goin' so damn much."

He looked at me.

With a collar around my neck, I was an obvious target for his contempt, but I was probably no more connected to organized religion than he was. It's what made my position ironic. From an early age, I'd had an intense spiritual hunger and an idealistic desire to help humanity, but had never felt comfortable or spent very much time within the structure of organized religion.

Daniels pressed the two flyers into Potter's chest. "Know anything about these?"

While Potter examined the flyers, Daniels and I looked

around the room. Between the exposed pipes running along the unfinished ceiling and the bare concrete of the floor, there was mostly open space with only a TV suspended from a bracket on the wall opposite us and a desk for the PM sergeant near the door.

Every sound reverberating in the open space of the two-story bare concrete building ricocheted around the room like a racquetball, and the air was filled with the stale depressing smell of confinement—sleep, sweat, and the lingering acrid odor of cigarette smoke.

I scanned the solid metal doors of the twenty-eight cinder block cells. With all the food tray slots closed, I could only see the inmates who were standing directly in front of the glass.

Potter's radio announced that two inmates were returning from medical, and they appeared at the door. He nodded them toward their cells, which popped open as they approached them, and then he turned his attention back to the flyers.

"It's bullshit," Potter said.

"What?" Daniels asked.

He nodded toward the flyers. "We got this place locked down tighter than the warden's black asshole. Every cell door is shut and locked. We've got complete control over all movement."

From somewhere near the staircase, an inmate asked Potter if he could be released to attend the service.

"See," Potter said. "Complete control."

Potter then radioed Pitts and asked him to unlock cell 203. The buzz of an electric lock sounded, then a click, and Chris Sobel, Justin Menge's boyfriend, emerged from the cell and walked over toward the folding chairs. Before he reached them, Potter motioned for him, and he walked over.

"Sir?" Sobel said.

His eyes were red and puffy, his face splotchy, and I wondered if he had been crying. His hands and hair were damp, the label on his uniform was missing, and he wasn't wearing shoes.

"Are you okay?" I asked.

He glanced at me and gave me a small twisted-lip frown and a quick nod.

"Next time I call for service, you either go right then or not at all," Potter said. "Understand?"

"Yes, sir," he said. "Sorry, I fell asleep."

Potter didn't say anything else and Sobel made his way over to the back row of chairs and took a seat. Almost as soon as he sat down, Potter called him back.

"Where the hell're your shoes?"

Sobel looked down at his socked feet. "This is now holy ground. It's my tradition."

"I got some traditions of my own you gonna find out about if you don't go git your goddam shoes on."

"Yes, sir," he said, and quickly headed back to his cell.

"Complete control," Daniels agreed with so little sarcasm that Potter didn't pick up on it.

"Damn straight," Potter said.

I scanned the small crowd of inmates for Justin Menge, but he wasn't among them. Though an outspoken critic of the Catholic Church, as far as I knew he never missed Mass.

Potter raised his eyebrows as if a thought had just occurred to him. "If we did have a murder down here . . . wouldn't be a bad thing."

Daniels started to comment, but Potter's radio sounded the return of another inmate from the library.

Daniels's eyes grew wide when the inmate appeared at the door by himself. "Where the hell's his escort?"

"They just bring 'em as far as the front door of the dorm. Officer in the wicker watches them from there."

"When he's there," Daniels said, shaking his head.

We fell silent for a while as Father James continued his homily. Eventually, Sobel came back with his shoes on, though he had missed most of the service.

The dim light coming from the high ceiling of the quad seemed to obscure more than it illuminated, casting everything in a ghost-like vagueness that seemed far too appropriate for the anticipation of murder.

Potter's radio sounded again and Pitts told him he was going to do a visual walk-by of the cells, which he promptly came and did, his dark skin shining in the dull light of the quad. Even from a distance, it was obvious Pitts was athletic. His casual, yet crisp movements demonstrated his comfort with and confidence in his body. After he made his rounds, Pitts gave Potter the thumbs-up gesture and returned to the wicker.

As the service continued, I looked around the quad, bowing my head periodically as Father James prayed, preparing to serve the Holy Eucharist.

"Pray, brothers, that our sacrifice may be acceptable to God, the almighty Father," he said.

His small congregation responded more or less in unison, "May the Lord accept the sacrifice at your hands, for the praise and glory of his name, for our good, and the good of all his Church."

"Lord Jesus Christ, you said to your apostles, 'I leave you peace, my peace I give you.' Look not on our sins, but on the faith of your Church, and grant us the peace and unity of your kingdom where you live for ever and ever."

When I looked up again, Potter was shaking his head, but he stopped when Father James held up the elements.

"This is the Lamb of God who takes away the sin of the world. Happy are those who are called to his supper."

I looked around the dorm some more, and though I was prepared for what came next, I still shuddered slightly when Father James said, "The body and the blood."

I glanced over at Daniels and Potter. They both looked pale.

When nothing happened, it was as if the collective breath being held was exhaled, though what followed was only a slight release of tension, not a complete exorcism of our uneasiness.

As Father James came around the table and presented the sacraments, the inmates stood and began filing down the center aisle to receive Holy Communion.

Father James held the bread in one hand, a chalice filled with grape juice (wine wasn't allowed) in the other, and in an atypical, unorthodox manner, each inmate would tear a small piece of bread from the loaf, dip it into the chalice, and drop it into his mouth.

"The body that was broken for you. The blood that was shed for you."

This continued for a long time under the scrutiny of Daniels and Potter, both of whom had moved closer to get a better view.

"The body of Christ. The blood of Christ."

Since Daniels was watching the Holy Eucharist so closely, I decided to concentrate on the rest of the quad. I looked down each wall, pausing at every cell, beginning where I stood and scanning slowly to the other end.

"The body that was broken for you. The blood that was shed for you."

I looked down the wall closest to me first. Nothing was out of order. There was no movement. No sound, but echoes of the priest's haunting words.

"The body of Christ. The blood of Christ."

I examined the wall opposite us. First the upper level, and then the bottom. Moving across each cell, beginning with the end closest to us and working my way back down to the far end near the door.

And that's when I saw it.

"The body that was broken for you," the priest was saying. "The blood that was shed for you."

I began moving toward it, but before I reached it, I knew what it was.

"The body of Christ. The blood of Christ."

It can't be, I thought, but knew it was.

There on the bare concrete floor, seeping from beneath Justin Menge's cell door as if from an open wound, was an expanding pool of blood.

CHAPTER FOUR

"How the hell did this happen?" Daniels yelled.

I didn't respond.

"We saw him come in just a few minutes ago," he said. "We've been here the whole time. Watching."

We were standing in front of Justin Menge's cell, carefully avoiding the blood puddle at our feet. Every inmate at the Catholic service and the few that were in their cells had been strip-searched by Potter and Pitts and then escorted to the empty quad on the other side of the dorm where they would stay locked down until the investigation was completed.

"How the *hell* did this happen?" Daniels said again, each time emphasizing a different word, as he continued to look around every visible inch of the quad.

Satisfied the crime scene was secure, he withdrew latex gloves from his coat pocket and handed me a pair. After we put the gloves on, the first thing we both did was pull on the cell door.

It was locked.

This massive metal door fronting the 6 × 9 foot cinder block cell was the only possible entrance or exit.

"Shit," he said.

"I know."

He shook his head. "It's locked and he's alone inside."

Like a coach yelling at his players during practice in an empty gymnasium, Daniels's voice echoed through the cement quad, bouncing around the room like an overinflated basketball.

I reached down and pulled on the food tray slot. It was also locked.

He took a step back and motioned up to the officer in the wicker to unlock the cell door.

Then he looked back over at me. "I asked you a question."

"You did?"

"How the hell did this happen? We just saw him come in. He's in a locked cell. Alone. And he's only been in—what? Twenty, twenty-five minutes?"

I shrugged. "Maybe less."

"Could it be suicide? It's got to be, right? I mean, of course. That flyer's got me thinkin' crazy, but it can't be murder. He had to do it to himself. No one else was in here."

As the electronic lock on the cell door clicked, Daniels pulled it open and the smell of wet copper rushed out and filled our nostrils. Taking a step inside the cell, he reached over to his left and reconnected the disabled light.

The lights inside the cells in G-dorm consisted of small halogen tubes with white plexiglass covers. The covers were held in place by four recessed screws—the heads of which were round and had a small flange hanging down. Using part of the cylinder of a large ink pen that had been cut to fit the opening, inmates often unscrewed the covers to disable the lights or hide contraband behind them.

There was no contraband in Justin's. The concealment in this instance had been the cell itself—the cover simply removed, the light merely disabled.

"Picked a hell of a time to be sober," he said.

My eyes darted around the room, unable to find focus, my mind rejecting the images they were sending. I had seen my share of crime scenes, but I had never gotten used to them, and I had never seen anything like this. I took a step back and looked away for a moment. And that's when what I had just seen finally registered.

On the floor inside the cell looked to be most of the blood from Justin Menge's body. It was dark maroon and black with pale yellow around the edges. But it was just his blood. His body was beneath the covers on the lower of the two metal bunks that hung from the pale gray cinder block wall, the gaping wound on his neck partially visible.

The sheet and blanket surrounding the body had very little blood on them compared to everything else—not soaked in blood like I expected them to be. Most of the blood was on the floor.

"The body and the blood," I said.

Daniels's eyes grew wide as he looked over at me. "Just like the fuckin' flyer. His body's in one place and his blood's in another."

We were both quiet a moment, the fact that the horror we were witnessing had been foretold sinking in more forcefully, and I wondered what I was going to tell Paula.

"The flyer," I said.

"Yeah?"

"Doesn't strike me as a suicide note."

"Oh," he said, nodding absently. "You're right." He shook his head, the lines in his face and forehead deepening. *"Fuck."*

I looked around the cell again. There were faint sprays and splatters, but none were heavy or concentrated on anything. "There's no real arterial spray."

He quickly looked at all four walls. "It's as if he was just drained."

"This much blood," I said, "you'd think something's got to have arterial spray on it. I bet the murderer's shirt is covered with it."

He glanced down for a moment and took a deep breath.

I followed his gaze. The outline of Menge's body was faint, but visible in the blood covering the cell floor. And there was something else.

"Look at that," he said, nodding toward two shoe prints in the blood. "You're right. Not suicide after all."

Looking at the nearly perfect set of boot prints before the outline of the body in the tacky substance, I realized that some of the blood had already begun to clot. Yet a lot of it had not. It didn't make sense.

"What if his throat was cut while he was laying face down on the floor?" Daniels said. "All the subsequent blood could be covering the bulk of the spray and splatter patterns."

I raised my eyebrows at him and nodded. "That could be it."

"How the hell did he get from the floor to the bed?"

I looked at him, wondering if I had misunderstood what he meant. It seemed so obvious to me. "The murderer must have moved him."

He was distracted, genuinely perplexed, and didn't answer right away. "Huh? Yeah, you're probably right."

"Though it was risky as hell to wait here while most of the blood drained from his body," I added.

He nodded, still staring down, his eyes shifting back and forth between the body and the blood.

"We've got to get FDLE in here to process this as quickly as we can," I said, thinking that the rate at which the blood was drying would help them to establish time of death more accurately.

"I've already called them. They're on the way," he said, "but it'll be at least another hour."

I shook my head and frowned.

"How can the blanket only have smears on it?"

Stepping over the blood and pulling back the covers with his gloved hand, he exposed the pale, purplish body of Justin Menge.

Except for a few patches of blood, the sheets were clean.

He ran his glove along the sheet beside the body. "Just smears."

Unlike the sheets, Justin's shirt was saturated with blood.

"Lift his shirt up a little, would you?" I asked.

He did.

Beneath the smears of blood on his skin, the front of Justin's body was deep purple. Daniels then rolled him over. In contrast to his stomach, his back was nearly the color of the sheet.

"Lividity," I noted aloud.

"Yeah," Daniels said. "Killed face down on the floor, then left there a while before being placed on his back on the bed."

I nodded. "But how was there enough time?"

Daniels then made another noise that sounded like a distressed grunt.

"What is it?"

"No weapon," Daniels said.

I quickly took in the rest of the cell.

"What's that?"

I moved over to the right side of the cell and carefully lifted the blood-stained inmate uniform wadded up in the front corner. Stretching it out revealed that it was smeared, not soaked, with blood, and that it belonged to Menge.

"No arterial spray on it," he said. "Killer must've used it to clean up—maybe to dry off after he washed up in the sink."

I nodded, and returned the uniform to its original spot.

When I glanced back at Menge, I noticed that the label on the shirt he was wearing had been ripped off, leaving a blue square with far less blood on it than the rest of the uniform. It looked like a small rectangular stencil that had been spray painted with blood.

"His name tag's been ripped off," I said. "After he was killed."

A white label with the inmate's name, DC number, and bunk assignment was sewn on every inmate uniform at the institution.

"It's right there." He pointed to Menge's plastic ID badge lying on the bed beside him.

In addition to the label sewn onto their uniform, inmates were required to wear a photo ID badge through a loop in their shirt or on the lapel of their jacket.

"Not the ID badge, but the name label sewn on his uniform. It's missing. But the ID badge is strange, too."

"I don't follow."

"It only has traces of blood on it."

He didn't say anything.

"Presumably the label is covered with it," I continued, "and it's missing."

"Oh, yeah," he said. "I thought you meant something else. I've already noted that."

He sounded defensive, as if he didn't know what I meant but wasn't willing to ask, and for a moment the old Tom Daniels was back.

"The yell we heard when we were talkin' to Potter," he said, "think that's when it happened?"

I shrugged. "It didn't sound like that kind of yell—not a scream or a cry for help. We were so on edge about the flyer, we'd've come running if it were a scream."

"You're right. It was definitely a yell, not a scream. At the time I thought it was just the usual inmate outburst."

"Still," I said, "we should've checked it out."

He frowned and nodded.

Closing my eyes for a moment, I took in a shallow breath through my mouth, trying not to smell the blood any more than I had to. I wasn't sure why, but I was finding this more difficult than I usually did. It was probably a complex mixture of things—like the shock and horror of the excessive violence and bloodletting, the fact that Justin, every bit the sensitive, talented artist, seemed far more vulnerable than most inmates, that I had told his sister I would check on him, and the fact that I had been warned, had been so close when it happened, and was still unable to prevent it.

"It doesn't make sense," I said.

"None of this does."

"Good point."

Carefully turning Menge's head, Daniels examined the enormous gash in his neck. As he moved the head, what had to be the last of Menge's blood oozed out of the gaping red and black wound.

"Doesn't look self-inflicted," I said.

We fell silent a moment, the raw violence of the situation resting heavily upon us, and I realized I had not said a prayer for Justin Menge nor mourned his death. I closed my eyes and briefly prayed for him and his family, especially Paula. The mourning would have to come later.

When I opened my eyes, Daniels was shaking his head, and I could tell something awful was dawning on him.

"What is it?"

"My case. There goes my whole fruckin' case against Martinez." He looked over at me, eyes blazing. "I know you're thinking about Menge and I should be too, but, dammit, I was so close."

"I understand. I'm sorry."

The more he seemed to think about it, the more it registered, the more disconsolate he became.

"I can't catch my breath," he said, his voice trembling, his hands shaking. "Do you know how many hours I've put in on this thing? How bad I wanted to get the bastard?"

I nodded. "You'll find another way."

He waved it off with a blood-covered gloved hand and looked away. He stood there quietly for a moment, staring at nothing, while I moved over and began looking through Menge's things.

Next to a black plastic comb on the stainless steel sink sat a small travel-size tube of toothpaste with the cap off, a blob of white oozing out of it. Next to it was a new bar of PRIDE soap.

The top bunk didn't have a mattress, and several books and notepads were stacked on it.

Among the books was *Catechism of the Catholic Church, Ceremonies of the Modern Roman Rite, The Road Less Traveled, A History of Art,* a bible, and a few paperback mystery and romance novels. Next to the notepads, several dozen drawings Justin had done were in small stacks grouped by periods: impressionists, post-impressionists, cubists, post-modernists, abstract expressionists.

Daniels moved over beside me and began thumbing through the notepads.

Lifting the lid of his footlocker, I squatted down beside it, and began carefully sifting through its contents. There wasn't much to see—a couple of bags of chips, two Butterfingers, socks, underwear, some personal hygiene products, some family photographs, and the colored pencils and sketch pads he used in lieu of the paints and canvases that were considered contraband. One thing I couldn't be sure about was his uniforms. One was on him, one wadded up in the corner, but I'd expect to see at least one more folded with his other things. He may just have had two. Some inmates did. Others had several. It'd be difficult to find out how many he actually had.

"There a notebook in there?"

I shook my head.

"It's not up here either."

"What?"

"Pad he used for his journal and statement against Martinez. It's gone. It was here earlier. I saw it." He shook his head. "Dammit. That fuckin' little . . ."

"You think Martinez . . ."

"Who else? I don't know *how* he did it. Still can't figure out how it was done, but yeah, I'd say he should top our suspect list."

Our? Was that just habit? Was he referring to the department? Or was he saying I would be involved in his investigation?

We were silent a moment, while I looked around one last time and thought about how it might have been done. Daniels continued to shake his head, seemingly on the verge of tears.

On the pale gray cinder block wall between the bunks, each dangling by a small strip of stolen Scotch tape, hung two different drawings of *La Grenouillere*.

In 1868, Claude Monet and Pierre-Auguste Renoir had set up their easels side by side and painted the frog pond or *La Grenouillere* with quite disparate results. Justin Menge had recreated them both with amazing accuracy, especially considering he was limited to a medium-size pack of colored pencils. He had lavished such care on them, risked so much to display them.

"Seen enough?" Daniels asked.

"One more thing."

Stepping over to the body, I carefully lifted Justin's shirt, and used my gloved index finger to press the purple patches on his lower stomach. The area beneath my finger turned white. When I moved my finger the discoloration returned.

"Blanching," I said.

"Yeah?"

"If he was killed the moment he came back into the dorm, how long's he been dead?"

He looked at his watch. "Over an hour and a half now."

I shook my head. "The blanching, lividity, and rate of blood clot just don't add up."

"None of this shit makes any sense. Maybe crime scene can tell us what the fuck's goin' on."

CHAPTER FIVE

Within an hour, the crime scene crew had arrived, and I stood back and watched as a FDLE technician snapped pictures, the brilliant flash washing out all color in the cell, turning crimson to pink and white. The crime was so surreal, the capturing of it so dramatic, that I half expected to hear the whine of the old flashbulbs, as if mourning the images they were illuminating.

While a female technician gathered evidence and put each piece into its own plastic or paper bag or envelope—depending on what it was and if it had blood on it—a male technician examined the doorjamb and lock mechanism for toolmarks. When the scene had been completely photographed, the blood splatter patterns were examined and sketches of the entire scene were drawn to scale.

"Obviously, I want your help with this thing," Daniels said.

Obviously? He had never wanted it before.

I thought about how weary I was, how spiritually unwell. I knew being involved in a homicide investigation, even in a limited way, would only make things worse. I knew all this, yet I couldn't resist.

"You're a good investigator," he continued, "and I need someone who can move around inside here among the inmates and the staff. No one does it better. Plus, you were here. You saw the whole thing go down. You willing?"

"What about FDLE?"

"My investigation. They're assisting. I know I've been a real pain in the ass when we've worked together before, but I'm different now. Hell, I'm sober."

I thought about Paula Menge and how I'd waited too long to do what she'd asked me to do. Thought about Justin and the progress he'd been making—how abruptly all his work had been cut short.

I nodded.

"I'll clear it with the warden. Anybody gives you any shit, you let me know."

"Everybody's pretty used to it by now . . . though we do have a new colonel."

"I'll break it down for him."

I cringed inside. He certainly had the authority. What concerned me was his approach. When this was over, he'd return to Central Office and I'd be left to deal with all the people he had angered and offended.

"Now that that's settled," he said, "let's talk to the two fuck-ups in charge down here."

He had Potter and Pitts brought down to us so that we could observe the crime scene being processed while we talked to them.

Michael Pitts was in every way Billy Joe Potter's opposite. He was smart, alert, caring. Whereas Potter was short and dumpy, Pitts was tall and lean, Potter soft and pale, Pitts hard and dark. In contrast to Potter's ill-fitting and wrinkled uniform, Pitts's crisp and clean uniform looked as if it had been tailor-made for him.

"What the hell happened here tonight?" Daniels asked.

"That's what we'd like to know," Potter said. "This ain't our fault. We're shorthanded. We do the best we can. A hard job that pays shit. Nobody can blame us."

"*I* damn sure can," Daniels said. "So shut the fuck up and

answer my questions. I don't give a good goddam who your family is."

Daniels leaned into Potter, daring him to respond. When he looked down, Daniels said, "Now walk me through exactly what happened from the time Menge returned from his visit."

"Yes, sir," Pitts said. "I'd just completed count in quads one and three and was returning to the wicker to call it in to the control room, when Officer Stanley arrived back at the dorm with an inmate. I sent him to quad two and returned to the wicker where I called in the count and buzzed his cell door open."

"I still don't see how this coulda happened, anyway," Potter said. "I mean we all saw him go in the cell and it was locked when we found him. Can any of you explain that? It couldn't've happened."

"Okay, Potter," Daniels said, "that's what I'll put in my report. This murder couldn't've happened."

"Well, I'm just saying—"

"Well, don't. Just shut the fuck up."

The FDLE agents in and around the cell stopped what they were doing and looked at Daniels. Potter shut up.

"Please continue, Officer Pitts," Daniels said. "What happened next?"

"Well, after I buzzed Sobel into his cell. I logged in count and movement—"

"Menge," Daniels said.

"Sir?"

"You mean Menge," he said. "You said you buzzed Sobel in, but you meant Menge."

"I thought it was Sobel," he said. "Sorry. They look a lot alike."

Behind Pitts and Potter, the two FDLE agents working inside the cell were gathering trace evidence with tweezers and putting

47

it into tiny coin envelopes and plastic bags. Outside the cell, three other agents were busy labeling and tagging each item of evidence that had been recovered.

"That's what happens when you're married long enough," Potter said. "You start to look alike. Those two butt-fucks have been together longer than me and my old lady."

"This is important," Daniels said, ignoring Potter. "Who did you buzz in?"

"It was Menge," Potter said. "You buzzed Sobel out a little while later for church and then you saw him again when he went back to his cell because I had to make him go put his shoes on."

Daniels looked at me. "Shoes?"

I nodded.

"That's right," Pitts said. "It was Menge. I'm sorry. I don't know what I was thinking. I was there when Stanley brought him back and I walked straight up and buzzed him in."

"What about the shoes?" Potter asked.

"We got two bloody footprints in Menge's cell," Daniels said. "So?"

"So maybe Sobel didn't wear his shoes to the service because they had blood on them," he said, then looking back at Pitts, "What happened next?"

"While I was updating my logs," he continued, "Sergeant Potter called the cell numbers of the inmates attending the Mass and I unlocked those cells and then a few inmates from medical came back and I buzzed them into their cells and then it was pretty quiet until . . ."

"Until Menge was served up as communion," Potter said with a sophomoric smile.

Menge's cell had now been cleared of all the agents except for the thin man dusting for prints. I watched as he methodically pointed his small flashlight in several directions at varying angles until he found what he was looking for. He then held the light with his mouth as he twirled the brush between his palms, dipped it into the powder, and then brushed the dust very lightly onto the surface that held the prints.

"Didn't Menge always go to Mass?" I asked.

"Yeah," Potter said. "He used to argue with the old priest during his sermons. Take up the whole damn hour sometimes."

"Okay," Daniels said. "I'm not here to bust anybody's balls. You were understaffed and that's not your fault. You were having to do too many things at one time. I understand. But I've got to figure out how this was done. Okay? So, tell me the truth and I'll handle the heat."

Pitts nodded.

"Could you've hit Menge's cell button when you were letting the others out?"

Pitts thought about it.

"He always goes," Daniels said. "You do it automatically. Same inmates every time. And you just hit the button. Coulda happen to anyone."

Pitts looked up, squinted, and thought about it, then glanced over at Menge's cell.

Having found and dusted another clean print, the FDLE agent was now pressing tape down onto it. Next, he lifted the tape in one quick motion that sounded like a Band-Aid being ripped off and pressed it down on the lift card. He then labeled the card and went off in search of others.

Pitts shook his head. "No, sir," he said. "I'm not here all the time. I'm in D-dorm some too. So I wouldn't've expected him to go—or anyone else for that matter. And I'm real careful over the cell door buttons. Real careful. Especially after Inspector Fortner told us about the threat."

"And the truth is," Potter said, "the cell doors are usually left open until lights out. This is a self-contained quad. It's not confinement. The inmates come out and watch TV or play cards or go to church service. Only reason we were on lock-down tonight was because we were told to. So no one would've been used to opening any cells for church anyway."

Daniels nodded. "Okay," he said. "I believe you. Is there any way the inmates could've opened it—either from inside or out?"

"Once that door is locked, they can't get it open."

"So you've never had one open before without you doing it?" I asked.

"Well, sure we have," Pitts said. "Almost every time we have a thunderstorm, some of them open. The lightning shorts the locks out or something. I'm not sure."

"But there wasn't any lightning tonight," I said.

"We've had a couple of inmates keep their cell doors from locking before," Potter said.

"How?" Daniels asked.

"By putting a plastic spoon between the lock and the latch," he said.

Daniels raised his eyebrows.

"But we haven't used spoons down here in over a year," Pitts said. "No one down here would have one."

"Yeah," Potter said. "I'm sure of that. Anyway, I checked all the doors when I went by for count."

"When was that?" Daniels asked.

Potter shrugged. "Right after the priest got here and just before you and the chaplain came down."

"Wait a minute," Pitts said, his face suddenly lighting up. "You said Sobel went back to his cell to get his shoes."

Potter nodded. "Yeah?"

"I didn't buzz him back into the cell," Pitts said.

"You sure?" Daniels asked.

"Positive."

"Then just how the hell did he get back in?"

CHAPTER SIX

It was the morning following the murder, and though I had yet to sleep, the adrenaline in my blood, the questions in my brain, and the shower I had just taken made me feel awake and alert.

I was walking down the compound with Anna Rodden to interview Chris Sobel. She was his classification officer.

If happiness is not wanting to be any place other than where you are, then I was truly happy. Happy to be in prison. Happy to be alive. Happy to be in the presence of Anna. I have that same thought every time I'm near her. It's as certain as the dread I feel as our time together approaches its end.

The early morning air was chilly and damp, the unseen sun illuminating the vibrant colors of the tender young flowers all around us, their delicate petals drooping beneath the weight of the thick dew. Inmates in pale blue uniforms assigned to inside grounds were already busy working on the only source of beauty—besides Anna—and their greatest source of pride in this desolate place. The care they lavished on the small, vulnerable plants showed in their abundance and lushness.

As usual, the inmates on the compound stopped what they were doing to watch Anna. They did the same thing every time an attractive woman was on the compound, but more so with her. The inmates gawked like teens who didn't know any better, but in fairness, most men and many women stopped to watch Anna—we just weren't as obvious about it.

"Does it bother you?" I asked.

"Whatta *you* think?"

I knew it bothered her. What I really meant was how much, but I didn't pursue it.

There was far more to Anna than what the inmates were seeing, her true attractiveness having more to do with qualities that couldn't be seen. Or, if they could, it was only intangibly, through their effects—the way she held herself, the way she moved, the way intelligence and compassion blazed through her bright eyes.

Had I been sober I would have married her back when we were both single. As it happened, I moved off to Atlanta after high school and the next time I saw her she was married.

When I moved back to Pottersville a little over a year and a half ago, thinking I was divorced, being around Anna was excruciating, and now, finding myself still married didn't make it any easier. Being so close to her was torture—cruel and unusual punishment. And there was nowhere I'd rather be. By definition I was a happy man.

A pang of guilt, unbidden but not unfamiliar, rumbled inside me like distant thunder, and I wondered how I could be happy so soon after Justin Menge had been so violently murdered. How could I be so glad just to be in the presence of a woman not my wife?

"How are things with you and Susan?" she asked, as if reading my mind.

"Good," I said. *Very good actually.* "We're different—and so's our relationship."

She nodded and smiled as if she knew something I didn't. "You think this is it?"

Unless you tell me it's not. "It could be. Who would've ever thought?"

"Not me."

The silence that followed accompanied a change in her

posture and presence. Without breaking stride, she stiffened slightly and withdrew from me somehow.

After a year of thinking I was single, it was nice to find myself back on a more emotionally level battlefield with this woman who in love was both enemy and ally. In some stunted sophomoric place inside, I felt a tiny bit triumphant at being able to make her feel some semblance of what I had felt in the recent past, and it disturbed me to be confronted with how shallow and immature I could still be.

After a while, she said, "Will you be moving back to Atlanta?"

I hesitated. "I'm not sure. I came running back here as a failure, not knowing where else to go. I've got a broken down mobile home and a downwardly mobile job, but . . . I love it. Love the space and solitude. Love the stripped-down way I live. Love being here with you. I've never been happier."

I was wearing a charcoal-gray suit with a thin pinstripe and a black clerical shirt with full collar. Anna was wearing a black sheath dress. We looked like a couple, or given our matching chestnut-colored hair and dark brown eyes, like brother and sister. Either way, we looked like we belonged together.

So why weren't we? I wish I knew. It was complicated and had a lot to do with timing.

Growing up, Anna had been my older sister Nancy's best friend. In high school, when our attraction began to blossom, the two years that separated us seemed insurmountable. After graduation when Nancy fled our family, Anna left for college. Four years passed before I saw her again and, by that time, she was married. I was devastated.

Several years later, following the breakup of my life and what I thought was the breakup of my marriage to Susan, I came home, began rebuilding, and not coincidentally became the chaplain at the same prison where Anna was a classification officer.

"I love having you here," she said. "Actually look forward to coming in here every day because most days I get to see you—be with you. But I can't see Susan living in Pottersville."

"I know."

Susan was a city girl, unsuited for my rural, Spartan existence.

"Certainly not the *way* you're living."

"And she shouldn't have to," I said.

She turned her head and looked up at me with raised eyebrows. "I guess Sarah shouldn't've had to follow Abraham into the wilderness either."

"Not the same thing."

She held up her arms and gestured to the prison around us. "You saying this ain't the Promised Land?"

Many of the inmates marching in orderly lines all around us were able to convey their contempt for life just in the way they moved, their careful avoidance of Anna as conspicuous as those ogling her.

"Seriously," she added, "you *do* believe God called you here, don't you?"

Lured is more like it, I thought, *and guess who she used for bait?*

"You're the one who told me you gotta go through the wilderness to get to the Promised Land?"

I nodded. "No other way to get there. Thanks for the reminder. You give good argument."

She smiled, something flickering in her eyes.

"That come from being married to a lawyer?"

"No," she said with a mischievous smile, "from having Sarah envy."

"What can you tell me about him?"

We were seated in the interview room of G-dorm, waiting for an officer to escort Sobel to us.

As Sobel's classification officer, Anna was responsible for classifying and managing him as well as writing his progress reports, determining his custody level and work assignment.

"He's got good adjustment," she said, using the vernacular of her position. "Hasn't given me one minute's trouble. Quiet. Sticks to himself—except for Menge. He's in on a drug charge and he's really worked hard on recovery. He's in AA and NA as well as the drug treatment program."

I nodded.

"He's very religious," she said. "Catholic. But I'm sure you know that."

"I was surprised when he showed up for Mass late."

"You think it's because he was busy killing Justin?"

"It's crossed my mind."

The interview room was roughly the size of a cell, most of which was used as a storage closet. A rickety folding table sat at its center, two rusted folding chairs on each side. Laundry lockers ran along one wall, shelves lined with bottles of cleaning chemicals on another, and a damp, musty smell emanated from the mops and buckets in the back corner.

"He's short, too," she said, which was prison speak for an inmate with very little time remaining on his sentence. "He's only got about sixty days left."

"Unless he killed Menge."

"Do you really think it's possible?"

"Do *you?*"

"You mean is he capable? Who can ever say? But my intuition says no."

"Well, that says a lot," I said. "Did you know they were lovers?"

"Well, not *know* know, but yeah, I'd heard they were. That's not something either of them would ever tell me. In here love's a crime."

She was right. But I had never thought of it in quite that way.

"But I could be wrong," she added. "I'm not saying he didn't do it. And if he's using again, then I'd say it's quite possible he did. What have you got on him?"

"Their relationship for one," I said. "This kind of crime is usually committed by someone close to the victim."

"We hurt those we love," she said playfully, but then quickly grew quiet.

We were silent an awkward moment.

"Do *we* hurt each other?" she asked.

"Faithfully."

We fell silent again, each of us retreating into our own interior worlds.

Eventually, she said, "What else?"

"He didn't come to the service until after it had started. He wasn't wearing shoes—and somebody's shoes have blood on them. Since he had to go back to get them, he passed Menge's cell several times. And Pitts never popped his cell door—or so he says. Pitts also said it was Sobel and not Menge he let into the cell the first time. Only changed his story later after Potter persuaded him to."

"Pitts could be setting Sobel up," she said.

"Sure. Or Potter. And there were other guys who passed by his cell, but we've got to start somewhere."

The door opened and Chris Sobel shuffled in, cuffed and shackled, and sat down in the chair across the table from us.

"Chaplain, Ms. Rodden. I'm so glad to see you both. I'm really scared. I mean *really*. I haven't even been able to be upset about Justin because I'm so frightened."

"Of what?" Anna asked.

"That whoever killed Justin is either going to kill me or set me up for killing him."

"You think you're being set up?" I asked.

He nodded.

"How?"

"I'm not sure. It's more a feelin' than anything. But I'm perfect for it. Everyone knew we were in love. My cell's close to his. I overslept Mass. I've never done that before. I think maybe someone drugged my food. 'Course, I don't even know *how* it happened. Maybe I'm way off base here."

It was amazing how much Chris Sobel looked like Justin Menge. They weren't twins, but like Anna and me, they probably could've passed for siblings. He was thin, with little muscle and no fat, and his inmate blues hung loosely on him. His eyes were light brown with a faint metallic quality like rust in water set beneath full, coarse hair of the same color.

Anna leaned over and whispered, "Are you sure he's Chris Sobel and not Justin Menge?"

Chapter Seven

"You're *not?*" I whispered back to her, looking at him again.

"I'm not," she said. "I never realized how much they looked alike before they started wearing their hair the same way. Could Menge have killed Sobel and taken his place because he's about to get out?"

"Prints say no. It possible their records were swapped?"

"It's next to impossible."

It occurred to me again just how many of the inmates look alike. Like the girl "band" in Robert Palmer's iconic video of "Addicted to Love," very disparate-looking people can look nearly identical when dressed and made-up alike. With inmates, it's even more extreme. Not only do they have the exact same uniforms, but they all have the same bad haircuts, pale skin, and the thickness that comes from too much starch and too little exercise. But for all the similarities of inmates in general, the particular likeness of Chris and Justin was staggering.

Like all couples, the time Chris and Justin had spent together enhanced their similarities. Not only did they look alike, but their mannerisms, voice, speech, gestures, expressions had all become eerily identical.

It was like talking to a dead man.

"You know you don't have to talk to us," I said to Chris.

"No, I want to. I really do."

"Okay. Start with why you *really* missed the first part of Mass."

"I told you. I was asleep. I've never missed Mass before—"

"Exactly. On the one night you miss most of the service a murder is committed."

"I know how it looks, but I swear. That's why I think someone's setting me up."

"I can't help you if you lie to me."

"I'm not. Please."

"And what was that shit about holy ground? You've never attended the service without shoes before. Now all of a sudden you decide the ground is holy and you can't wear shoes to Mass."

"Ah, I'm, I'd been reading about Moses. I know it sounds crazy, but I really did have a sense that God was meeting with us in that quad and that I needed to hallow the fact."

I shook my head. "Even if I believed that, which I don't, I'd expect you to wear your shoes to the service, then take them off when it started."

He didn't say anything.

"You sayin' the whole quad's holy ground?"

"I don't know. I's just trying to honor God."

"Think about the timing. You did this on the night that Justin was murdered. Never before. It means you passed by Justin's cell at least three times. That's more than anyone else."

He shook his head, appearing frustrated. "I know how it looks, but I swear I didn't kill him."

"We're going to test your boots for blood. Sure you don't want to tell me now?"

"I don't have boots, just tennis shoes, but they don't have blood on 'em. I swear it. I went back, put them on, and then came back to the service. If they had blood on 'em, I'd've tracked it out onto the floor."

"We're checking it, too," I said.

"Well, if you find any, it won't be from my shoes. I loved Justin. We were planning on spending our lives together. Hoping to get married someday soon."

"That's great. And I'm sorry that won't happen now. I truly am. But your story doesn't add up. Sure you don't want to change it to the truth? It'll go a lot better for you, if you get in front of this."

"I can't believe you don't believe me," he said. "I'm telling the truth."

"Then, tell me this. Officer Pitts didn't buzz your cell open when you went back for your shoes, so how'd you get in?"

He opened his mouth to say something, then closed it. Tears formed in his eyes and he began to shake.

"Tell me."

"Just believe me," he said. "I didn't kill him."

"I'm gonna need a little more than your word."

"I can't," he said. "I just can't. I'm sorry."

When he'd left the room, Anna sat tapping a pencil against her pursed lips for a long moment. Finally, she said, "Whatta you think?"

"He's not giving us much," I said, "and lying about what he is. Gonna have to figure out a different way to come at him."

She nodded, then, dropping the pencil down on the table, stood up and said, "What's next?"

"I've got to go tell Paula Menge her brother was murdered, and—"

"How're you able to switch gears between investigating and ministry so easily?" she asked, shaking her head.

"You didn't let me finish."

"So finish. You're going to tell Paula Menge her brother was murdered *and* . . ."

"And ask why it happened on the only night she's visited him in the past four years."

As I pulled up in front of Paula's house, my phone rang.

It was Susan.

"Morning handsome."

"Morning," I said.

"How'd you sleep?"

"I didn't."

"Because I'm not there? That's so sweet."

"Can I call you back in a little while?"

"Sure. I miss you."

"I miss *you*," I said, and as I walked up Paula's driveway, I thought about just how much.

Having a second chance with Susan was a grace, and I was doing my best to be truly grateful for the opportunity. I was falling in love with her all over again, feeling in many ways like I had when we were newly together—except far more mature and selfless, far less desperate and needy.

Chapter Eight

"I knew something was wrong," Paula Menge said. "It'd been a long time, but I could still tell."

One of the more difficult parts of my job involved death notifications. As the chaplain, I notified inmates of deaths in their families and families of the deaths of inmates. Each had its own ministerial challenges, but when the bereaved was also a suspect it was especially difficult. I still had yet to find a way to fully integrate the seeming incompatibility of compassion and suspicion.

I was seated in Paula Menge's small living room in the soft glow of the early morning light streaming in through the windows.

Her house was small, but in the right neighborhood not far from downtown Panama City, and very nicely decorated with spotless white carpet and exquisite furniture with surfaces so polished they looked like mirrors.

Both the house and furniture looked inherited. Nice, but old—not old enough to be antique and too uniform to have been bought piecemeal recently.

"I'm so sorry," I said. "I can't help thinking that if I'd just checked on him sooner . . ." She shook her head.

We sat in silence for a moment, tears trickling down her cheeks.

She was wearing long white silk pajamas, her delicate tanned feet gathered up beneath her in the chair. Only the tips of her toes were still visible and I could see that the perfectly applied pink polish matched that of her fingernails.

Not for the first time I regretted not carrying a handkerchief. "Can I get you some tissues or—"

I broke off in mid-sentence, my awestruck eyes coming to rest on the painting across the room.

She turned and followed my gaze.

The white frame on the white wall held Chagall's "White Crucifixion."

Oil on canvas, the painting stood over five feet tall. At its center, an unblemished Christ is on a cross, a prayer shawl wrapped around his waist. He is surrounded by revolutionary red flags, a Nazi desecrating a synagogue, Ahasverus, the wandering Jew stepping over a burning Torah scroll, refugees in a boat, as figures from the Hebrew Bible hover overhead, lamenting in the desolation and darkness.

"You like it?" she asked, wiping her cheeks.

"It's my favorite Chagall, and I *love* Chagall."

"At first I thought it didn't provide enough contrast for . . . but now—"

"It's perfect. It's not the—"

"Original? No."

"It looks like it."

"Justin did it," she said.

I shook my head. "I knew he was talented, but I had no idea he was . . ."

"He can paint like anybody," she said. "But to me, his own stuff blows them all away. I own a small gallery downtown, you should drop by. I have a lot of Justin's work."

Interviewing women was never easy, but when they were beautiful, bereaved, and vulnerable—and wearing white silk pajamas, it was virtually impossible.

"How do you have so many of his paintings?"

Her brow furrowed. "I don't understand."

"You said you hadn't seen him in four years. I didn't think you were close."

"I had them before he went in. Justin's not one to hold a grudge. He's written me this whole time—even when I wouldn't write him back. Even when I wasn't sure whether he was guilty or not, he still let me be the exclusive rep of his work. I guess if I had more integrity I wouldn't have been making money on a man I thought might be guilty of child molestation, but . . ."

She sniffled.

"I was going to ask you if I could get you a tissue or . . ."

She shook her head.

"I would imagine his paintings will bring far more now."

She frowned as she nodded.

I waited, but she didn't say anything.

From out of the kitchen, an elegant all-white Turkish Angora cat strolled into the living room and over to Paula's chair. The white fur coat covering the animal's thick body was so shiny and silky it didn't look real. As the cat approached, Paula put her feet back on the floor, and with one graceful motion, the cat leapt into her lap.

"You suspect me of having something to do with his death, don't you?" she asked, her gaze leveled at me, her green eyes narrowed and intense.

I shrugged. "Haven't ruled anyone out."

She smiled. "I appreciate honesty, but I was nowhere near the institution when it happened. And it didn't happen in the visiting park, but in the PM unit where I've never been nor could ever go."

She didn't seem too upset, didn't seem like she was capable of getting too upset over anything, so I decided to press her a bit.

"Doesn't mean you didn't have something to do with it."

"And I'm the one with the money motive."

"Are you?"

"His half of this house, his half of the gallery, his place in Pine County, and all his art."

"People've killed for less," I said.

"A *lot* less. A conservative estimate would be over two million, and if his paintings take off like I think they will, it could be ten."

"That's a lot of cat food," I said.

She smiled, and seemed to purr contentedly, though I was pretty sure I was just imagining that.

"You haven't even told me how it happened."

I rectified that.

She listened to me intently, resting the full weight of her attention on me. She had a sultry, sleepy quality about her, a seeming unapologetic languidness that heightened her beauty and allure.

"So *you* don't even know *how* it happened. Not really."

I shook my head. "Not really."

"Well, I didn't have anything to do with it. Would you find out *who* did? For me."

"Why would you ask *me?*"

"Justin told me all about you. Said you used to be a cop and if I ever needed anything or if anything ever happened to him you were the one to call. He trusted you."

I felt a pang of guilt for not doing more for Justin—and not just last night.

"Why didn't you mention that when we spoke last night?"

She pulled back from me, body tensing, eyes wide, looking like a child in trouble. "I wish I had. I guess I just thought . . . well, Justin always had a little of the drama queen in him, you know? I just didn't take it as seriously as I should. I *did* ask you to check on him."

I nodded. She had and I had not—at least not soon enough.

"Will you find his killer for me?" she repeated, absently stroking the cat.

"I'll try to help . . . where I can."

"Thanks. I feel better already."

"Talk to me about him. I'd like to hear about him, his case, anything from your perspective."

"He was gay. I say that first because he would. It was often the first thing out of his mouth. He was very comfortable with it—with himself. Please don't hold that against him."

"I don't."

She studied me for a long moment, her eyes narrowing as her head came forward slightly.

"You don't, do you? I thought . . . I mean as a preacher I'd expect you to . . ."

"I'm not that kind of preacher."

"But—"

"I wish a minister was the last person you'd associate with judgment and condemnation."

"He was like that, too. Full of love for everyone. That was part of his downfall. He was too trusting. Thought everyone was basically good. But they're not, are they?"

"No," I said. "They're not."

"He was caged up with some real animals. At first, I was glad to hear he was in that protective unit thingy. At least until. . . . It didn't protect him, did it?"

She lifted the cat, shifting her weight in the chair in order to reposition her legs, and as she did, I was reminded again that all her movements had a distinctive feline quality. Sitting there together, animal and owner, the two favored in ways that could only be the result of spending an enormous amount of time together.

"He said that he was about to get out. Was gonna testify, get a reduction in his sentence. He was nervous about it—no, that's not it. Well it is, but there's more to it. He was nervous about testifying. But he was scared, too. He said if anything happened to him to tell you that it would be related to him testifying. I could tell he didn't want to do it. But someone he loved was getting out soon and he wanted to be with him."

"Did he tell you his name?"

"Chris."

"You're sure?"

She nodded.

"Last night you said he didn't seem like your brother. Is it possible that he wasn't?"

Her face lit up. "You mean Justin may not be dead?"

"Sorry. I meant during your visit."

"I didn't mean it literally. He was just so different." She paused for a moment, then locked her eyes onto mine. "Is there any chance that Justin's still alive?"

I shook my head slowly. "I would've never come here and told you he was dead if I wasn't sure. I even had FDLE compare his prints with his file after what you said about him being so different."

She nodded and looked away.

"If you still have any doubts or think it would help, I can arrange a viewing for you."

Without any warning, the cat leapt out of her lap and onto the floor next to me. Then, in one fluid motion, she stretched out and rolled over on her back. When she looked up at me, I took it as a signal that I was supposed to rub her, which I promptly did.

"That won't be necessary. It was him."

"You're sure?" I asked.

"Well, maybe I better. I don't want to, but it'll be the best way to get it out of my head."

"I'll set it up."

"Thanks."

"You know what he was testifying about?"

"No. He wouldn't tell me."

"Is there anything else you can think of?" I asked.

"Rest of the time we spent catching up on personal stuff."

Every time my hand neared the cat's head, she lowered her nose and nuzzled it, pressing her head hard against it. Anytime I stopped rubbing, she would tenderly drape her paws across my hand for a few moments, then nudge her head against my hand until I started caressing her again.

"What can you tell me about his case?"

"He was innocent. Set up by the sheriff of Pine County. Howard Hawkins—corrupt son of a bitch."

Something in the way she hissed the words made me think of a cat.

"It's why I wasn't happy about him being in the protective unit. He was in on a sex offense. But he was set up. Hawkins's own grandkids were the victims. I think it was somebody in the family, and Hawkins, homophobe that he is, set up Justin to take the fall because he wanted him out of Pine County. Justin was getting quite renowned—he couldn't just run him out or kill him without attracting a lot of attention."

"I've heard rumors about Pine County over the years. Why would Justin live there if it's so—"

"My mom's dad left him some land and a small house there. I told him to sell it and put the money toward a place somewhere else, but it was a beautiful place to paint—and he had been so happy there as a kid. It was my grandfather's place. Been in the family a long time."

"You really think he was innocent?"

"I've spent a lot of time checking things out. Even hired a PI who found out a good bit before taking off with my retainer. I know it in my heart, but I couldn't prove it. Not in court. It's Howard's brother. He's lost several jobs and now his family over it. But Howard protects him. *Protection*. I can't believe they put Justin in there with . . ."

"With who?" I asked, expecting to hear the name Juan Martinez.

She gave me a strange look. "I hear they keep all ex–law enforcement in there."

"Most. Yeah."

"Mike was a deputy."

I tried to recall an inmate named Mike in the PM unit, but was unable.

"Howard's son," she said. "Mike Hawkins."

At first, I couldn't respond. The whole reason for protective management was to keep inmates like Mike Hawkins and Justin Menge away from each other.

"You sure?"

She nodded.

We sat in silence a moment as I wondered how something like this could've happened.

Eventually, the cat got up and slowly sauntered out of the room and into the kitchen.

After a while, she said, "You don't do Catholic funerals, do you?"

I shook my head. "Pope won't let me. He's got this whole rule about having to be Catholic. I figured Father James would do it."

She shook her head, her jaw clenching, anger burning in her eyes. "He actually told Justin the Catholic Church would be better off if he were dead. I know it sounds crazy, but I keep thinking if Hawkins didn't kill Justin then that evil old priest did."

Chapter Nine

"Will you hear my confession, Father?" I asked.

"Why?" Father James asked, the medicinal smell of mouthwash on his breath. "You thinkin' about converting?"

There was movement in the other side of the dark wooden box confessional and with it the smell of cheap cologne.

"Call it professional courtesy. Besides, confession's not just good for the Catholic soul—and I'm part Catholic."

The morning sun was a soft pink glow illuminating the stained-glass depiction of the crucifixion above the choir loft, but the sanctuary was cold and dim except for the small flickering light of a few votive candles near the altar.

"Which part?" he asked.

"I can tell you which part it's *not*. It's not the celibate one."

He let out a small, forced laugh. "Okay," he said wearily. "Let me have it."

I did.

Afterward, he said, "Say five Our Fathers and ten Hail Marys."

As the sunlight grew, the pink glow was replaced by orange beams that pierced through the windows, driving the darkness from the sanctuary and breathing life into the now seemingly animated glass images. The confessional was less like a coffin now, though Father James was still a disembodied voice in the darkness.

"That *it*?" I asked.

"You're not exactly the last of the big-time sinners," he said. "I mean really, John, your life's pretty dull."

Often abrupt and off-putting, Father James lacked the social grace to be a parish priest anywhere much larger than Pottersville, and whether it was the result of too many years in the military, too many years of living alone, or just too many years was a source of speculation among both members of his church and the community.

Like me, he was rumored to have a drinking problem, but, unlike me, he didn't have much of one—or one at all—and I'd always guessed the rumor was more small southern town Protestant prejudice than anything else.

In the momentary silence, the loud creaks of the massive oak beams supporting the roof reverberated through the empty church.

I looked up at it.

"The roof's not going to fall in," he said.

"I don't know," I said. "I don't often darken the doors of . . ."

"A Catholic Church?"

"*Any* church."

"Why's that?"

"I work in an institution, but I'm not fond of them."

"The institutional church has much to dislike, but it's not all bad."

"Wasn't saying it was."

"Then what is it?"

"It's not just one thing—and it's me, it's not—"

"Just give me a few."

"Individuality, creativity, free thinking's not always encouraged."

"True. What else?"

"Answers. Too many answers. An answer for everything. Not enough questions. I prefer questions."

"Well then, go ahead and ask me yours. You're here to question me about the murder last night, right? Come on, let's get out of this box."

We stepped out of the confessional and took a seat on a pew near the back. The morning light filtering into the sanctuary was bright enough to reveal several coarse dog hairs on his old ill-fitting black suit. He wore a black clergy shirt that was a noticeably different shade from his suit, but without the white tab that made it a Roman collar. Whether the missing tab was intentional or not, it contributed to his unkempt appearance.

"Can you think out here?" I asked with a big smile.

A look of confusion on his red, puffy face was quickly replaced by widening eyes and a smile. "No wonder you don't fit. Too much of a smartass."

From the side door near the front, an elderly woman with a curved back hobbled in, genuflected as best she could, lit a candle, and knelt down to pray.

"So," he said softly, "whatta you want to know?"

"What can you tell me?"

"Not a damn thing."

"That's the spirit," I said. "Cooperation."

"I was concentrating on Mass. I didn't leave the altar during that time."

"See anybody around Menge's cell?"

"Chris Sobel went by a couple of times. I think maybe he stopped one time, but I'm not sure. I saw him in front of it, looked away . . . a moment later when I looked back he was still there, but maybe he'd been to his cell and he was passing by again."

"Or in Menge's," I said.

"He was acting so strange—coming so late, not wearing his shoes."

"What about Menge? Were you surprised he wasn't at Mass?"

"Yeah, but I was relieved, too. He's such a little pain. . . . He hated the church, but wouldn't leave it—and he hated it for all the wrong reasons. He was always interrupting me. I always dreaded goin' in there."

"Why do you?" I asked.

"Because," he said. "The little busybody wrote the bishop and demanded it. I don't have time for it. I'm serving three parishes as it is. None of 'em're very big, but they're spread out in three different counties. I spend most of my time in the car."

"Will you stop doing it now that he's dead?"

He nodded. "It's why I killed him. Nah, if I were willing to kill to get out of doing Mass, I'd be a mass murderer."

"Cute," I said.

"Better than your lame 'think outside the box' thing."

I shrugged. "Maybe."

The flickering candles backlit the elderly woman as she prayed, making her movements clipped and jerky, highlighting her deformities, and she looked like a minor character in an old, undercranked horror film.

"Did you go around to the cells prior to the service?"

He nodded. "Always do. Walk by each one so that everyone can see me. Let the regulars know I'm there. They're usually open."

He was right. Though the quad door always remained locked—or was supposed to—the cell doors for PM usually stayed open. In theory PM inmates weren't a threat to each other or the staff as much as they were threatened by the rest of the population. The only reason one of G-dorm's quads was used for PM inmates was because of how easy it was to isolate them from the rest of the population.

"They were closed and locked last night because of the threat I received," I said.

"Didn't do any good, did it?"

"You see anything strange when you walked by Menge's cell?"

He shook his head. "Didn't see anything. It was dark."

"Darker than the other cells?"

He thought about it. "Yeah, I guess it was. I really didn't think about it at the time."

"But you looked in?"

He nodded. "It was empty."

"Did you look at the floor?"

He shook his head. "I never walk right next to the doors. So I can only see from about the waist up. Plus the windowpane is so narrow."

I looked back at the elderly woman in the front. Even at this distance and in candlelight I could see that the fingers fondling the rosary were disfigured and arthritic.

"Anybody else outside the cells?"

"The man with you. Officer, the white one, and—"

"Potter?"

"Yeah. He was all over the place. Seemed hyper or upset about something. And a woman."

"A *woman?*"

The elderly woman looked back at us for the first time.

"Yeah," he whispered.

"Sorry," I said. "This is the first I've heard of a woman being down there. Was she an officer? In uniform? What?"

"No. She had on pants and a blouse."

"Was she staff? Wearing a DC name badge?"

"Not that I saw, but I only saw her from a distance."

"What'd she look like?"

His face contorted into a questioning frown. "Not sure exactly. I try not to look at attractive women too closely."

"So she was attractive?"

"Yeah. Kind of exotic. Cuban maybe. Do they grow this far north?"

"And this was all prior to Inspector Daniels and myself coming in?"

"Just before."

"What about the flyer? How long you been using it?"

"Couple of weeks."

"Who printed it?" I asked.

"I did. On my computer. Why?"

"One announcing the murder looked identical to it."

"How could an inmate do that?"

"Not sure," I said with a shrug. "Maybe one of the inmates in the PRIDE printing program did it for him. Even so, don't know how he'd get it into PM. Don't know how any of it was done at the moment."

"Then you're wasting a lot of valuable time."

"Oh yeah?"

"How can you hope to figure out *who* did it if you don't even know *how* it was done?"

CHAPTER TEN

"I still can't figure out how it was done," Pete Fortner, the institutional inspector, was saying. "I mean, it seems impossible. He's alone inside a locked cell."

Tom Daniels and I were sitting across from Pete in his office inside the security building of the institution. Tom had just given Pete the butt-chewing of his correctional life for not taking the flyer about the murder in PM seriously, and to make up for his negligence Pete was now trying to be helpful.

"It's just impossible," Pete added.

Daniels nodded. "That's what I'll put in my report, Pete. Inspector Fortner says it's impossible."

A short, pudgy man with unruly hair and a bushy mustache, Pete Fortner wore glasses, which he blinked behind a lot, out-of-date and too-tight slacks, and black athletic shoes left over from his former life as a coach and teacher at the local high school.

"What if somebody reached through the door?" he offered.

"Reached *through* the *door?*" Daniels said. "Solid steel?"

"Through the food slot. If Menge—"

He pronounced it as if it rhymed with hinge.

"It's Menge," I said. "Like thingy."

"If Menge was bent over or squatting down near the food slot the way they do, someone could've slit his throat while walking by."

"Sure," I said, "then Menge lies on the floor, bleeds out, then hops up and gets on his bunk."

I felt sorry for Pete, but his incompetence also made me angry. Perhaps if I weren't so sleep-deprived and frustrated I could have shown more patience, but as it was I had none of my usual restraint.

"Well, couldn't he?" he asked. "I mean not bled out all the way, but—"

I shook my head. "He was dead before he was moved to the bed—and had been for a while. Lividity was fixed."

"Besides," Daniels said, "the food tray slot was locked. We checked it."

"It could've been locked afterward," Pete said.

"You mean after the guy reached through with his eight-foot Stretch Armstrong arms and lifted the body onto the bed?"

"You're right. Sorry."

Slumping in his chair with his head down added extra chins to Pete's fleshy neck and made him look as if he had C-cup size breasts.

"It was a good thought, Pete," I said. "We've just got to keep tossing them out and working through them until we find one that'll fit."

Pete's office, like most of those in the prison, was cramped and nondescript. Four square cinder block walls painted pale gray, cold tile floor, one window, one door, one desk, one filing cabinet, and three chairs. He was seated behind his dented metal desk, which had been painted pea-green to match the two uncomfortable chairs Daniels and I sat in across from him.

Pete cleared his throat. "Did Potter tell you about the spoon thing?"

"Yeah," Daniels said. "But it's irrelevant. We know inmates got out of their cells to go to church. Getting out's not an issue. How the killer got *in* Menge's cell is."

"What if a spoon was used to keep his cell door from locking?"

"Yeah," Daniels said. "Menge came in and before he slammed his cell door shut, he put a spoon into the locking mechanism so he could get murdered. So you're saying I gotta charge him with conspiracy and as an accessory?"

Fortner started to say something, but stopped, blinked a couple of times, pushed his glasses up on his nose, and looked down. When he looked up again, he said, "Maybe he was supposed to meet someone. Let them into his cell briefly on their way to church or later that night after lights out."

"We were right there," Daniels said, jerking his head toward me. "We'd've seen."

Pete sat up a little and adjusted his glasses. "I still think it's the food slot," he said.

"That's because you're an idiot, Pete," Daniels said. "Even if he was killed through the food slot, which he wasn't, how was the body moved from the floor to the bed?"

Pete suddenly lit up.

"You havin' a thought or a wet dream?"

"What if the sister slipped him something during the visit? Some kind of poison that made him bleed through all his—"

"He only bled through the big slit in his neck."

"What if it wasn't a slit from the outside, but the poison eating a hole in his throat from the inside?"

Daniels sat up, his face growing animated. "I think you're onto something," he said.

Pete smiled and sat a little straighter.

"But what if rather than poison, she impregnated him with some sort of alien that gestated awhile before bursting out of his neck. Remind me to have someone check the cell for aliens."

"You think there could be more than one?" I asked.

Daniels nodded.

I thought about how often Daniels, Pete, and I had sat in similar circumstances discussing a case, tossing out ideas, and how tense it used to be. This was different. Daniels was different. Everything, including his anger and frustration with Pete, was out in the open. There was none of the usual subtext or underlying tension. It was refreshing. I was actually enjoying working with him, and it gave me real hope for my relationship with his daughter. Maybe we could be the family Susan wanted after all.

"Anything else you want to run past us, Pete?" Daniels asked.

"How about my resignation?"

"No, you hang around a while and take your medicine. A man is dead because you didn't take the threat seriously. I'm not saying we could've stopped it, but the chaplain shouldn't've been the only one who tried."

"You're right. I'm sorry."

"Okay," Daniels said. "We know the door was locked when Pitts checked it."

"No," I said. "We know that's what he says."

"Good point."

Pete smiled.

"And why'd he leave the officers' station and come down to the quad to do a walk-through during the service when you, me, and Potter were already down there?"

"Good question."

"Maybe he was coming down to lock the door," I added. "It's possible that the killer had an accomplice. It's a somewhat sophisticated crime."

"God, I hope an officer's not involved," Fortner said.

"We know when Menge arrived back at the dorm and went into his cell," Daniels said. "We saw him. What else do we know?"

"That approximately twenty-five minutes later he was found

murdered alone in a locked cell," I said.

"Yeah?" Daniels said.

"That's it."

"Then we don't know shit," Fortner said.

"Yeah," I said, "but at least we're used to it."

"We also know who went anywhere near his cell," Daniels said, pulling a folded piece of paper from his coat pocket. "Inmates: Chris Sobel, Milton White, Jacqueel Jefferson, Carlos Matos, Juan Martinez, and Mike Hawkins. Staff: Tom Daniels, John Jordan, Michael Pitts, and Billy Joe Potter. Volunteer: the priest, James McFadden."

Pete smiled. "The priest did it."

"I hear there wasn't any love lost between them," Daniels said.

"You say Hawkins?" I asked.

"Yeah. He came in from medical while we were there and went to his cell. Why?"

"Menge's sister said Mike Hawkins was a deputy in Pine County where his dad's sheriff and that they're the ones who set Justin up."

Daniels narrowed his eyes and shook his head slowly, then turned to Fortner. "Did you know that?"

"No, sir."

"Why the hell not? How could you not know a cop was in the same unit with a man his department put away?"

"Only way I'd know is if an investigation had been initiated by a classification officer because one of the inmates involved requested it."

"Well, whoever missed this can kiss his correctional career goodbye."

Please don't let it be Anna, I thought.

"Did Martinez know Justin was going to testify against him?" I asked.

Daniels shrugged. "I didn't think so, but there's really no way to know for sure. We have to consider it a possibility. After all, the notebook with his notes and written testimony was taken. As far as I can tell, that's the only thing missing from the cell."

I nodded. "So Hawkins, Martinez . . . and we know Sobel had a connection with him."

"Of the most intimate kind," Fortner said.

"There're probably all kinds of connections we're not even aware of yet."

"We've gotta divide 'em up and do interviews," Daniels said.

"But it doesn't really matter who's got a motive," Fortner said, "if none of 'em have means or opportunity. We still don't have any idea *how* it was done."

"That's true," Daniels said, "but the chaplain's working on it."

"I am?"

"At least we know *when* it was done. And just maybe we can find out *who* did it by the time we find out *how* they did it." He looked over at me. "You know how they did it yet?"

"Not quite. Give me another minute."

"We've got to figure out how that cell door was unlocked," Pete said.

"And how it was locked back," Daniels said.

"And how a room full of people, including the inspector general of the department, didn't see it," I said.

We grew silent a moment, and a possible scenario occurred to me.

"What if the door wasn't unlocked after Menge went in?"

"Huh?" Pete said.

"Maybe the killer didn't have to get in at all—merely get out."

Daniel's eyebrows shot up.

"Maybe the killer was already in the cell waiting for Menge to return."

"All the cells were open earlier in the day," Pete added.

"Speaking of which," I said to Daniels. "Did you see a woman in the quad when you were in there earlier?"

He shook his head. "Why?"

"Father James said there was one down there."

"Whoever she was, she didn't come out of Menge's cell while we were there."

"Still like to talk to her."

"Sure, but you were saying the killer was waiting inside Menge's cell when he got back from his visit. He kills him, then when it's time for Mass, he calls out the cell number and goes like everybody else."

"Just thinking out loud, but it doesn't fit."

"Why not? It's the best theory so far."

"If an inmate had been in Menge's cell rather than his own, count wouldn't have cleared."

"Could've been faked," Daniels said.

"Maybe."

"Officer counting could be an accomplice."

"The killer would've been covered in blood. Besides, Potter didn't call out Menge's cell number."

Pete said, "If it was the woman the priest saw, there any way she could've snuck out while you guys were looking at something else?"

Daniels shook his head. "One of us was watching the area the whole time."

I added, "Couldn't've gotten past *all* of us, through the quad door *and* the dorm door without being seen."

"Empty cells on the end," Pete said. "She could have slipped into one of them."

"Yeah?"

"Could've waited until later and slipped out of the dorm."

Daniels pulled back and considered Pete. "That's not bad. You trying to make up for your earlier stupidity?" He looked at me. "Whatta you think?"

I smiled at Pete. "It's possible she's still hiding in there right now. I'll go check."

CHAPTER ELEVEN

Ducking beneath the crime scene tape, I entered the PM unit to find Merrill Monroe inventorying the property in each man's cell. A light sheen of sweat covered his dark brown skin and glistened in the light when he moved. He held a clipboard with one hand and a pen in the other, and his massive biceps stretched the short sleeves of his light brown uniform as he worked.

" 'S up?" he said, looking up from his clipboard.

"Not the life expectancy of PM inmates."

One of my favorite people on the planet, Merrill Monroe was the best friend I'd ever had. Our friendship had been forged over two decades of being outsiders in our own homes and town. Though we'd known each other nearly all our lives, and his mom had kept me for a while when I was a child, it wasn't really until early adolescence that we gravitated toward each other—neither of us fitting in with the rednecks, thugs, geeks, or jocks.

"You haven't seen an exotic woman in civilian clothes hiding out down here, have you?"

"Exotic women don't hide from me."

"What I've heard."

"What's her story?" he asked.

"Priest said he saw one last night."

"And you think she's still down here?"

"Not really. Mind if I look around?"

"It's your crime scene," he said with a smile. "I just work here."

I walked slowly around the quad, the events of last night drifting up from my subconscious—fractured images, out of sync and sequence, flickering in the dark theater of my mind.

I saw Justin Menge walk from the quad door to his cell. Heard the electronic buzz and metallic pop of the lock. Saw him walk in. Heard the cell door clang closed behind him. Saw his blood seeping out from beneath the cell door.

How? How could I've seen and heard all that? But I had. I knew I had.

Justin Menge had died alone in a locked cell. How could it be murder? But it was.

I became aware of being stared at, and looked up through the inside glass wall of the quad and into the wicker beyond to see the day-shift officer eyeing me suspiciously.

I waved to him.

He returned my wave and went back to work.

Michael Pitts had been up there—well, some of the time—with a better view than anyone involved. Had he seen more than he had let on?

In addition to Pitts's God's-eye view, Potter, Daniels, Father McFadden, and I were right here in the quad. The killer took an awful chance committing the crime when he did. Why? Was it the risk that excited him? Was this crime as much about how he did it as who he killed?

Walking over to Justin's cell, I stood staring at the blood-stained floor. How had his blood wound up in one place and his body in another? Was there religious significance to the crime as the flyer suggested or was that just a cover?

Glancing over at Chris Sobel's cell, I thought again about how suspiciously he'd acted—coming to Mass late, shoeless, taking so long to get his shoes that he missed most of the service. Had Pitts really not unlocked his cell door? No one was closer to Justin—physically or emotionally.

I became aware of Merrill standing beside me. At six feet, I wasn't a small person, but standing next to Merrill I felt like one. And it wasn't that he towered over me. He was only a few inches taller than I was. And it wasn't his broad shoulders, narrow waist, and enormous muscles. It was his presence. His strength—not limited to his physique—was palpable.

"Got it figured out yet?" he asked.

I smiled and shook my head. "So many problems to work out."

"Like what?"

"Like the procedures Pitts and Potter followed—well, failed to follow—are they involved or are they really that incompetent? Why do it when we're all down here? Must've wanted an audience, but why? And how did Menge, Martinez, and Hawkins wind up in the same quad? Was that just an oversight? Not to mention I can't figure out for sure *how* it was done."

"Whatta Martinez and Hawkins got to do with it?"

I told him.

"I'm surprised Daniels ain't arranged for Martinez to slip in the shower and fall on a shank or something. Mike Hawkins is Howard's son?"

"You know the esteemed sheriff of Pine County?"

He nodded. "Menge may've been innocent after all."

My eyebrows arched.

"Just 'cause it usually a person of color Howard be fuckin' over, don't mean he don't know how to do it to a white boy."

Merrill's speech patterns confounded most people. He was capable of nearly flawless formal register *and* pitch-perfect rural South Ebonics, and he shifted between them effortlessly, often to punctuate a point or to be funny, but occasionally for no discernable reason at all.

"So he's not down with the brothers?" I asked.

He shook his head. "More into keepin' a brother down."

"How well you know him?"

"We've had a run-in a time or two. Wouldn't mind renewing our association. He's got that whole absolute power, absolute corruption thing goin'. Small county. Do what the hell he want. Never been caught doin' shit—how the hell he let his son get caught?"

I shrugged.

"To make sure when Menge got out it in a bag?"

"Could be."

"How the hell they both wind up in PM?"

"I'm trying to find out."

We were quiet a moment.

"Why they got you searching the cells?" I asked.

"You know," he said with an elaborate shrug and an attempt at nonchalance.

Because of an investigation he had helped me with last spring, Merrill's correctional career had stalled. He was paying the price for something I did, but what bothered me even more was that Merrill not only accepted but expected it. Injustice was part of his existence. It was his worldview, forged in the fires experience, hammered into him day after day by a nation that dared to affirm his equality with a straight face.

"Sorry," I said.

He shook his head.

I gestured toward the quad. "Found anything interesting yet? Anything out of the ordinary?"

He looked down at his clipboard. "Sobel's missing his boots and a shirt."

I nodded as I thought about it.

"A clue?"

"Just might be," I said. "Menge missing anything?"

"No, he got all his shit. 'Course, don't mean shit to him now."

CHAPTER TWELVE

Beneath tall, twisting oak trees, their roots spreading out in all directions, disappearing into sandy soil, I sat on a wooden-slat bench eating shrimp creole out of a Styrofoam cup from the Cajun Café.

Above me, the oaks' enormous branches created a thick canopy, from which Spanish moss waved in the breeze.

I was having a late lunch alone in the lakeside park near the center of town.

Lunch options in Pottersville for a bachelor who didn't cook were limited to a no-name café featuring traditional southern fried fare; Rudy's, a cross between Waffle House and the no-name café; Sal's Pizzeria, and now, the Cajun Café, a taste of New Orleans.

Unlike the other restaurants in town, the Cajun Café could make it anywhere—not just in a small town with limited dining options, but, thank God for her mercies, the local lady who operated it only wanted to live in Pottersville.

The midday sun had burned the chill off the morning air and heated up the day, but beneath the tree branch canopy it was cool and comfortable.

Numb inside and weary even before Justin was murdered, I was now sleep deprived and frayed. Beside me on the bench was Thomas Moore's book *Dark Nights of the Soul,* which, not for the first time, I was rereading. I was in need of help, of spiritual nourishment, and few people had provided that for me over the years as much as Thomas Moore. His gentle approach was soothing, but like most things these days, it didn't seem to be penetrating, getting past my mind, down to the deeper parts of my being.

I had come to the park in search of silence and serenity. I had come to the right place. Now, if I could just let them in.

Before me, beyond the swollen bases of the cypress trees encircling it, the water of the lake was still and smooth. Behind me, the slow-moving traffic on Main Street created a breezy resonance that sounded like the tide intermittently rolling to shore. To my right, stay-at-home moms watched their toddlers playing on the enormous jungle gym, their laughter and squeals rising to meet the twirps and songs of birds in the trees.

I took in a deep breath, held it, then let it out very slowly.

The creole was hot and spicy, thick with chunks of onion, tomato, bell peppers, and large Gulf shrimp, the sun-dappled park peaceful, the breeze cool and refreshing, the moment perfect in every way . . . until my dad and brother walked up.

"Eating alone's bad for the digestion," Jake, my younger brother, said.

"I'm not alone."

He rolled his eyes.

He assumed I was talking about God, and, though I had been referring to the living Eden in which I sat, ultimately I didn't see much difference, so I didn't say anything.

Two years my junior, Jake was a couple of inches shorter and about fifty pounds heavier. Though he was in his early thirties, his thinning hair and soft body gave him the hayseed in middle-age look so many of the guys around here had.

"How're you doin', Son?" Dad asked.

Jack Jordan, the sheriff of Potter County, had somehow managed to have a son as different from him as if I'd been adopted. Though it couldn't have been easy, he'd been extremely understanding my whole life, but his recent verbal jabs let me know he was beginning to resent my differences and independence. He appreciated me as an investigator—though he couldn't understand why I wouldn't work for him, and I knew it hurt him—but he couldn't understand me as a minister, a prison chaplain. To his practical way of thinking, I was a fanatic, a wishful thinker—a daydreamer who spent too much time on frivolous things that didn't matter.

As different as I was from Dad, I was far more so from Jake.

"I heard about the inmate who was killed last night," he added.

"Why didn't you say anything to us?" Jake asked.

Dad said, "FDLE notified us after they were well into the investigation. We always cooperate, and they would have processed the scene either way, but it seems like I'm always the last to know anytime there's a crime committed in the prison. Any idea why?"

I shrugged. "I honestly think it's just lack of coordination. Not intentional. I should've called you, but this is the first time I've even paused since it happened, and I figured someone else already had."

He nodded and thought about it.

As sheriff, Dad was the chief law enforcement officer of Potter County, and was normally the first called in when a crime was committed. Ordinarily, there was a lot of interdepartmental cooperation—crime scene and lab work was processed by FDLE, crimes on the river or in the woods always included the Florida Fish and Wildlife Conservation Commission, but the sheriff's department was always involved, usually in charge.

"FDLE's letting Tom Daniels run with it," I said.

"Your other *daddy?*" Jake said.

A redneck who could hold his liquor, and often did, Jake had always seen my addiction as a sign of my weakness, and I think a lot of his anger toward our alcoholic mother came out as disdain for me. It'd explain the rage he continually directed toward me much more adequately than sibling rivalry.

"You helpin' him with it?" Dad asked, ignoring Jake.

I nodded.

"Do me a favor and keep me informed. Seems like I'm the sheriff of this entire county except for the land the prison's on."

I nodded again.

"People're beginning to talk. Election's only a year away."

One of the things I had always most respected about Dad over the years was that very few of his decisions were dictated by political expediency, but lately that seemed to be changing, and I found myself looking at him differently, wondering if it was because he was getting older or the talk that he might have real competition for the first time in a couple of decades.

"What've you got so far?"

I told him.

"You were there when it happened?"

I nodded.

"Any idea who did it?"

"Don't even know *how* it was done. Yet."

A loaded log truck raced by on Main Street, its enormous diesel engine protesting the grinding of its gears. The sun ducked behind a cloud, and the day turned dark, the wind coming off the water cold.

To our right, a kid who looked big enough to be in school began banging on one of the metal support poles of the jungle gym with a stick. The noise was loud and annoying.

Jake turned toward the playground. "Hey, kid. Cut that shit out."

Dad winced, but ignored him. "You need to let us help you," he said.

"How?"

"Starting with a little piece of information for background. My department would be a valuable resource for you and the prison if you'd just let us."

"I know. I do."

"We responded to a call from Michael Pitts's house less than a week ago."

My raised eyebrows asked the question.

"Call came from his wife. Nothing much came of it, though it should've—I didn't know about it until after the fact."

"Happenin' a lot lately," Jake said.

"They extending him a little law enforcement courtesy. Said it wasn't nearly the worse case they'd seen, but there was no doubt that it was a case of domestic abuse."

CHAPTER THIRTEEN

Michael Pitts was maybe one of five of the very best football players Pottersville had ever produced. A quarterback with an amazing arm who was even more dangerous on the run, it was Michael's field generalship that most impressed the college scouts. He won the state championship for 1-A schools two years in a row with a team that shouldn't have made it past the district playoffs.

In high school, Michael Pitts was a living legend, the hero of every young boy—boys who had no doubt he would finally put their small town on the map.

But all that seemed like a lifetime ago now.

I found Michael Pitts where he spent every fall afternoon— sitting alone in the bleachers of the high school football field intently watching boys with a fraction of his talent practice half as hard as he had.

He nodded at me when I walked up, but continued to focus on the practice without saying anything. Beside him, I sat in silence, waiting until he was ready to speak.

On the field before us, six enthusiastic men tried to motivate twenty-six teenagers who were not. Only three of the men were coaches. The others—a hardware store owner, a banker, and a father—were merely attempting to be close to what the boys unknowingly had in abundance.

Next to me, Michael Pitts shook his head.

"All the talent in the world can't make up for attitude," he said. "But attitude go a long way in making up for talent."

I nodded.

"As things get better for these kids, they get softer, attitudes get worse. Got no motivation. Want the easy way outta everything. Everything's somebody else's fault. Everybody owe 'em somethin'."

He was right of course, but I knew that much of the anger he expressed was at the injustice of his own unfulfilled promise, and not merely at the blatant lack of character in the boys before him.

I studied him again sitting in this place that must be haunted for him. Did he hear the roar of the crowd? Smell the sweat and dirt and hamburger grease as it dripped down from the patties and sizzled on the charcoal? Did he taste the blood and bile and Gatorade? Was he thinking the best part of his life was over?

"Try to talk to 'em, but they won't listen."

We didn't either when we were their age, I thought.

The last of the setting sun backlit the small figures in practice pants and old torn and ripped jerseys, the plastic smash of their helmets and pads reverberating through the stadium like cheers on game day.

"You ever think about coaching?" I asked.

He shook his head. "I can do it," he said, continuing to stare straight ahead at the practice, "or could, but I can't teach somebody else how to do it."

I nodded. "It wasn't something you were taught."

He nodded.

The something that he hadn't learned—the gift—had been taken from him just as quickly as it had been given. Cruelly, it had been his just long enough to make him dream.

During the last game of his last season, Michael Pitts had broken his ankle. One wrong step and the road less traveled was no longer his to choose.

God created the world out of chaos, I thought, *and sometimes the chaos shows through.*

"Do you like being a correctional officer?" I asked, though I knew of no one who did.

He shook his head. "Hate it."

I didn't ask the obvious question, but he answered it anyway with a question of his own.

"What else'm I gonna do?"

Most correctional officers I knew would ask the same question.

"Before I started," he continued, "I was roofing with my uncle. Minimum wage. No benefits. No security."

Limited options, I thought. *Why they build prisons in rural areas.*

One of the coaches blew his whistle and the players lined up on the goal line and started running wind sprints. No one, not a single player nor any of the adults, had acknowledged Michael Pitts's presence the entire time I had been here, and I wondered if it was that way every afternoon.

"I hear you're a good officer," I said, just to be saying something.

"Compared to assholes like Potter. Look, I'm gonna tell you some things 'cause I know you're gonna hear 'em sooner or later anyway."

I nodded.

"Like I said, one day I'm roofing, six months later I'm walking inside a prison. I don't know exactly what I expected, but—well, let's just say I wasn't ready. Wasn't prepared for what I found inside."

"None of us are," I said.

"In training—what little you can get in six months—the main thing they taught us was to hate inmates. They brought a lady in to teach us CPR, but as soon as she left, the officer training us said the way to give CPR to an inmate was to remain standing, stomp on his chest with your boot, and blow air down at him. But I don't hate inmates. And I actually did CPR on one. Saved his life."

He took in a deep breath and let it out slowly.

"Something other officers'll never let me live down."

Wind sprints completed, the players took a knee around the coaches at center field, the other men standing close by.

"I didn't go in hating inmates, but the longer I'm inside . . . way they act . . ."

"Not all of them."

"Some actually act like human beings. But most of them act like animals. I don't know how much more I can take."

He didn't start out hating inmates, but that had changed. The abyss was looking back at him, and in the process of working with monsters he was becoming one. Maybe slowly, but inevitably we all were.

Eventually, practice ended and the stadium was once again as empty as the dreams it held.

"What you afraid I'll hear?"

"Sometimes we have to give an inmate a tune-up. Amazing what a little attitude adjustment'll do. Only thing some of them respond to."

I nodded.

"When I first started administering them, it was almost surgical. I never did it when I was angry, but more and more I's always angry. Grew to hate the men more and more, the tune-ups I gave them got worse and worse." He turned to me suddenly. "I'm not a bad man."

"I know that."

"I've done some bad things."

"To Menge?"

He nodded.

"Did he retaliate?"

97

He nodded again.

"How?"

"Got me on video. Blackmailing me with it."

CHAPTER FOURTEEN

"How the *hell* a inmate make a video of a officer?" Merrill asked.

I had run into him at Sal's Pizzeria, a small storefront next to the Dollar Store with a kitchen and a takeout counter, the three round tables placed next to the plate-glass window an afterthought. It was noisy, dusty from yeast and flour, and cramped. Sal preferred carry-out customers.

Merrill and I, the only patrons in the establishment, were sitting at the center of the three tables near the front window.

"How the hell an inmate video *anything?*" he said again.

I recounted Pitts story to him.

About a year ago, video cameras were placed throughout the institution to record all use-of-force incidents because of the number of inmates alleging abuse and retaliation by correctional officers. What they captured was intended to corroborate the written reports and witness statements that had previously been all that was entered into evidence.

Permanent surveillance cameras were mounted only in confinement—one on each end of the hallway, showing the front of the cell doors but not inside them. Every other post in the institution was dependent on handheld camcorders, which were kept, along with blank discs and batteries, in a case with a seal on it in a secure location. Each week the seal was broken, the camera and battery checked, and the broken seal submitted along with an incident report to Central Office.

Of course, only a few of the cases of use-of-force can be

predicted. Most erupt with little warning and no time to wait for a video camera to be retrieved from a secure location. Consequently, most of what was captured was after an inmate had been subdued. But once the camera was out it must follow the inmate through his post use-of-force medical exam and his placement in an appropriate cell. And occasionally, as in the case of tune-ups, the officers involved delayed the retrieval of the camera until what it captured wouldn't get them indicted.

Still, they had to video at least some portion of every use-of-force, which was how Justin Menge caught Michael Pitts in the act.

Justin had orchestrated every aspect of it from the very beginning, but he had to have help to accomplish it, which Chris Sobel, Jacqueel Jefferson, and Milton White gladly provided.

Pitts had taken Menge into the empty shower cell, which was where most tune-ups took place so any blood spilled could be washed down the drain. The door to the shower cell, unlike the others, consisted of bars—bars through which Menge's cuffs had been threaded.

Leaving an officer in the wicker, Potter had brought the video camera down into the PM quad and sat it on the table to wait until, at the end of the tune-up, Pitts would uncuff the beaten and provoked Menge and video him fighting back.

But while Pitts was busy with Menge, Potter got distracted by a fight between Milton White and Jacqueel Jefferson just behind the quad on the small PM rec yard. The staged fight provided enough time for Chris Sobel to grab the camera and video Michael Pitts beating, some would say torturing, Justin Menge.

"Real smart sons a bitches working G-dorm," Merrill said, shaking his head.

"It was a good plan."

"Not if it got his ass killed."

"True."

Sal had finished Merrill's pizza before mine, and he offered me a slice while we talked, but, being the purist I am, I declined. A pizza should have meat—preferably pepperoni and bacon—but no vegetables, and certainly no form of fruit, and I told him so.

"You think the disc really exists?" Merrill asked.

I shrugged.

"Sounds like prison legend to me."

"Maybe," I said, "but the scenario he described seems plausible. And if there's not a disc, why would Pitts make it up? An inmate trying to deflect suspicion off himself onto Pitts, sure, but why Pitts? Why tell a lie to implicate yourself?"

Outside, a woman in a faded flowery housecoat, soiled white tube socks, pink slippers, and a white straw cowboy hat with a Rebel Flag button pinned to it pulled up in her motorized wheelchair, which she drove around town in like a car. Her sun-damaged skin was wrinkled and leathery, making her look far older than she was, and she had the soft, shapeless mouth of a person with no teeth.

"So where's the disc now?" Merrill asked.

"No one seems to know. Pitts thought he'd confiscated it from Menge's cell during a shakedown, but later when he tried to watch it at home it was a National Geographic disc about gorillas."

Merrill smiled appreciatively. "Even money Pitts and Potter missed the message."

I nodded.

When the woman in the wheelchair reached the door, I stood and held it for her, and she spoke to me by name as she rolled into the restaurant. Like many people around town, I knew of her, knew quite a bit about her, but couldn't recall her name—if I ever knew it. Years ago, perhaps before I was even born, her father had kicked her out of their house at the age of seventeen because she was in love with a young black man. Her dad had died recently—without ever having reconciled with his daughter, though thirty years later she and the young man he hadn't approved of were still together.

"Where you think the disc is?" Merrill asked as I returned to the table. "I've been over every inch of G-dorm."

I shrugged. "Don't know, but I bet it turns up before this thing is over."

"You think Pitts coulda killed Menge?"

I nodded.

"Why tell you about the disc?"

I shrugged. "Preemptive strike? May think we already have it or figures we'll find it eventually. If he killed Justin, it was a smart move."

When I got home that night, the Prairie Palm II, the abandoned second phase of a planned mobile home community I live in, was still and quiet. That was just the way I liked it—which was a good thing since it was rarely anything else. The trailer I lived in was the only one in the failed park. I picked it up cheap when I first moved back down here after the divorce—or what I thought was the divorce—and it had steadily grown on me since.

Now that I had a few more options—just a few on a state prison chaplain's salary—I could move if I wanted to, but I didn't want to. There was something very appealing, and appropriate I felt, about living in a rundown house trailer that hadn't been nice even when it was new. I liked that I, who so often felt like a failure, lived in a failed subdivision. I liked the peace and quiet, and much of the time, I liked the solitude.

After putting the pizza box, half a pizza still in it, into the refrigerator, I carried Thomas Moore's *Dark Nights of the Soul* to the living room and collapsed onto the couch with it. For a long moment, I just laid there, clutching the book to my chest, my weary mind trying to process thoughts, my slow, steady breathing the only sound in the room.

All around me were stacks of books—on shelves, on the floor, on the tables, and I felt comforted just being back in their presence.

For a while I thought about the counseling sessions I had squeezed in between the first steps of the investigation today. I had been distracted, preoccupied with Justin's murder and the pursuit of his killer, and I felt guilty. Much of the time, I felt like an adequate enough chaplain, and there were many inmates and staff members who told me I was good, but when I was involved in a homicide investigation I was nearly useless.

Murder cases were overwhelming. They had a tendency to engulf every facet of life, and I knew Justin's would be no different. I also knew I'd be involved—and would've been even if Daniels hadn't asked me. I'd put a temporal mystery ahead of my work helping people investigate and experience eternal ones. I'd be neglectful of many of my duties and distracted while performing the others, and I'd feel guilty, but I wouldn't stop. The best I could hope for was a quick resolution to the case so I could return more of my attention to the needs of my wayward flock.

But when I did, what would I have to offer them?

I felt dead inside—and did before Justin's murder, my missed night of sleep, and all that had transpired today. I had gone through periods like this before, the winter seasons of my life and relationship with God, but this seemed different, more severe, more a state than a season. I was concerned. I opened the book hoping Moore could give me some encouragement, reassurance, and answers, and was asleep before I had reached the end of the page.

★ ★ ★ ★ ★

I was aware of the phone ringing a few moments before I could resurface into consciousness and answer it.

"I wake you?"

It was Susan. Even in my groggy state, I was instantly happy. Just hearing her voice did something deep inside me. Buoyed me up somehow.

"I was reading."

"In your dreams?"

"Sorry I haven't called you back."

"But you've been too busy reading?"

"I love you."

"I'm so glad we got another chance," she said.

"Me too. Not many people do."

"I know. I've been thinking how lucky we are. I mean really, *really* lucky."

We were quiet a moment.

Eventually, I said, "We're gonna get it right this time."

"Already are. Now, go back to sleep. Talk to you tomorrow."

CHAPTER FIFTEEN

When I reached the chapel the next morning, Daniels and Fortner were waiting for me. Like mine, Daniels's bloodshot eyes had a glazed look underscored by dark circles. He moved slowly, like a man with a hangover, which I hoped was just the result of sleep deprivation. Pete just looked his normal unkempt self, his ill-fitting clothes slightly wrinkled, his curly hair all over the place.

As we neared my office, I could hear my phone ringing.

"Hello, handsome," Susan said when I answered it.

"Hey."

With Pete and especially Daniels present I was guarded and restrained, and I wondered if she could hear it in my voice.

"Are you naked?" she asked.

"You wouldn't want me to be. One, I'm in a prison. And two, I'm with your dad."

Mentioning Daniels to Susan in his presence caused a palpable tension, though I wasn't sure if it were in the room or just in me. There was something about their relationship, an undercurrent beneath the overt and often demonstrative love—something found in the dynamic between most addicts and their children—a contradiction between the text and subtext that gave me a dull ache deep inside.

Part of the problem was that Susan had never been completely honest about her feelings. In fact, I often thought her fierce loyalty and effusive affection were the result of the guilt she felt at what seemed to her to be betrayal.

"He said you two were working together again. How's that going?"

"Better than usual."

"That's not saying much."

"Far better."

"I so want you two to get along."

"I'll do what *I* can," I said.

"Hey, this investigation going to mess up our weekend together?"

"You'll have to ask the boss."

"You ask him."

I moved my mouth away from the receiver, but didn't cover it. "Is this investigation going to mess up my plans with your daughter this weekend?"

He shook his head. "I value my life too much to let that happen."

"Good," she said. "See you tonight?"

"Or tomorrow," I said, floating it out there to see what her reaction would be.

"Tomorrow?"

"And tomorrow and tomorrow and tomorrow."

"Good try, but you're not gettin' off that easy. I still want you to move back up here."

I didn't say anything.

"We'll talk about it this weekend. Don't wait until tomorrow. Come tonight. I love you."

"I love *you*," I said, and we hung up.

It felt awkward telling Susan I loved her in front of Daniels, but when I looked at him, he was smiling.

"Got the prelim autopsy results."

"Yeah?"

"And you're not gonna believe this. The victim bled to death."

"They sure?" I asked.

"Sometimes it's hard to tell with these things. That's why we have the professionals. They used words like death occurred as the result of excessive blood loss—"

"I'll say it was excessive," Fortner said.

"Due to lacerations of the jugular vein and carotid artery."

"So, he got his throat cut," Fortner said.

"Yeah," Daniels said. "It means he got his throat cut."

"What about time of death?" I asked.

"Say they can't be sure."

"What about the lividity and blanching? Condition of the blood?"

He shrugged. "Got an approximate time of death from what we saw. And it's a lot closer than they could've gotten if we hadn't been there."

I thought about it. There was something about the body and the blood that bothered me, but I couldn't quite figure it out. "Doesn't add up."

"It will. Soon as we figure it out. I mean, not everything will. It never does in a homicide investigation—you know that, but we'll know most of the particulars. But let's back up and get real basic. Why do people commit murder?"

Pete seemed to think about it. "Possible motives for murder are profit, revenge, jealousy, to conceal a crime, or avoid humiliation and disgrace."

"You forgot one. What about homicidal mania?"

"Always a strong possibility in here," I said.

"Exactly. Now how about some theories on how."

"One way or another the cell door had to be opened," Pete said. "Either somebody was already in the cell and had to get out after he killed him or he had to get in after Menge went in."

"And just because we didn't see it doesn't mean it didn't happen," Daniels said, looking over at me.

I nodded.

"I know we probably won't come up with something that'll answer all the questions, but I'd like to have a couple of working theories."

"You've got them," I said. "Someone already inside who had to get out or someone outside who had to get in and out again."

"Don't you think the first one is the most likely?"

I shrugged.

"Here's a theory," he said. "There's not one killer, but two—or a killer and an accomplice. The killer waits in the cell. Kills Menge. His accomplice opens Menge's cell door along with the others for Mass, even though its number is not called out. Then later, when he's doing a walk-by of the cells, he ducks in and moves the body to the bed. Count clears because the accomplice is the one doing it. Wouldn't that explain everything?"

I nodded. "Very nice."

"So that would make Sobel our prime suspect," Pete said, "and Michael Pitts his accomplice."

"I guess," Daniels said.

I said, "If so, they're heading up a long line."

"Martinez—my personal favorite—and Hawkins?" Daniels asked.

"Among others. Who put Hawkins and Menge in the same quad?"

"Hawkins was just put in there recently. Menge's been in there a pretty long time. George Dunn, the classification supervisor, is taking full responsibility. Says it was just an oversight. If either one of the men had mentioned anything to their classification officers or him, they would've special reviewed them against one another. Neither of them said anything."

"Was there blood on Sobel's shoes?" I asked.

"Not a trace, but he doesn't have any boots, just shoes."

Every inmate was assigned a pair of black brogan boots and had the option of ordering blue canvas tennis shoes through the canteen.

"He say why?"

"Says he wore out his last pair and is scheduled to get a new pair this week. And get this. The shoe prints we found in the blood were made by a pair of boots that belonged to Justin."

I thought about that for a moment.

"He wasn't wearing them when we found him," he said. "He had on tennis shoes. Boots were under his bunk."

I said, "So, what, he lost most of his blood, got up, stood in it with his boots on, then changed into tennis shoes before he got into his bunk?"

"This one's a dandy, isn't it? Can't imagine we'll ever figure out exactly what happened. Be daisies if we do."

My head hurt, I was tired, and the continual conundrums of this case were getting to me. After a while, I said, "He had on boots when he returned from his visit."

"You sure?"

I nodded. "I can still picture him walking in."

Daniels shook his head. "The hell we gotten ourselves into?"

"Did you talk to Hawkins?"

"Yeah," Daniels said. "Says he didn't do it."

"You cross him off the list? How many we down to now?"

"Says he came in from medical, went straight to his bunk, and went to sleep. Didn't even stir until the officer woke him up, searched him, and took him to a cell in the other quad. Said he knew about Menge, of course, but didn't work his case. Says if he did what they said he did, he's sick, but he wouldn't kill him over it."

"Compassionate guy. What about Martinez?"

"He was at Mass because he's been a good Catholic since he was a boy. He's very devout—when he's not committing murder and violating women. Says if Menge was gonna testify against him it's because I was settin' him up. Says he's an innocent man who'll be gettin' out soon and he wouldn't do anything to jeopardize that."

"I see a pattern emerging," I said. "Everyone's innocent and being set up."

"It's alarming. How could our criminal justice system have come to this?"

I held my hands up, palms facing him. "One mystery at a time."

I found myself relaxing around Daniels, enjoying his company. The very fact that we were able to quip and banter showed how far we had come. Previous times with him—both at family gatherings and in work situations—had been strained and humorless. If any humor had occurred it was mean spirited and at my expense.

"I should've talked to Martinez," I said. "I wasn't thinking. You shouldn't've had to do that."

"It's okay. I'm still gonna get him the right way. Now, if I saw him on the street . . ."

"Any word on the woman who was in there before the service yet?"

They both shook their heads.

I looked at my watch, then glanced out the window toward the sally port.

"We keepin' you from somethin'?" Daniels asked.

I shook my head.

"Be sure to let us know when we are," he said. "Wouldn't want a little thing like a murder investigation to get in the way of your plans."

"Thanks."

He shook his head. "How about you? You got anything?"

I nodded, and told them about Michael Pitts.

"There's Pitts's motive," Daniels said. "Concealment of a crime."

"We gotta find that fuckin' disc," Pete said.

"If it exists," Daniels said. "Sounds like penitentiary lore to me."

"Merrill thought the same thing," I said.

"You're talking with him about my case?" Daniels asked.

I glanced at my watch again, then nodded.

"I'd rather you not do that."

"I know."

"So you're going to stop?"

I smiled. "Right away."

I stood up.

"Where're you going?" Daniels asked.

"To see if I can find out about the disc."

"You need backup?" Pete asked.

"Not likely," I said. "It's Jacqueel Jefferson."

"Why don't we come anyway?" Daniels said, starting to stand.

"Because," I said, "there's a chance he might talk to a chaplain. There's no chance he'll talk to an inspector. If you really want to help, you can fill in here. Do some counseling, say some prayers, spread some love."

"Think my time would be better spent taking another crack at Sobel and Pitts," he said. "I'm pretty sure I'm goin' to hell, but if I did what you suggest there'd be no doubt."

CHAPTER SIXTEEN

"I didn't have any reason to kill him," Jacqueel Jefferson said. "Hell, I even help make that little home movie of his."

We were seated in the entrance of the security building while the transport officer pulled the van into the sally port. Jefferson was cuffed and shackled and would soon be transported to Broward County for an outside court hearing.

"I heard about that," I said. "Any idea where the disc is?"

He shook his head. "If I did, I'd tell you. I liked Justin. I didn't have any reason to kill him."

"Doesn't mean you didn't do it. Someone could've hired you."

"I'm not that type of ho. Someone did offer to pay me to eighty-six his narrow white ass, but I told 'em I'd rather earn my money the old-fashioned way."

Jacqueel Jefferson was so emaciated, his skin stretched so tightly across his bones, I wondered if he was terminally ill. He peered out at me warily from sunken eyes, his bald head gleaming in the dull fluorescent light. He was in his mid-twenties, but looked to be dead.

"How's that?"

"Blow jobs," he said with a big smile. "Takin' it up the ass. I make a good livin' in here eatin' sin. Didn't need his money."

I was sure his explicit comments were supposed to shock me, so I didn't even blink. It wasn't just that I heard far worse every day, I didn't want him controlling the interview.

"Whose?" I asked.

"Whose sin?" he asked.

"Whose money?"

"Mike Hawkins."

"You sure gave him up fast," I said.

He shrugged, his chains rattling against each other. "I don't like his racist ass. Lot of black folk go missin' in Pine County. Hawkins's old man done most of 'em, but I hear old junior's done his fair share."

Through the steel-reinforced glass of the door and the chain-link fence and razor wire of the pedestrian sally port, I watched as the front gate of the vehicle sally port opened and the transport van pulled in, the second gate never opening, never giving the inmates inside even a glimpse of a world without steel. The front gate then rolled back to its closed position as the officer parked and secured the van.

"So Hawkins wanted him dead? But who did it?"

He shrugged. "Don't know. I still don't know *how* they did that shit."

"Whose smart enough to pull it off?"

He shook his head. "Theys some dumb motherfuckers in this place."

I smiled. "Don't be so hard on yourself."

"You go ahead and think I'm stupid if it means I won't take the fall for cuttin' that cracker up."

"Anybody else we should be lookin' at besides Hawkins?"

"His bitch."

"Whose?"

"Menge's," he said.

"Who's that?"

"Sobel. What if he got tired of being the woman? Or what if Menge been lookin' at some fresh meat?"

"Had he?"

He shrugged. "Don't know. But he was one horny bastard. Wore Sobel's ass out. Shame, too. Such a fine ass."

"But as far as you know, they got along well?"

"Enough for con queens. I never heard either of 'em complain. And they never gave me the time of day. Guess they don't like dark meat."

"Anyone else?"

"Potter."

A loud electronic hum and click sounded as the new chief correctional officer of the institution, Colonel Rish, was buzzed into the holding area where we sat. He glanced at me when he walked by, but didn't say anything. He walked over to the door of the hallway that led to his office, but surprisingly, the officer in the control room became distracted with paperwork and forgot he was there.

"Sergeant Potter?" I asked.

He didn't answer at first. He was too busy trying to scratch his nose, which with his cuffed hands chained to his waist wasn't easy to do.

When the lock finally did buzz, the colonel snatched the door open, marched through it, and slammed it shut.

"He the dirtiest son of a bitch in here."

"Who?"

"Potter. Worse than any convict. Do whatever the hell he want. Gets away with anything."

"What does that have to do with Menge's death?"

"Menge wrote his ass up. Wasn't gonna take it no more. Justin never act like no inmate. Always fightin' for this or that. Potter threaten him all the time."

"Did you see a woman in the PM unit on the evening of the murder?" I asked. "Before the Mass."

He nodded.

Not many women went into the PM unit. It was probably a

classification officer, a psych specialist, or someone from the business office. There was a good chance he knew her.

"You recognize her?"

He shook his head, seemed uninterested. "Naw."

"She an employee? Someone you'd seen before?"

He shook his head, then looked over at the door.

The transport officer was buzzed into the holding area. "It's time to go, Jefferson."

"It's a convenient time to be going to outside court," I said.

"Yeah. The entire criminal justice system is conspiring to get me out of the institution so when you finally figure out I the one what killed him I'a be workin' on my tan in Miami."

"You had to know about this the night of the murder."

He raised his eyebrows in appreciation. "You may be right. But seriously, try to have this thing wrapped up by the time I get back. I hate confinement. Bein' alone all day. Nothing or no one to do."

"I imagine it *is* tough on a people person like yourself," I said.

CHAPTER SEVENTEEN

"I used to work for your dad," Brad Rish said. "Back before they built the prison. I hadn't been out of high school long. I was a deputy for almost three years."

Brad Rish, the new colonel of PCI, was a well-built man in his early forties with fine, wispy hair and a thin mustache. Almost the opposite in every way from the previous chief correctional officer he replaced, Rish was friendly, intelligent, and a native.

"Your dad's a good administrator," he continued. "I try to pattern my leadership style after him. He puts his people first and always backs 'em up."

We were under the small covered area behind the security building. Rish was seated on the aluminum bench, which, like all the chairs, benches, and tables in the institution, was bolted down. He was smoking a short cigar and watching as inmates came up to the property room window to send out packages or settle property disputes. I had been walking back to the chapel from talking to Jacqueel Jefferson when, without preamble, he had started talking to me.

For a moment neither of us said anything.

Finally, as if it had just occurred to him, he said, "Was inmate Jefferson botherin' you?"

Now we came to the real reason he had stopped me.

"We were just talking."

"About what?"

I shot him a look. The question was inappropriate, and I tried to let him know. "Various things."

He nodded.

The inmates in front of the property window were unusually quiet and orderly, the sergeant inside calmer and more patient. The colonel's presence, even while taking a smoking break, had a potent effect.

"You working the Menge homicide?" he asked.

"Just helping Daniels," I said. "His case."

He nodded. "He told me you were. You two're related somehow, aren't you?"

I nodded, but didn't say anything.

"They say you're a good investigator," he said. "You'd just moved to Atlanta when I went to work for your dad and all I heard from everyone was what a loss not having you was."

There didn't seem to be anything to say to that.

"But I'd think it'd be hard to be a good chaplain *and* conduct an investigation."

"Never said I was good."

"Everyone else around here does. Everywhere I go I hear how good you are—no matter what you do."

His voice had filled with what sounded like a challenge.

"Don't believe everything you hear," I said.

"I don't," he said, then smiled, but a hardness had changed the timbre of his voice. "And I wouldn't want you to lose that good reputation of yours."

"Well, thanks for looking out," I said, and started to leave.

"Wait," he said, standing and extinguishing what was left of his cigar. "Step in my office for a minute."

Without waiting for a response, he opened the door to the security building and walked in. I followed.

When we were seated in his office, he said, "I understand my predecessor gave you some trouble."

"He wasn't crazy about me helping out with investigations."

"Well, I just wanted you to know that as long as your chaplaincy duties don't suffer, you won't have any problems from me, and if I can ever help you I will."

Though he was responsible for the overall security of the institution, I didn't answer to Brad Rish—I worked with the assistant warden of programs and answered directly to the warden—and his comments were overreaching and challenging.

"I'll take you up on that. Officer Pitts and Sergeant Potter were both in G-dorm the night Menge was killed."

His forward-leaning face and raised eyebrows told me he wanted more.

"What can you tell me about them?"

"Nothing. I'm still trying to meet everyone. I wouldn't know them if I ran into them out of uniform."

Unlike the previous colonel, Rish kept his office clean and organized. Nothing was out of place. None of his many marksman trophies or numerous framed citations had even the slightest hint of dust on them. There were no piles of paper, no stacks of file folders, no indication that any work actually took place here, though I knew it did.

"Why was it just the two of them?" I asked.

"I asked the OIC about it . . . said it couldn't be helped. They were just so shorthanded they were operating in critical. He called several officers at home, but couldn't find anyone willing to come back in."

"I thought if it was critical they didn't have a choice?"

"Well, maybe they didn't answer their phones. Point is, he had to work with what he had. I'm sure if he spoke to officers that weren't willing to come in, he wrote them up."

"Did Menge write Potter up recently?"

His gaze quickly darted over to the grievance on the corner of his otherwise empty desk. Realizing his mistake, he quickly looked back at me, but it was too late.

"No," he said, but it lacked conviction.

"You sure?"

"Positive," he said.

"What about Pitts?"

He shook his head.

"There's a rumor of a video showing Pitts giving Menge a particularly brutal tune-up."

"I've heard."

"And?"

"I'd like to see it. But until I do, it's just a rumor. Prison's full of them. I've heard a few on you."

I smiled. "But you don't believe everything you hear."

"Let me tell you what I *do* believe. I believe in backing up my men. Just like your dad. The single worst thing for morale in such a difficult job is having a colonel who won't back you up."

I understood what he was communicating, and it contradicted what he'd said earlier about being supportive and helping me when I needed it.

"But there's a big difference between backing up and covering up," I said.

He twisted his lips, raised his eyebrows, and shrugged. "Sometimes not as big as you might think."

CHAPTER EIGHTEEN

When I stepped out of the security building, Merrill was waiting for me with a big smile on his face. His expression was one of genuine pleasure, and it made him look like the little boy I had known in childhood.

"Guess who's in the infirmary with cuts and scratches?" he asked.

"One of the inmates in the PM quad the night Menge was murdered."

"Yeah. Carlos Matos. And guess who lined up a little two-on-one interview with him?"

"You."

"And guess who gonna play the bad cop?"

"You again," I said. "It's a lot harder to pull off in a clerical collar."

"You good at this game. We need to get your ass on *Jeopardy* or some shit like that."

As we walked toward the medical building he said, "You goin' to Atlanta this weekend?"

"Leave later today."

"Things workin' out between you and your new old lady?"

"Better than I ever would've expected," I said.

The inmates walking along the sidewalk toward us split apart like the Red Sea for Merrill to pass through as if he were Moses himself, but it wasn't the rod of God they feared. Some of them spoke to him, but he didn't acknowledge any of them, just continued talking to me. I nodded to them, but it didn't seem to be any consolation.

"So you not gonna do anything about Anna?"

"What can I do?" I asked. "We're both married."

"What marriage got to do with destiny?"

I stopped, a broad smile spreading across my face in reaction to the man who never ceased to amaze me. "Romantic bastard, aren't you?"

"Some kind a bastard," he said.

"I'll always love Anna, but what I now have with Susan—or have the potential to have is . . ."

He nodded.

We walked along in silence for a while, both of us seeming oblivious to the prison and prisoners around us, though neither of us were. But as alert as I was, Merrill was more so.

"You need me to do anything while you're gone?"

"You could take a little closer look at Hawkins," I said, "find out what's going on in Pine County."

"I was hoping you'd say that."

"Habla Ingles?" Merrill said to Matos when we walked into the infirmary.

Carlos Matos was lying face down, his shirt off, on the first bunk of the otherwise empty infirmary. His skin, the color of tobacco stains, ripped and torn, was covered with a clear salve. He looked up in surprise and fear at Merrill.

"What?" he asked.

Speaking slowly in a loud voice, Merrill said, "Do you speak fuckin' English?"

Merrill had slipped into his bad ass CO persona. He would be brutal, uncaring, and unrelenting. He pulled it off as well as anybody at the prison. The difference between him and the others who also did it was that for Merrill it was a persona, a role—

one he could slip back out of again just as quickly and effortlessly as he had slipped into it. For many of the others, they
soon became the persona.

"English?" he asked.

"*Si*," Merrill said.

"Yes," Matos said. "*Si*."

Carlos Matos was about five and a half feet tall, thick and
meaty, but not quite muscular. His dark hair matched his eyes,
and his nose spread over much of his round face. His teeth were
small and very white with space between them.

"So you understand me when I ask who cut you the fuck
up?"

He nodded. "I fell in my cell. Scraped my back on the wall
and my bunk."

"How you say bullshit in Spanish?" Merrill asked. "I thought
you said you understood my question?"

"I did, *señor*," he said.

"I don't think so," he said. "Did I say fuck with me?"

"No, sir."

"Oh," Merrill said, as if he suddenly got it. "You just did that
on your own. You improvisin' and shit?"

"It is the truth."

"*The truth*. You don't tell me the truth, they gonna have to
call the doctor back in here."

All but the outside wall of the infirmary was steel-reinforced
glass, and though the nurse doing paperwork in the nurses' station could see everything, she kept her head down, conspicu-
ously paying no attention to us.

Carlos looked at me, fear in his eyes.

I shrugged and gave him an expression like *what can I do?*
This was Merrill's interview. I was just along for the ride. We
had different roles, different approaches, but we'd probably get

the same results either way—lies, misdirection, and misinformation.

"I look like I could stop him?" I asked. "I mean, without a gun?"

Merrill slapped Carlos on the back with his open hand. Carlos jumped and screamed in pain.

I winced, but neither of them saw me. Matos seemed so vulnerable, so helpless, it was easy to forget what he was capable of. A hardened gang member with assault and battery charges, among others, his current condition was deceptive. Merrill's approach was probably the best one to take with him. It was truly amazing how many of the men in here didn't respond to anything else, and I understood how having a strong, even menacing, warden and security presence ultimately made for a safer compound—which protected inmates as well as staff. I was just glad he was here to do it because I didn't think I could.

"Did that hurt?"

He looked at Merrill in obvious pain, sweat pouring from beneath his coarse and shiny black hair.

"Did that hurt?" Merrill asked again.

"*Si, señor,* very much."

His black eyes looked glazed and watery.

"Then you got what we call a low threshold of pain," Merrill said, wiping his hand on Matos's shirt and tossing it on the floor. "Now, what I'm gonna do to you next—well, let's just say it's made some tough motherfuckers cry, so I'm pretty sure it's gonna kill your sensitive ass." While Merrill continued to chat with Matos, I stepped into the nurses' office and called Daniels.

"They find anything under Menge's fingernails?"

"No," he said. "Evidently, he didn't put up much of a fight."

"What about blood? Anybody else's in his cell?"

"Looks like just Menge's. Just about all of Menge's, though. What's this about?"

"I'll tell you later," I said.

"Okay. Okay," Matos was saying when I walked back into the infirmary. "I tell you. I got into a fight."

"No shit," Merrill said. "Was it with Menge before you killed him?"

"No. No. I swear."

An extremely overweight nurse from the meds desk lumbered down the hallway toward the break room and the candy bars and chips it held. Gasping for breath from the effort required to walk, she alternated between glaring at Merrill and giving Matos a look of maternal pity.

"Then who?"

"I cannot say. Maybe he kill me."

"Maybe I kill you," Merrill said. "And I'm here."

"He got to Menge," he said. "You don't think he could get to me?"

"Who?"

"Juan," he said.

"Martinez?"

"*Si.* I refuse to kill Menge for him, so he had me cut. Teach me a lesson. I disobey him again, I die."

"You two part of the same gang?" I asked.

He nodded. "Juan is the leader."

"And he killed Justin Menge?" I asked.

He shrugged. "I do not know."

"But he wanted you to?"

"He wanted him dead before he could testify. He was tryin' to set up Juan on some bullshit charge for the chief inspector. He's really got a hard-on for Juan for some reason."

"If you've been lying to me, you're dead," Merrill said as we began to leave.

"Since I told you the truth I am dead. Either way I die."

Merrill smiled broadly and said, "Then next time somebody ask, say 'No *habla Ingles.*' "

CHAPTER NINETEEN

"You two've been up to no good," Anna said when we walked into her office.

I nodded as we both sank down into the chairs across from her desk.

"So tell."

"We had a little chat with Carlos Matos," Merrill said, still squirming around trying to fit his large frame into the average-size chair.

"Did he do it?" she asked.

From behind Anna's desk, on the shelf with all the ceramic angels, a small CD player emitted the smooth sounds of jazz. It was mood music. And it created a soulful, pleasant atmosphere that, like Anna, was out of place here. No wonder inmates lined up to get into her office, though I suspected they, like me, had other, more carnal, reasons as well.

"Don't ask me," Merrill said with a wry smile. "I just available for fisticuffs when needed."

"Fisticuffs?" I asked.

He shrugged. "Just tryin' it out."

Anna smiled and looked at me for a real answer.

I shrugged. "I don't think so, but . . ."

"I figured you'd have this thing solved by now."

"I keep telling you," I said. "I'm not nearly as smart as you think I am."

We all grew silent a moment and I considered again how

much the angels in her office reminded me of her. Like Anna, they were fiery and sensual, with a look of intelligence and simple unadorned beauty.

She cleared her throat. "Need me to do anything on the case while you're gone?"

"Mind doing a little background on the suspects."

"Sure. Who are they? Chris Sobel . . ." she said, reaching for a pad and writing his name on it.

"Yeah," I said. "Though you've probably already told me most everything on him. Mike Hawkins, Jacqueel Jefferson, Carlos Matos, Juan Martinez, and Milton White. They're the only inmates who went anywhere close to Justin's cell."

"You figured out *how* it was done yet?" she asked.

I shook my head. "Daniels has a couple of working theories, but we're not quite there yet."

"Well, *I* might just have it. And if I haven't, I know who does."

"Who?"

"Milton White."

"Milton White?"

"Oldest convict we've got. His DC number is in the sixties. And he's escaped from six different maximum security prisons, including FSP."

I was shocked. Inmates rarely escaped from within a prison, especially not Florida State Prison, the Florida prison most like an old-fashioned penitentiary. Most escapes were done by inmates who were already outside the prison—on a work squad, chain gang, furlough, or while being transported.

She said, "Who better to commit or plan the perfect locked-cell murder than an escape artist?"

Before I could respond, her phone rang.

"It's for you," she said, handing me the receiver.

I took the call while they continued to talk quietly about Milton White.

"Come on," I said after I hung up.

"Where?" Anna asked.

"That was Shebrica Pitts," I said. "Michael's wife. She wants to meet with me."

"So why're we going?"

"To put her at ease," I said.

"How exactly will *we* do that?" she asked, looking at Merrill.

"Just being ourselves," Merrill said. "You a woman and I a brother."

We met Shebrica Pitts in front of the Dollar Store in Pottersville where she worked part time as a cashier. She was a thick woman with dark skin and long straight hair in a heap atop her head, its thick strands coated with a wet substance that made it glisten in the sunlight. Her breasts were enormous, seeming to stretch her bra to the point of tearing, but for all their heft, her backside was even bigger.

"*Damn*," Merrill exclaimed when we pulled into the small parking lot. "Just follow the booty."

"Have you ever known him to do anything else?" Anna said.

"You think when she back that thing up you can hear those little warning beeps?" he asked.

"I thought brothers liked a sister with some backside," Anna asked.

"*Some*," he said. "*Sheeit.* They is such a thing as too much."

Merrill was in a particularly good humor, which was often the case when Anna joined us.

Shebrica Pitts was standing at the corner of the building lighting a cigarette when we walked up. Her forehead furrowed and eyes narrowed as she looked at Merrill, then Anna, then me.

"They're here to put you at ease," I said.

She looked confused.

"This is Merrill Monroe," I said.

"I'm black," he added.

"And Anna Rodden."

"I'm a woman," Anna said.

"We work together," I explained. "If they hear what you have to say now it saves me the time of having to tell them later."

She nodded as if that were reasonable.

Though her cigarette had been lit for a while now, she still hadn't taken a drag.

"We got to breathe that shit," Merrill said, "you might as well be enjoying it."

She looked at the cigarette in her hand as if surprised to see it. "I don't smoke . . . just like the breaks."

Beneath the overhang, the front porch of the Dollar Store was filled with several outdoor products including a barrel filled with rakes, hoes, and shovels, a stack of park-style benches, and plastic tables with matching chairs and optional umbrellas—all for what seemed to me a fraction of the cost of the materials it took to make them. The plate-glass windows behind them were filled with sale signs and Halloween decorations.

"I don't have long," she said. "Better get to it. Michael in trouble?"

I shrugged. "Could be. Right now he's a witness and a suspect in a murder investigation—but one of many."

I decided not to mention the possible assault charges should the video resurface.

"He *really* a suspect?" she asked in surprise.

I nodded. "So am I. Everyone who was there at the time is right now."

"He's been so different lately," she said, shaking her head. "It only started when he got on at the prison. And it's gettin' worse and worse."

"What is?" Anna asked gently.

"He's got no patience with me or the kids. Ten years of marriage, he never put a hand on me and only spanked the kids when he wasn't mad."

From the pocket of her Dollar Store smock, she withdrew a long, narrow sausage stick, peeled back its red and yellow wrapper, and began chewing on it. I thought about how trim and muscular her husband was, how different they seemed—and not just physically.

"And now?" Anna asked.

She swallowed. "He hits me . . . beats my kids."

Merrill's reaction—the change in his posture, the flexing of his muscles—was palpable, but he didn't say anything.

Across Main Street, the bell of the drive-thru liquor store dinged and the clerk slid open the window. Next to it, a man was coming out of the florist shop carrying a single rose in a bud vase with a balloon tied to it.

"How long has this been going on?" I asked.

"Been building for about a year now, but it's gotten real bad the past few months."

"Do you think he's involved in Justin Menge's murder?" I asked.

She took the last bite of the sausage, wadded up the wrapper, and stuck it in the pocket of her smock. "Who's that?"

"The inmate who died in the PM unit."

She shook her head. "I don't know. No, there's no way." Her eyes narrowed in concentration and she thought about it some more. "I ain't sure, but I don't think so."

"But you never thought he'd hit you either, did you?" Anna said.

"That's different."

"It ain't *that* different," Merrill said. "Man who a hit a

woman . . ."

"It's not like that," she said to him, then turning to me added, "That's why I wanted to talk to you. I want you to help him."

"If he wants me to," I said. "But he's got to—"

"It's that damn job," she said.

Paula's question reverberated through my mind: *How much does prison change a man?*

I had heard this so many times before—from spouses, children, parents, friends, even the officers themselves. The hostile, negative environment, the continuous assault on their sensibilities, the constant lack of civility, humility, even humanity, resulting in the captors acting like the captives they loathed.

This was nothing new. What was, and what concerned me more, was the way I was feeling, the change I was experiencing. How could I, as their spiritual leader, offer them an alternative if I were no different? How could I help them deal their demons when I was continually being defeated by the same ones?

There were so few opportunities in rural areas like this one, which, of course, was why the state built prisons in them. And now, with a soft paper market, there were less and less logging jobs. One paper mill had closed and the other was struggling. With such rampant poverty, many people took any position the prison offered—as much for the insurance as the money.

"That's all it is," she continued. "That damn prison. I wish he'd go back to roofin'."

School was out. I could tell by the new clientele. Now, teachers—nicely dressed women, their walk intentional, their pace certain, who normally shopped in Panama City or Tallahassee—dashed into the Dollar Store, and unlike their mid-day counterparts, didn't browse or do their week's shopping, just picked up an odd item or two and left.

"He won't?" Anna asked.

"Say he won't."

Evidently the Dollar Store didn't have an intercom system. From inside the open door, a woman with a low, heavily accented voice shouted, "Shebrica open up register two, please. Shebrica."

"Listen," she said, extinguishing her cigarette, "I don't think he killed nobody, but if you find out he did, I need to know."

"What will you do?" Anna asked.

She shrugged. "Don't know, but I've gotta look out for my kids. Will you talk to him, try to help him?"

I nodded.

"You think he did it?"

"I think he could be dangerous," I said. "I have no idea whether or not he was involved in the murder."

"I can't afford to leave him right now even if I had to," she said. "But in a few months . . ."

"What changes then?" Anna asked.

"I finish my correctional officer training," she said, without the slightest hint of irony in her voice, "and I can get on out at the prison myself."

CHAPTER TWENTY

"I've got a big surprise for you," Susan said. "And you're gonna love it."

It was late Saturday afternoon. We were riding in her black BMW on 285, the under-produced, cheaply recorded sound of indie alt rock playing softly through her speakers in the back. The sun was setting, the dusk air cool and crisp, the weekend traffic light.

It had only been three days since Justin had been murdered. As usual, things were moving quickly—they almost always did at the prison—and I didn't want to leave, but Susan and I had been planning this for a long time, it was important to her, and I was sure the break would do me good. It was for that reason that I was determined not to talk about—and if possible not to even think about—the case this weekend.

I had felt so dry lately, so numb inside, as if I were in a spiritual wasteland, and was hoping time away from the prison would help.

I said, "I couldn't love it any more than last night's surprise."

When I had arrived last night, she had met me at the door wearing only her earrings.

She smiled, and though it was spectacular, it wasn't quite the same with her clothes on. "You'll love this surprise, too. Just in a different way."

I nodded.

"By the way, how's it going working with Dad?"

"Like things with another Daniels I know," I said, taking her hand in mine. "Surprisingly well."

"I'm glad to hear you say that."

"Why's that?"

"The third surprise."

"There's a *third* surprise? But I haven't even gotten the second one yet."

"You may not think the third one's a good surprise. Mom and Dad are coming up tonight."

"What? Why?"

"To visit. Get away for a while. Mom needs a change of scenery. Trust me, the second surprise is so good it'll make up for the third one. It's why I told you about the third one first."

"You could always just give me the first surprise again," I said.

"Oh, *I* will. And again. And again. And again."

She sounded like the insatiable wife every husband wanted, which, when we were married before, she hadn't been. Had she changed? Was it that we were older now? Were we still in the inevitable infatuation-induced ecstatic period of a new relationship? Or was she just trying to do and say all the right things?

"Who's this playing?" I asked, nodding toward the sound system.

"You like them?"

"I do. They've got a good sound, but their lyrics . . ."

"I know. I knew you'd appreciate what they have to say."

"What's their name?"

As we turned onto 75 North and drove through downtown, I realized for the first time in a long time just how much I missed the city. The mammoth Turner Stadium dominated the landscape on our right, and I longed to see the Braves play in person again. Seeing the old familiar sights of Georgia Tech, the Varsity, MARTA, and the large illuminated sign on the Big

Bethel AME church on Auburn Avenue that read JESUS SAVES made me feel like I was home. Maybe moving back up wouldn't be so bad after all.

I realized what I was feeling was nostalgia, and I also knew how deceptive visiting a place could be. At the moment, I wasn't thinking about the realities of life here, the bad memories, the places that were haunted for me. Nor was I seriously considering how I would make a living or deal with the congestion that felt so claustrophobic to me.

"Why won't you tell me the band's name?"

"I'm doing some PR work for them."

"You are?" I asked, my voice rising in surprise. "That's so cool. I didn't know you did—"

"I keep telling you, I'm a whole new person since you knew me. Anyway, I'm trying to get them to change their name. You know how these indie bands are with their names. They pick one their friends think is clever or will stand out, but they don't really think it through."

"Damn. It must be pretty bad if you can't bring yourself to tell me."

"It's . . . Anal Seepage. And we're going to hear them at Chastain tonight."

"Anal Seepage?"

"As in, their music's so good, even if you take as directed it may cause . . ."

Ten minutes later, we were entering Chastain Park, picnic basket in hand, to see the group I liked to think of as Susan's as yet unsigned band perform beneath the stars.

"I think it's so cool you're doing this," I said.

"I told you I wasn't just a suit."

"I love you," I said, and pulled her into me with my free hand and kissed her on the neck, getting lost momentarily in her hair.

We found our seats and observed the time-honored Chastain ritual of spreading out gourmet takeout and candles on TV trays in front of us.

Just a mile from all the bustling and boozing of Buckhead, the Chastain Park Amphitheatre is an intimate outdoor stage at the bottom of a gently sloping hill, beneath the trees of Chastain Park.

Susan and I were sitting in the center terrace section on metal seats. Behind us, young people sat on blankets spread out on the grass of the hillside. Before us, near the stage, small groups of middle-aged patrons sat around tables, drinking wine, eating gourmet takeout, and laughing.

Unlike the general admission blanket sitters on the Lawn, the gray-haired, living-the-good-life season ticket holders sitting around Plaza tables weren't here for the music.

Most of the acts who performed at Chastain were older, even iconic. Susan had booked her band in here at the last minute when Moody Blues had to cancel, thinking it was a great opportunity for good exposure, but I wasn't so sure. Too many of the ticket holders in attendance were not the target audience for a band like this one—even when they were no longer known as Anal Seepage.

As it grew dark, bringing out the stars in the sky and the future stars on stage, I looked up at the vast expanse and gave thanks for such experiences, which I knew to be a foretaste of what was to come when the one who created the stars, the moon, the music, and the love I felt made all things one again.

The music was good. The band gave a great performance, their lack of pretension and cynicism making up for any deficits in musicianship.

It was a perfect night—good music and food, me with my new wife bathed in magic and moonlight.

Perfect . . . right up until the thunderstorm started.

"I don't want us to leave," Susan said. "They'll come back out when it passes. I don't want to miss it."

"I don't want us to miss the rest of our lives. These are metal seats and they're inside a giant target on the side of a hill."

"We can go to the car, but we're not leaving."

By the time we reached the car, it had stopped raining, but rather than being pulled back to the concert, we were pulled by a much greater force into the back seat.

Soon our wet clothes were on the floorboard, and we were making love to a soundtrack of dripping raindrops, frogs and other post-rain, nocturnal noises, and the live music of an energetic, enthusiastic band.

Our lovemaking was tender, but intense and passionate, and as sacred as the rain or the music or the magical night. Through the open window, the moon bathed our bodies in a soft light as the windswept raindrops baptized us into a renewed matrimony that was truly holy.

Afterward, we had dessert at a twenty-four-hour bakery on Peachtree Street with the sweet taste of each other still in our mouths, and then we went home and made love again, careful not to wake Tom and Sarah Daniels who we hoped were fast asleep down the hall.

CHAPTER TWENTY-ONE

"I need to talk to you," Susan said.

We were lying in bed, having just made love, the soft light of morning spilling onto our still entwined bodies, the smell of sleep and sex lingering in the air of her plush bedroom.

"Now would be a good time," I said with a satisfied smile. "Whatever you ask I will give you to the half of my kingdom."

"*Half?*" she asked in mock outrage. "*Half?* Hell, I was gonna get half if I divorced your sorry ass. If I'm stayin', I want it all. Besides my kingdom is like five times as big as yours."

"Still, now's the best time to ask."

"Even to move back up here?"

"Probably should've asked me that during," I said.

She smiled.

Susan, the naked stranger and not so ex-wife in bed beside me, seemed to be experiencing a sexual-spiritual awakening, and I was reaping the rewards. Not only had she met me at the door naked Friday night, except for the concert, she had been mostly naked ever since. It was a very nice naked, too. Susan's body was even better than I remembered—if she were going to be compulsive about something, there were worse things than diet and exercise.

She had always liked, even needed, sex, but unlike the Susan from a lifetime ago, this Susan wasn't nearly as needy. She was nurturing, withholding nothing. She was generous with her body and her soul. She was passionate and abandoned. This time it seemed more about love and pleasure than manipulation and control, but it was far too early to tell for sure.

"Seriously," she said. "Is this it? Are we officially married again? I mean I know we were never officially unmarried, but in our hearts we were. What about now? Are our hearts one again?"

I thought about all we had shared, all the loneliness I so often felt, how much I had missed making love and sharing a life with someone, and my apprehension and ambivalence seemed worlds away.

I tried not to think of Anna. But, of course, that was impossible, so I told myself that I had been critical of Susan even as I had idealized Anna. Both had to stop now. It wasn't fair to any of us, but especially Susan. She deserved better. She deserved all of me.

It felt so good with her now, so right.

"They are," I said.

"They are, aren't they?" she said, looking up at me with smiling eyes from where her head rested on my chest. "How can we stay as one with you in Florida and me up here?"

"The Internet?"

She slid her fingers up along the inside of my thigh and took me in her hand. "I can't do this on the Internet."

"Good point."

"I don't just want to have cyber sex with you, or phone sex, and it's not just about sex—"

"*Sure,*" I said.

"It's not," she continued, her dark brown eyes deep and intense, "though it's a lot about sex—don't forget how well I know you. But it's also about sharing a life together. I want to share your life, and I want you to share mine."

"I don't think so. I don't think you want to share mine. I think you want me in *your* life."

Rather than getting defensive, she just shrugged. "I guess

you're right. I *do* love you, but not necessarily how or where or the way you live."

"But that's *who I am*. And it's not you. Look at this place."

We both looked around at the fruits her labor as a corporate tax accountant and burgeoning PR maven had produced. Her second-story bedroom was enormous. The bed we were lying on was a massive antique oak with four large spiral posts and a plush tapestry comforter above silk sheets. The dresser and chest of drawers were antique oak topped with marble. Large tassels hung from several of the drawer pulls of the dresser and Victorian picture frames holding old photos of us sat beside a china trinket box and various crystal perfume bottles, two stately oak and iron framed mirrors suspended from the wall behind them.

Walls of mirrors enclosed a dressing area with two walk-in closets and a sitting area, beyond which was a lavish bathroom about the size of Pottersville. Thick, expensive carpet that didn't show traffic ran across the floor and under rich tapestries draped over large windows that looked out onto the other enormous homes and the perfectly manicured lawns that surrounded them.

"Don't try to make me feel bad for how I live," she said, removing her hand from me as she pushed up on her elbow.

"I'm not. Not at all. I'm just pointing out how different we are. It's not that it's wrong. It's just wrong for me."

My family had always had money. We had never been wealthy, but we had always been upper-middle-class comfortable, which in poverty-stricken Pottersville was seen as wealthy. But I hated the current culture of greed, took very seriously Jesus' message about justice and compassion and sharing what we have, taking care of the poor.

I didn't live in a trailer and pastor in prison because I couldn't live better or have a higher paying job, and in this I wasn't sure Susan and I were compatible.

"Is this about money?" she asked, her forehead wrinkling as she squinted in incomprehension.

"Not money, but class and prestige and pretension. No matter how much money I have, which will never be much, I could never live like this."

"They're just things," she said, her eyes filling with tears. "Besides, every time I buy something I'm helping someone make a living."

She looked so vulnerable with her hair falling down around her face, her bare breasts hanging loosely, their nipples grazing my arm and side. My heart ached for her.

"It's not the things."

She sniffled, and I could see that she was tearing up. "So I've got to move to Pottersville and live in a house trailer to be in your life?"

I gently wiped away her tears with my fingertips. "It doesn't have to be me here or you there, you living the way I do or me living the way you do."

Perking up a bit, she sniffled and wiped away the last of her tears. "I'll start thinking about alternatives."

I took her by the chin and lifted her face to mine. "We'll figure this out."

"You sure?"

"Positive."

Her face lit up. "Good," she said, " 'cause so was my test."

CHAPTER TWENTY-TWO

She'd saved the biggest surprise of all for last.

When I staggered out of the shower, the smell of bacon and coffee filled the air. After throwing on some clothes, I stumbled down the stairs with wet hair to find Sarah and Susan tripping over each other to cook breakfast as Tom sat at the table reading the *Atlanta Journal*.

We had decided to keep our news to ourselves for now, but I knew Susan thought it would do Sarah good to know she was going to have a grandchild.

I wondered if my shock showed. Could Daniels tell something was going on? It wasn't that I didn't want to have children. I did. I just wasn't sure we were ready. We had just gotten to the place where we felt married again. We weren't even sure where we were going to live, but ready or not . . .

When I walked in, Tom looked at his watch, then looked at me. It was late, and evidently they had been up a while. "Can't really call this breakfast, can we?"

"Late night. Long drive back."

His expression and nods said, *Yeah, yeah, yeah.*

"Important investigation," I added. "Demanding Inspector General."

"Hey, baby," Susan said and gave me a kiss. "Hungry?"

I nodded and pulled back from her.

She didn't often call me baby, and I wondered if she were being cute or passive-aggressive. I couldn't help but feel blindsided by what she had told me and the way she had done it. With as fragile as our reconciliation was, and with as much sex as we were having, we had discussed birth control early on, and she assured me she was on the pill. Not only did I have her assurance, but we had a history of unsuccessful attempts at pregnancy when we were trying to salvage our marriage the first time. I was pretty sure she had to try to get pregnant, and she did so without ever talking to me about it. In one sudden turn, I'd gone from euphoria to anxiety, from options to obligations. I now felt trapped, imprisoned by paternity. Not that I wanted out or away from Susan, but now I didn't even have that choice. I could never have children without being an integral part of their lives.

"John," Sarah said, "get her to go sit down with you. I'll have everything finished in no time."

"Why won't you let her cook breakfast?" I asked.

Susan whispered, "I was in the middle of making us all breakfast when she came in and took over."

Tom folded his paper down and softly said, "Let her do it. She needs to."

"You two don't have much time left," Sarah said. "Go be together."

Susan's eyes widened in exasperation at her dad. Sarah's need to control seemed to have intensified, but perhaps it was merely her method that had changed. Before she had been raped, her attempts at control had been passive and manipulative, now they seemed far more aggressive and domineering.

His raised eyebrows, shrugged shoulders, and cocked head conveyed his helplessness.

Susan sighed loudly. "Come on," she said, taking my hand and leading me out.

"Oh, and John," Sarah called without looking up from her culinary ministrations.

"Ma'am?"

"It's good to have you back in the family."

"Actually," Daniels said from behind his paper, "he was never out."

"Every time he tries to get out," Susan said in her best Godfather voice as she extended her hands and drew them back again, "we keep pulling him back in."

Tom laughed, but I couldn't—at the moment, it felt too true—and Sarah, moving frantically through the kitchen, missed it altogether.

Susan led me into her game room, closed the door, pushed me against the pool table, dropped to her knees and began unzipping my jeans. She was using sex as a distraction, and it made me angry. She was doing anything she could to avoid the inevitable confrontation about Hemingway's white elephant in the room with us.

"Is your mom okay?" I asked.

"You're about to get a second helping of Sunday morning sex—a blow job no less, and you're asking about my mother?"

"Seriously," I said, anger at the edge of my voice.

She paused for a moment and said, "She hasn't been okay since it happened."

I nodded and thought about how Sarah was acting. "She seems to be getting worse. We need to get her some help."

"We will," she said, running her hand inside my jeans, "you can see all about her in just a few minutes, but right now your wife's tryin' to give you a goodbye present."

"I don't understand why you're not more concerned."

She let out an angry sigh. "It's been over a year. She's not getting better because she doesn't want to. I know what happened to her is horrible. I'm not minimizing it, but she's using it to manipulate us. I'm not saying it wasn't devastating, or that she doesn't need help. I just know how she is. I can't let her suck me back into the old dynamic. She'll find help when she really wants it."

I understood what she was saying, how she felt. I'd seen the same rigid resolve in many recovering people, but I knew how dangerous it could be.

In my own feeble attempts at recovery, I had removed myself from my family and its sick dynamic as far as I could without completely severing all ties, and though I was occasionally close to them in proximity, I rarely was emotionally. At least Susan was trying to maintain her relationship with her parents—and maybe her rigidity and seeming coldness were just the costs involved. I wasn't sure, and it still bothered me, but I also knew that I couldn't very well judge her when I was doing so little for my own mom.

She said, "Can we kick my parents out of our bed now? Please."

Early in our prior relationship she was this same way—sexually aggressive, inventive, imaginative. It was only later that she lost interest. And even then she would have moments like these when she was wanton and brazen, but they became rare and had seemed more and more mechanical.

"Were you trying to get pregnant?" I asked.

That stopped her. She let go of me and dropped down onto the floor. "What?"

"Did you mean to get pregnant?"

"You're not happy? I thought you always wanted—"

"I did. I do. It just seems a little soon. We're just barely back together. We've got a lot to—"

"Do you think I'm trying to trap you? That it?"

"John," Sarah yelled from the kitchen. *"Susan. Breakfast!"*

Susan stood up and walked out of the room without saying anything else.

I followed her back into the kitchen to find far more food

than we could possibly eat. Tom had put down his paper, and they were both seated, waiting on us.

"Let's eat before it gets cold," Sarah said.

"I'm not hungry," Susan said.

Typical for the child of an alcoholic, Susan showed far more overt anger and resentment for her sober parent than her addicted one. After all, it had been Sarah who had actually been her parent all those years that Tom was passed out on the couch in "his" room. Being a single parent was difficult enough, but when you felt abandoned, powerless, afraid, and were having to both cover for and enable your husband's addiction it made you the easy target for a child's anger and blame.

"You need to eat somethin', darlin'," Sarah said. "Breakfast is the most important meal of the day."

Susan rolled her eyes.

Sarah started passing dishes in both directions, and we each loaded down our plates with eggs, grits, bacon, sausage, toast, pancakes, and fresh fruit.

"Eat up," Sarah said. "Oh, first, John would you say a blessing?"

I said I would, and I did. I wasn't sure if they noticed, but it seemed to me that it sounded stale and stilted, as if rote and formal for a distant deity I suspected wasn't really listening anyway.

We all began to eat, but not eagerly enough for Sarah, and she let us know it. She talked faster and more than I had ever heard her before.

"This is good, Sarah," Tom said. "Very good. Thank you."

By his words and actions I could tell Tom Daniels was doing for his wife what she had done for him for so many years. He was taking care of her. Their role reversals was ironic, and I wondered if that, more than anything else, was responsible for his sobriety.

Now I understood why he wanted to get Juan Martinez so badly and why he was taking Justin Menge's death so personally. Sarah Daniels was no longer her calm caretaking self.

"You two think it's gonna work this time?" Sarah asked.

I nodded.

"*Mom,*" Susan said, her tone scolding.

"You thinkin' about moving back up here, John? Or can you help persuade our girl to finally come home to Florida?"

"We're in negotiations right now."

"Well, don't waste too much time," she said. "I'm ready for a grandchild."

Susan smiled to herself.

"Not right away, but before I'm too old to be any help with it. Come on, guys, eat up. I didn't spend all morning doing this just to throw it away."

She began passing dishes again, though our plates were still full.

Tom took one of the dishes, pretended to dip more eggs onto his plate, them began to eat in earnest, occasionally glancing at Susan apologetically.

All the while, Sarah Daniels continued to talk. "John, you eat like a bird. Here, have some more grits."

"No thanks. I'm full. It was all so good."

"You can't be full."

"I've eaten a lot. And it was very good. All of it."

Without saying anything, Susan pushed away from the table and stood up.

"Where're you goin', honey?" Sarah said. "You need to eat some more. Here, have some more eggs."

"I don't want any more goddam eggs," Susan yelled, and rushed out of the room.

I started after her, but Sarah, jumping up, said, "Let me. I'm the one who upset her."

When both women were out of the room, Daniels said, "You see what that cocksucker did to my wife?"

"Who?"

"Martinez."

I nodded.

Tears formed in his eyes and his next words were said through soft sobs. "John, the ways he violated her." He shook his head, wiping at tears. "She'll never be the same. We've got to get him. You better help me get him . . . because if we don't I'm gonna kill him."

"We will."

"Sorry we crashed in on you two this weekend, but I don't know what to do with her."

"She needs to see a counselor."

He didn't respond.

"She needs to see a counselor," I said again.

In another moment, the two women came back into the room the best of friends, acting as if nothing had happened, pretending to be one of those happy families Tolstoy said were all alike, instead of the uniquely unhappy family they were.

CHAPTER TWENTY-THREE

On my way back from Atlanta that afternoon, I drove through downtown Panama City and stopped by Paula Menge's art gallery for an exhibit of Justin's work.

Her gallery was just off Harrison Avenue behind the old Martin Theater. The crowd was small, but the art was extraordinary.

Justin Menge was a gifted artist with an eye for the spirit of the people and places he captured on canvas. His specialty was beach landscapes and children. Though not strictly an impressionist, Justin was obviously influenced by the movement. His landscapes brought to mind Monet's water lilies, his children, Degas's dancers.

He painted the Gulf Coast's beaches to perfection, capturing the great curves of powdery white sand and blue-green waters in a still frame that seemed to move somehow. His depictions of the Gulf were more accurate than any I had ever seen, finding the delicate balance between its beauty and danger, its transparency and mystery.

The children in Justin Menge's paintings seemed alive, their soft skin and innocent eyes animated by the peculiarity of personality. His powerful paintings did nothing less than expose the young souls to the voyeuristic adults who found the distant wonder of childhood only faintly familiar.

It was no wonder he was so easily convicted of lewd and lascivious acts on a minor. I was sure his art alone was enough to convince a Pine County jury, but these weren't abused or exploited children. He understood them. He loved them. He didn't harm them, not in any way—not if you believed the truth of his art. And I did.

As I studied one painting in particular of a small girl running naked in the incoming tide, her blonde hair spun gold against the rich green of the sea, the actual little girl of the picture, older now, walked up with a woman who seemed to be a taller version of her.

"There it is, Mommy," the little girl said. "There I am. See? That's me."

"Yes," the woman said softly. "It's beautiful. *You're* beautiful."

"Where's Justin?" the little girl asked. "I don't see him. I want him to do another one."

"He's not here, honey," the woman said. "He had to be somewhere else today. But we'll see him again real soon. I promise."

"It really *is* magnificent," I said.

"Thanks," the woman said. "You a fan of his work?"

"Quickly becoming one."

"I'm Katherine Kirkland and this is Emily."

"Hi, Emily. I'm John. You sure are pretty. That's one of the most beautiful paintings I've ever seen."

"Justin did it."

"Do you know the artist well?" I asked Katherine.

She nodded. "We went to school together. He even took me to the prom. He was great back then, but he just keeps getting better and better. Do you know him?"

I nodded.

I wasn't sure whether or not I should tell her he was dead. I couldn't believe that she didn't know. Daniels had done a great job of keeping it out of the media. I decided not to reveal his secret.

"I'm the chaplain of Potter Correctional Institution."

Across the room, I saw Paula slink in, head down, shoulders up, and look around, as if for prey. When she saw me, she waved. I waved back.

"Oh," she said in surprise. "Wow." She hesitated a minute, studying me more closely. "Well, how's he doing?"

I shrugged and gave her my best as-well-as-can-be-expected look.

"I can't imagine what a place like that is doing to a sensitive soul like his."

Beside her, Emily twirled around in a small circle, humming to herself, and I saw the same free spirit Justin had somehow managed to freeze in a single frame of time and space with paint and canvas.

"I hope he can survive intact," she continued. "Not let it change him. Not let it change his heart—his art. That would be the greatest crime of all."

"Did I hear Emily say she was going to work with him again?" I asked.

Behind us, a steady but small stream of people slowly walked past, each glancing from the program in their hands to the paintings on the wall, many of them gasping when they saw the painting of Emily by the sea.

She nodded. "I hope so." She looked up at the painting of Emily hanging in front of us. "Don't you think she should?"

Looking at the painting, I nodded. "But what about what he was charged with?"

Three overweight elderly ladies passed by us in too-tight dresses, their pinched expressions indicating how seriously they took art.

One of them whispered: "I heard he's not here today because he's in prison."

"Really?" another one said. "How exciting."

Katherine shook her head. "It's not possible. If there were

any chance, I wouldn't let Emily go anywhere near him. But there's not. Trust me. Justin Menge is one of the purest souls I've ever encountered."

I looked down at Emily who had stopped twirling and was now studying the parade of adults around her. Her fine blonde hair outlined her small round face like an expensive gold frame, her deep green eyes the color of the Gulf in the painting.

"But—"

"I'm a psychologist. I've worked with abused kids and those who've abused them. Believe me, I'd know."

I nodded.

"Just look at his work. You can see for yourself."

After Katherine and Emily had wandered away, Paula walked up. "Thanks so much for coming."

"It's incredible . . . and your gallery's great."

"That's sweet of you to say. But I'm about to redo it. Come back in about six months, it'll really be something then."

"Justin's work selling well?" I asked.

She smiled. "Actually, everything I was willing to sell sold before the show began."

"What?"

"A collector from Sarasota bought them all when she heard Justin had died."

"Everything?" I asked, looking around.

She nodded and smiled. "Come on. I'll buy you a cup of coffee."

"You can certainly afford it."

We walked up to Harrison Avenue to a new coffee shop. At the end of Harrison beyond the marina, the sun sat low in the sky, casting a soft rose-colored glow on the buildings lining both sides of the street.

I had coffee and a slice of coconut cake. She had a large Java Royale, quiche, and a bagel with cream cheese. I paid.

We sat at a table outside.

"I haven't eaten anything today," she said. "I'm starving."

There was very little traffic on Harrison, and a Sunday evening hush rested on downtown. The shops were closed, the visitors few, the cool air calm and quiet.

She ate without inhibition, enjoying every bite, yet shoveling it in as fast as she could.

"Most of the people at the gallery didn't seem to know about Justin," I said.

"It's not public knowledge," she said, wiping her mouth with a small paper napkin. "And I didn't tell them."

"How'd the collector who bought all his paintings find out?"

"She didn't buy them all. Just the ones I was willing to part with. I called and told her. She had acquired several of his pieces before, and I knew she loved his work. She had the means to buy the collection I was offering."

I nodded, wondering again at her lack of grief.

"A lot of the people there today were friends or regular customers," she continued. "If they'd known Justin had died, they would've tried to buy something, but it would've been awkward because they couldn't have afforded it."

"You seem to be doing good."

"I have my moments, but, yes, overall I'm doing fine."

"When's the funeral?" I asked. "Have you made the arrangements yet?"

Her eyes grew wide. "Did you want to come? I'm sorry. I decided just to have a memorial service. He's just going to be cremated when they release his body, and I didn't want to wait 'til then for all of us to get closure. It was earlier this afternoon."

"*I'm* sorry. I would've been there."

"I should've let you know. It was just me, Mom and Dad, a few cousins, and Justin's partner, Chris."

"Chris *Sobel?*" I asked.

She nodded. "Said they let him come since he was minimum custody with very little time left."

"But he's also one of the leading suspects in your brother's murder."

"Really? Chris? I can't believe it. He wouldn't do—he loved Justin."

"How'd he even know about it?"

"I made sure he knew. I know how close they were."

I said, "I thought you hadn't talked to Justin in four years?"

She shook her head. "I hadn't *seen* him for four years, but he never stopped writing me, letting me know everything that was going on in his life. He told me all about Chris in his letters, even sent me a picture of the two of them together."

"Didn't you think he and Justin looked like twins?" I asked.

She squinted and looked away as she seemed to consider it, then shrugged. "I guess they favored some in the picture, though it was a long time ago. Now, it's hard to tell since he doesn't have hair."

"Who doesn't have hair?"

Her expression was one of confusion. "Chris. He shaved his head."

"That's something new," I said, wondering if it were a sign of grief or an attempt to alter his appearance in order to escape. "Was he cuffed, shackled, and in the custody of a sheriff's deputy?"

She shook her head. "His brother was able to sign him out."

My heart started racing. One of our leading suspects was out of prison, and I doubted he would ever come back again—not willingly anyway.

"Did he tell you when he had to be back?" I asked, hopping up from the table.

She shrugged. "Sometime tonight . . . before count, I think."

CHAPTER TWENTY-FOUR

When I pulled into the PCI parking lot, Anna was waiting for me.

"What is it? What's wrong?"

I'd called her on my drive back and asked her to meet me, but was unwilling to tell her why on the cell phone since a favorite Potter County pastime was listening to cell and cordless phone conversations on emergency scanners.

"Chris Sobel," I said. "Did you approve him for a furlough?"

Her face grew alarmed, then angry. "Of course not."

"He went on one."

"There's no way."

On the rare occasions furloughs were approved for inmates who had a nonviolent charge, a minimum custody level, and very little time left, they were only granted for the funerals of immediate family members.

"He went to Justin's memorial service, according to Paula Menge."

Turning toward the control room, she said, "Let's find out just what the hell's goin' on."

When we reached the control room we were greeted with a wave by the officer and the sergeant inside.

Lifting the lid of the document tray, Anna said, "Hey, Sarge, are there any inmates out on furlough right now?"

He nodded, glancing down at the log. "Two. A Russell and a Sobel."

155

"Chris Sobel?" she said, concealing the alarm I knew she felt.

"Yes, ma'am."

"Who approved Sobel's furlough?"

He shrugged. "I don't know. He left before I came on duty."

"What time is he scheduled back?"

He glanced at the log book again. "Six."

I looked at the clock on the back wall of the control room. It was five-forty-five. He should be pulling up any minute—if he were coming back.

"Who's the OIC on duty right now?" Anna asked.

"Captain Weaver."

"Would you please radio him and ask him to meet me up here?"

"Yes, ma'am."

While he did, Anna turned back to me. "Fifteen minutes. Whatta you think?"

"I think it could be fifteen days—wouldn't matter."

She nodded.

"Somethin's way off about this whole thing," I said.

Before she could respond, Sergeant Bryan said, "Ms. Rodden, Captain Weaver's in the VP. He said for me to send you two on back."

And so, without our ID badges, he buzzed the gate and we walked in the institution when we were off-duty—something we were never supposed to do.

We found Weaver sitting with Rosetta Jackson, the sergeant in charge of supervising visitation, at a table in the corner of the visiting park.

The PCI visiting park was a large room, maybe 50 × 75, with cinder block walls and a tile floor. Folding tables with plastic chairs around them filled the center of the room and vending machines lined two of the walls. For safety and security, there were separate bathrooms for inmates and visitors and the pavilion out back was enclosed by its own fence and razor wire.

Anna told Weaver what was going on.

"Don't know anything about it. I came on at three, but we can step in my office and call Captain Weeks."

I stayed behind and talked to Rosetta Jackson at her request.

"Merrill said I should talk to you," she said.

"About what?"

"I worked in PM for two years before makin' sergeant."

And though I figured she was about to tell me what I already knew, I said, "Yes ma'am?"

"Inmates in PM the worst kind there is," she said. "They in PM 'cause they made too many problems for theyselves with the other convicts on the 'pound."

We were surrounded by inmates and their loved ones, who were talking, but not touching, smiling, but not laughing, as they ate junk food they had gotten out of the vending machines. Seeing them eating the candy bars, chips, and microwave sandwiches made me wonder if Justin and Paula had eaten anything during their visit that might help us better establish time of death. I made a mental note to talk to Paula and Daniels about it.

"Most of 'em pissed off another inmate and now they hidin' from him," she continued. "It's usually over gamblin' debts. Sometimes sex. They play games like the rest of the convicts, but then when it's time to pay the bill, they skip out on the check."

At a table in the back corner, a young Latin woman slid her hand up an inmate's thigh and began giving him an on-the-clothes hand job beneath the table.

Who said Florida no longer has conjugal visits?

I wondered how long it would take the other officers to spot it. Probably longer than it would take him to reach climax. I started to say something to Sergeant Jackson, but just couldn't bring myself to.

"You know how irresponsible and immature all these men are?" she said. "Well, just multiply that by about a thousand and that's a PM inmate. They come runnin' to us, say somebody tryin' to rape them or some shit like that and all along they just owe him money."

When I looked back over at the Hispanic inmate in the corner, he had a smile on his face and he looked far more relaxed than before. Beside him, his Latin under-the-table lover seemed thrilled to have been of service.

"There's ex-law enforcement," she said. "And a few baby-rapers or high-profile cons, but for the most part it's the lowest scum in the prison pond."

"What about the inmate who was killed?" I asked.

"Menge? He was one of the better ones. Quiet. Stayed to himself mostly. Never gave me no trouble. And paint. That boy could paint."

"Any ideas about who could've killed him?"

She shrugged. "Take your pick. Like I said, it coulda been any of them and it coulda been over a card game or pack of cigarettes. Or just because one of those other sorry bastards owe him some canteen. Or he owe them. Whatever it was, it wasn't over much. I can tell you that. It's the way PM inmates are. Whoever did it, it won't take you long to find out. They all snitches. Every damn one of 'em. They'll sell each other out for a smoke. Or less. Just a few weeks ago, we noticed they were all requesting Sudafed. It was allergy season—hell, it's always allergy season 'round here—but it was suspicious. Sure enough they were all requesting it and selling it to this one dude so he could get high. Thing is, we didn't even have to threaten them. All we had to do was ask. They told us. No fuss. No muss."

I nodded.

"Half of 'em down there're homosexual," she said. "That's

part of the reason they like being in there. They get to be with each other. Shit, they have more sex than we do."

"Speak for yourself," I said. "I'm on my second honeymoon."

"Then what the hell you doin' here?"

"Good question."

An elderly inmate with a half halo of white hair around a reddish bald head sat at a table surrounded by his children and grandchildren, two of whom sat in his lap. They looked happy together. Not as happy as the Hispanic inmate, but happy nonetheless. It made me sad to think of the old man spending his later years in a place like this, seeing his loved ones, at most, eight hours every other weekend.

"Who was on duty down there the night Menge was killed?" she asked.

"Pitts and Potter," I said.

"Well, add them to the list of suspects. At least Potter—he'll do anything if the price is right. He been bringin' drugs in here for years. I don't think Pitts does anything like that, but he not very bright, so no tellin'. I'm just glad I'm not down there anymore. That's the biggest bunch of—"

Before she could finish, Anna appeared at the door and motioned for me.

"I'm sorry," I said. "I've got to go."

Her eyebrows shot up. "More honeymooning to do?"

When I reached her, Anna said, "Six o'clock and no Sobel."

"Probably just running late."

We were buzzed out of the security building, through the sally port, and out of the prison. We sat down on the aluminum bench under the covered area in front of the control room and alternated between watching for Sobel and watching the clock.

"What'd Weeks say?" I asked.

"Sobel's attorney showed up with an order from a federal judge saying Sobel could go to the funeral."

"What?"

"Yeah."

"Why would a federal judge—" I started, but broke off as headlights shown on the road leading up to the prison.

"It's not him," Anna said.

The car parked in the lot and an officer got out.

I glanced back at the clock. It was six-thirty.

By seven all the visitors had left, the inmates returned to their dorms. By seven-thirty, the citizen volunteer who was doing the Sunday night worship service had entered the institution. By eight, the food service staff had gone. By nine, FDLE had been contacted, Sobel's escape reported, and an APB posted. By eleven, the shift change was completed. By midnight there was still no sign of Sobel, which was no surprise. Over seven hours earlier, we had known there wasn't going to be.

CHAPTER TWENTY-FIVE

I loved to watch Anna work.

Actually, I loved watching her do anything, but seeing her work was something special.

Like everything she did, it consumed her. Her concentration was amazing, her focus complete. She was confident without being cocky, tenacious without being tyrannical, persistent without being pushy.

She was on the phone, the federal judge's order allowing Sobel to go to Menge's funeral on the desk in front of her. Trying to reach the judge who had issued the order, she was getting transferred from one end of Atlanta to another—and not liking it.

Refusing to relent, she continued to speak calmly, saying the same thing over and over to different people as if it were the first time she'd said it.

When I'd entered her office on this rainy Monday morning, she looked up and smiled, but quickly returned to the task at hand. Now, still consumed, she picked up the court order from her desk and tossed it to me.

I looked at it. It looked real to me, but I wouldn't have known if it weren't. Anna, soon to finish her law degree, said it looked legit to her.

Finally, after nearly an hour, she got through to the chambers of the judge who issued it. While she talked with an assistant, Tom Daniels walked in.

He looked tired and stressed, but still sober.

Anna hung up.

"We go away for a weekend and y'all can't keep track of our prime suspect."

"Don't look at me," she said. "I'm just a girl."

Anna had always accused Daniels of being sexist, which he was, though seemingly less so these days. The recently sober Tom Daniels was far less racist, sexist, and homophobic. In fact, he was generally just less of an ass. It was probably less a result of a change of heart than the return of inhibitions, but whatever the cause I was in favor of it. Maybe fake it 'til you make it could work for tolerance too.

"Fuckin' feds," he said.

Expecting his faux-tolerance to extend to feds was just too much to ask.

" 'Scuse my French," he said to Anna.

"No," she said, "I agree."

"What'd you find out?" I asked.

She closed her eyes and shook her head. "It was issued on Friday by Judge Joe Paul in response to Sobel's attorney's petition."

Daniels shook his head. "I'd like to know what the hell he was thinkin'."

"Well, you never will. He died on Wednesday."

"Two days *before* he issued the order?" I said.

"Yeah," she said.

We each sank back into our seats in silence.

"How the hell do they explain that?" Daniels asked.

"I faxed a copy of it to Judge Paul's secretary," Anna said. "It didn't come from there—before or after he died. It's a forgery. A very good forgery, but forgery nonetheless."

"That'd take some juice," I said.

Anna nodded. "His secretary said it was almost good enough

to fool her. And there's something else. Chris Sobel doesn't have a brother."

I nodded.

"With what's happened, doesn't come as much of a surprise," Daniels said. "Just who in the hell is this Chris Sobel?"

"I plan to find out," Anna said.

"Any thoughts?" Daniels asked, looking over at me.

"None worth mentioning," I said. "If she's willing, I think we should let Anna continue to work Sobel's past while we work the other aspects of the case."

"Yeah," he said, "just because he escaped doesn't mean he killed Menge—he could just be scared."

"Would you mind?" I asked Anna.

"You kidding? I'm gonna do it anyway. No reason for both of us to."

"Thanks."

Almost to himself, Daniels asked, "Why do it now when he was so close to getting out?"

"Well, either he killed Menge," I said, "or he's afraid of who did and he's trying to get away from him."

"Maybe he didn't plan to escape at all," Anna said.

Daniels looked puzzled.

I thought about it. "Someone could've gotten him out just so they could get to him," I said, nodding. "That's good. If it were just an escape, why go to the memorial service?"

"Exactly," Anna said.

"Of course," I said, "he could've loved Justin so much he was willing to risk it."

Daniels said. "Are we sure he did?"

"So far I only have Paula Menge's word for it," I said. "But I felt like she was telling me the truth."

"*Felt?*" he asked.

I nodded and smiled.

"His intuition is as good as mine is," Anna said.

Daniels frowned.

"If Sobel's out of the picture Paula gets everything," Anna said.

"Oh," Daniels said, reaching into his pocket and pulling out a small pad. "With all the excitement about Sobel, I forgot to tell you. We found a uniform with blood on it."

Anna and I exchanged wide-eyed looks.

"Inmate or officer?" I asked.

"Officer," he said.

Beyond the streaks of rain on Anna's window, the rose bushes in the beds between classification and the center gate were rocked back and forth by the force of the wind, their leaves curling, their rain-soaked petals tearing off and littering the soggy ground beneath.

Because of the weather, the yard was closed, the inmates locked in the dorms. We had all the time in the world.

"Where?"

"In a garbage can in the parking lot of the institution. Blood's same type as Menge's."

The effects of Daniels fully immersing himself in the case and maintaining his sobriety were obvious. His eyes were clear and bright; his clean-shaven face, taut and still tanned.

"Who found it?" I asked. "When?"

"Outside grounds crew officer named Melvin," he said. "Friday afternoon."

"And you didn't mention it this weekend?"

"I promised Sarah I wouldn't say a word about work. I'm too worried about her right now to risk—well, anyway, she means more to me than any goddam case."

I realized the real reason he hadn't retaliated against Martinez. He was too worried about her to risk getting caught. She was in no condition to lose him after having lost so much.

"So," Anna said, "a CO uniform with Menge's blood on it—does that mean Sobel didn't escape because he did it?"

Daniels shrugged.

"It doesn't make any sense," I said.

"What?" he asked.

"Any of it. If an officer killed Menge, why leave the uniform here?"

"Keep blood out of his or her car."

"Her?" Anna asked.

"Why not?" Daniels asked.

"Because there wasn't one down there."

"There was *one*."

"She wasn't wearing a uniform," I said.

"She could've been when she was killing Justin. Put it over her clothes to keep the blood off. I don't know; it feels like a woman to me."

"*Feels?*"

"You're rubbing off on me."

"Thank God," Anna said.

"I keep coming back to Paula Menge," he said. "She was here. She could've done it. Maybe even worked with Sobel and is now double-crossin' him. We know she benefits the most from her brother's death."

"She already has, but there's no way she could get down to the PM unit from the visiting park. Besides, we were down there. Did you see her?"

"We didn't see anybody do it, but somebody killed him. So the fact that we didn't see her doesn't mean she didn't do it."

"She was leaving the institution when I was coming back in," I said.

"Doesn't mean she did," he said. "Besides, she could've just come in to slip her brother a drug or somethin'."

"I'm not ruling her out," I said. "She might even be behind

it, but no way she could actually get down there to do it. It'd be next to impossible from the VP. It's impossible from outside the front gate where I saw her when I was coming back in. No way a civilian got through the four gates and three doors required to kill Menge in PM."

Daniels said, "Dorm *and* the quad doors were unlocked."

"Still got two gates," Anna said.

"Sure," Daniels said, "but if she had a uniform on. . . . It was a very dark night."

"Speaking of her drugging him," I said, "was there anything in his stomach that might help us establish time of death?"

He shook his head. "He hadn't eaten anything since lunch, so if she did drug him it went to work fast."

"Too early for us to have tox tests back, isn't it?" I asked.

He nodded. "They've finished the presumptive, but the confirmatory will be a while longer."

When testing for drugs, toxins, or poisons, most labs follow a two-tier approach. They do initial screenings known as presumptive tests, which are faster, easier, and cheaper than those of the second tier. If the first tier tests are negative for a particular substance, further tests are unnecessary. If any of them are positive, indicating that a particular substance is possibly present, then confirmatory testing is done. The second tier testing is more accurate, but more expensive and time-consuming—and though a lot had happened, we were still less than five full days from the murder.

"So the screening showed something?" I asked.

"Guy was real vague. Used the word 'possibly' a lot. Doesn't want to commit to anything until he's finished, but yeah, my guess is they've found something. We should know for sure by the end of the week. Of course, I hope we're finished with this thing before then."

"If Justin was drugged it'd explain a lot."

"Yes it would."

We were quiet a moment, and the raindrops pelting the window seemed suddenly louder.

"You realize that whether it's Michael Pitts or Paula Menge helping him," he said, "we still keep coming back to Sobel."

I nodded.

Anna's phone rang, and we waited while she answered it. As she listened her eyes grew wide. When she hung up, she spoke very softly. "Maybe it wasn't Sobel *or* Paula."

"Why?" I asked.

"Because," she said, "they just found the shank they believe may be the murder weapon in Mike Hawkins's cell."

CHAPTER TWENTY-SIX

"I'm bein' set up," Hawkins said. "Which means somebody's fuckin' with the wrong white man."

I was locked in Mike Hawkins's cell with him, but a short Asian correctional officer with wet-looking spiky black hair was just outside the door. Thinking I would get further with Hawkins alone, Daniels was having FDLE test the blood on the blade while I did the interview. Anna was waiting for me by the quad door.

"Excuse the language, preacher, but I'm mad as hell right now. I know it ain't you, but you're a part of this corrupt system, and that big black boy that killed the white officer is a good friend of yours."

The weak light from the gray day filtering through the narrow pane of thick glass was inadequate to illuminate the cell and only added to its illusion of colorlessness. The only advantage to the cell being a pale gray haze was that the absence of light also deemphasized its smallness.

"You think there's a racial motivation behind your being set up?" I asked.

"He *is* the one who searched our cells."

"Sergeant Monroe didn't find the weapon. Another officer did."

"I didn't say he found it—how would that look? I'm saying he planted it. The views of my family and the good people of Pine County aren't exactly a secret. Now, don't get me wrong, we don't go lookin' for trouble, but if it comes our way, by God, we know how to deal with it."

Mike Hawkins was maybe five inches shorter than my six feet, with a stocky build and a full face and neck. His inmate haircut was worse than most with nicks and gashes that revealed virgin white scalp. His eyes were big and dark, but not really a color I could define in the dim light. They were hard and slightly crazed.

"What's the black population in Pine County?" I asked.

"Enough to cut the grass, clean the houses, and keep the jail full."

I shook my head in disbelief. Unlike many of the things inmates said to me for shock value, he was expressing genuine sentiment. He was actually serious.

"My family and I never miss church," he offered. "I'm a bible-believing Christian. I do all I can to usher in the kingdom of God."

He was smiling now, being both charismatic and charming. He didn't look like the devil. Listening to him I was reminded of how many seemingly decent people were just as racist, though not as up-front about it. I recalled an incident from childhood and how sick it made me.

When I was in the third grade, my Cub Scout troop met at the Baptist Church. We had one African-American kid whose mom made him come, though he obviously didn't enjoy it. I'm not sure any of us really did. At one of our meetings a kid fell into the aluminum covering of a return air duct and bent it. When two of us were sent to the parsonage to tell the preacher what had happened, his son, a kid just a few years older than us, answered the door. His first words were, "Did that nigger do somethin'?" I was so shocked I couldn't speak.

I can't understand racism. It's hard for me to truly believe people like the Hawkins family exist—and I wouldn't if I weren't confronted by them on an almost daily basis.

"When the kingdom comes," he continued, "it won't be filled with a bunch of blacks and Jews."

"You just left out nearly everyone in the Hebrew Bible and everyone in the New Testament, including Jesus, the most famous Jew who ever lived."

"You oughta be careful how you talk about our lord and savior."

I found myself amazed again that two people so different, so diametrically opposed as the two of us, could both consider ourselves in some sense Christian.

Mike Hawkins and the well-meaning, more subtle racists like him proclaimed in the name of Jesus everything that Jesus was against, and it nauseated me. But I was as likely to change his worldview as he was mine, so I decided not to cast any pearls before this swine.

"If it wasn't Sergeant Monroe, how do you think the weapon that killed Menge got into your cell?"

He thought about it for a moment. "You tell me. They moved us outta there as soon as it happened. I've been over here ever since. Anyone coulda put it in my stuff. Any one of the officers, that is. All the PM convicts've been over here locked down twenty-four-seven."

"Anyone in particular you think it might've been?"

"Well, if not Monroe, then Pitts. He hates my white ass too."

"Why's that?"

"Jealousy."

I was able to keep from laughing, but I couldn't suppress the smile on my face.

He shook his head. "You're a real disappointment. I expect more from a man who calls himself a minister."

"More what? Racism, hatred, ignorance? What exactly?"

"I'd be careful I was you. My daddy not a man to mess with,

and he has a lot of powerful friends in this great state."

I was surprised. "You *like* Florida?"

"Until about Orlando," he said.

"Menge was in here for sexually assaulting a member of your family," I said.

He shrugged.

"What?"

"Got nothin' to do with me. My fuck-up brother's kids. I could give a damn. Him, his kids, or his whore dog wife. None of 'em're any good. Hell, I think he musta been adopted."

"So you didn't have a score to settle with Menge?"

"If he'd a killed the little rugrats, he'd've been doin' our family a favor. Whatta I care he felt them up a little?"

I didn't respond to his hollow bravado.

"Let me give you a little piece of advice. Stay out of this. Back off this whole thing. You seem like a pretty good guy. I've never heard of you doin' anybody wrong. So, it'd be best just to get away from those messin' with me, 'cause, well, you know what the good book says: eye for eye, tooth for tooth."

I nodded. "I figured you an 'eye for an eye' man."

"Can't argue with the book."

"You *can* read it carefully. If not, you make it say whatever you want it to. What about turning the other cheek?"

The change in him was as severe as it was surprising. In an instant his charming, nice guy persona was discarded, the snarling rage of the wolf beneath revealing its teeth.

"That's *not* how I read it. Somebody fucks with me, I'm gonna fuck with them. Somebody fucks with my family, my family's gonna fuck with them."

"That's a convincing argument," I said.

He nodded as if it were obvious, his sense of pride and superiority palpable, but he stopped smiling when I added, "For why you'd kill Justin Menge."

CHAPTER TWENTY-SEVEN

The new quad the PM inmates were housed in was filled with cigarette smoke. It curled up into the thin shafts of light coming from the narrow second-story windows and hung there like smog. The dank, smoke-filled air made me choke, and I began coughing as soon as I stepped out of Hawkins's cell.

The smoke was laced with sweat and urine and the thick pungent smell of unwashed bodies trapped in a confined space with very little air flow.

"You gonna make it, Chaplain?" Milton White asked as I continued to cough.

He was seated with two other inmates in plastic chairs, watching a local fishing show. On the opposite end of the quad, four other inmates sat at a table playing cards. Everyone else appeared to be in their cells.

"I'm not sure," I said as I continued trying to catch my breath.

"You ought to have to live here with asthma," he said.

"Can I talk to you a minute?" I asked after I had quit coughing.

"Sure," he said, standing up slowly and hobbling over to me.

He moved the way most old men with stiff and swollen joints do and winced as if his bones were grinding with each movement.

"Mind if I sit down?" he said.

"Not at all."

He eased over to the steps and slowly lowered himself down

onto the third one. I stood in front of him, my right foot resting opposite his on the first step.

"Tell me why God allows us to get like this," he said.

"Like what?"

"Old and feeble."

"I can't."

"Good man. I've no tolerance for easy answers—or anything that explains everything."

I nodded. Milton White was a pleasant surprise.

"Why're some of the men locked in their cells and some are out in the quad?" I asked.

"They're letting a few out at a time. Rotating. Everyone gets a turn."

Milton White, sometime philosopher of the PM unit, had been a gentleman thief in his youth. His specialty was large heists without weapon or accomplice. He had taken over a million before he'd ever gotten caught—and that was back when a million was a lot of money.

"I'm sure there's a valuable life lesson in old age," he said. "But I doubt I'll learn it."

"Maybe this won't be your only chance."

"I don't think it will be, but I'm sure you didn't come down here to talk about the afterlife with me, did you?"

I shook my head.

"You want to know if I killed Justin Menge. I didn't. I didn't have any reason to. I liked him. He was a good kid. He and Chris mainly stuck to themselves. Always polite. Quiet. So rare in here."

"Any ideas about who might have?" I asked.

He looked up at the wicker. "He and Potter had a lot of problems. Potter persecuted him 'cause he was gay. The truth is, I think Potter's got latent tendencies. It got pretty bad. I mean, Potter knew they were having sex, but he could never catch them. They were much too smart for him—which only made things worse. Finally, Justin wrote him up."

"And you think Potter retaliated?"

He gave me an elaborate shrug. "Could of been anyone. Don't take this for more than it is, because it's probably nothing, but I think he and Chris had been having trouble. Chris was about to get out. That may have had something to do with it."

"Why do you think Chris ran?"

He gave me another shrug. "The obvious implication is that he's guilty—why else do it with so little time left?"

"Did you know he was going to?"

"Had no idea. I'm not saying I would've told if I did, but I honestly didn't. And I'll tell you something else. No one else knew either."

"Because they'd've said something now that he's gone?" I asked.

"Exactly. You understand the men down here."

"Oh, I wouldn't say that. Anybody ever ask you how to do it—get in or out of a cell?"

He shook his head. "Well, I mean they ask me that stuff all the time—how did I do it, could I do it again, could I show them how. But I didn't tell anybody anything. Not really. Certainly nothing they couldn't've figured out on their own."

"Who'd you tell the most to?"

"Mike," he said. "But it was a long time ago and it was about escaping."

"Hawkins?"

He nodded. "But it was about someone escaping from his dad's jail, not—" He stopped abruptly.

"But he could use the same secrets to break *into* Menge's cell, couldn't he?"

His eyes grew wide in recognition as he nodded his head very slowly. "He has such a short sentence. I knew he wasn't planning to escape."

"How was it done?" I asked. "How did the killer get in?"

"There's a hundred ways. Short-circuit the lock, pick it—but he'd have to be good and it'd take some time to do it."

"But *you* could do it?"

"I could do it. In about thirty seconds, maybe less if my arthritis wasn't acting up. It could've been done with an inmate ID badge—or staff ID for that matter, but they probably wouldn't need to do it that way. It could be done with a fork."

"A fork?"

"*I* could do it with a fork." As he talked, he moved his hands about in various demonstrations of what he was saying. At the end of his crooked and swollen fingers, his long yellowing fingernails came to sharp points. "Or a wad of toilet paper stuffed into the locking mechanism. Or a piece of tape. Cover the bolt or the hole in the doorjamb. The thing is, just an hour or two before, all the cells were unlocked—he could've disabled the lock then. So, when Menge gets back in his cell, the door's unlocked. On the way to Mass, or on the way back to the cell from library or medical, pop in, pop him, and pop out."

I looked over at the cell that was in the same position as Menge's in the other quad. The stairs were close to it. In fact, they partially hid it from us the night of the murder, but the door was still visible and couldn't have completely hidden someone trying to disable the locking mechanism.

"Or he could've even gotten Justin to do it," he continued, shifting his weight from one hip to another, wincing in pain and whistling as he did. "Maybe Justin trusted him. Maybe they were going to meet for something—a transaction, a quickie, a discussion. So Menge disables the lock and lets him in. Then the guy double-crosses him."

I nodded as I thought about the implications of what he was

saying. That seemed much more plausible than any other scenario we'd come up with so far.

"But the most likely way was for the guy to disable the lock early in the day, then while Justin was at his visit, sneak into his cell and wait for him. When he comes back, the guy cuts him first thing, then sneaks out to Mass or back to his cell."

"If you're right, all he'd have to do was call out his cell number for Mass—while he was still in Menge's cell—then instead of coming out, he'd slip into it."

CHAPTER TWENTY-EIGHT

When I walked up to Anna, she had a worried look on her face.

"What is it?"

"You seen Merrill?"

I shook my head. "Why?"

We were buzzed out of G-dorm, and, sharing an umbrella, walked up the sidewalk of the empty compound in the rain.

"Officer Ling said he didn't show up for work today."

When she saw my expression, she said, "What is it?"

"He was going to do a little poking around in Pine County this past weekend."

"Oh," she said, a look of concern crossing her face. "Well," she added, forcing a smile, "if he's still in Pine County he shouldn't be hard to find."

"That's true."

The chain-link of the center gate was wet and cold as I pushed it open. The officer in the state-issued clear plastic rain poncho who unlocked it for us was sitting inside the small wooden building in between the two gates in the holding area, his poncho dripping. The tiny building looked more like a bus stop than an officers' station and he looked about as happy as a kid waiting to go to school on a rainy day.

"Can you stop in my office for a minute?" Anna asked.

We had just stepped through the second gate onto the upper compound. On either side of us, the food service and classification buildings were empty, their windows coated with raindrops outside and condensation inside, the weather having driven in the little clusters of inmates who usually congregated around them.

"Sure. Everything okay?"

Thunder rumbled in the distance, and she waited for it to end before she answered.

"I've got some more information on the suspects."

We strolled through the empty halls, past Psychology and into Classification, our wet shoes squeaking loudly on the polished tile floor.

As we rounded the last corner, her wet heels slipped on the slick tile, and her feet went out from under her. I reached for her at the same time she fell into me, and we both went down. As we did, I was able to turn us so I would be underneath her.

Suddenly, we found ourselves in an intimate position gazing into each other's eyes, faces a fraction apart.

"You okay?" I asked.

"*I'm* fine. You're the one who's gonna have to be hospitalized from having an Amazon woman fall on top of you."

I gave her an incredulous little laugh and rolled my eyes. Though not a small woman, Anna was as far from Amazon as Pottersville was from the rainforest.

Neither of us made a move to get up.

"God, I'm so glad no one saw that," she said.

"Don't be so sure. Someone sees everything around here."

She looked around, her body rubbing against mine, but still made no attempt to get up.

"You know we're supposed to fill out an incident report in case we have to file for workman's comp later."

"Got too much pride."

As I felt my body responding to hers, I thought not only of Susan, but of her news that she was pregnant and how nothing would ever be the same again. There was something about being a family instead of a couple that made my desire for Anna seem even more like betrayal.

"I guess I should get off you," she said, but didn't move.

"What's your rush?" I asked. "Lay a while."

"I would, but you're a married man."

"Well, you were a married woman first," I said in my most childish voice and smiled.

"Which is why I have no right to resent your being happily married the way I do," she said, as she pushed herself off me and stood up.

There it was. The as yet unspoken truth. I admired her for saying it.

"You do?" I asked, joining her in an upright position.

"You know I do," she said.

"Now you know how I've felt for so long."

"*Felt?*" she asked.

"Feel."

"Let's change the subject," she said.

Without another word, she started toward her office. I followed after her.

As we walked down the hallway, I thought about what had just happened. In the past, most everything she said about us had been playful—honest, but partially hidden in humor. Now, without the lubrication of humor, there was a rawness to her honesty that I hadn't seen before.

When we reached her office, I used her phone to call Merrill. When he didn't answer, I called his mom. When she told me she hadn't seen him since Saturday, I called Dad and told him what was going on. He said he'd find him and let me know.

After I hung up, we talked for a moment about Merrill and decided that a day was too soon to get worked up over.

"Dad'll find him," I said. "He'll be okay."

She nodded. "No doubt."

Michael Lister

"So . . . what'd you turn up on the case?"

"A prison hasn't been built Milton White can't escape from. They say he's only inside now because he's got no place to go. He says he stays for the health insurance."

"I just talked to him."

"And?"

"It was helpful. He had some good ideas of how our guy might have gained access to the cell."

"This case," she said, shaking her head. "I mean, you think you'll be able to make one?"

I shrugged.

"What happens if you figure out how and who and can't prove it to a DA or a jury?"

"Not my department. Have to ask Daniels."

She shook her head. "I can't believe that creep is your father-in-law again."

I didn't have anything to say to that, so I said, "This is the type of case that'll be very difficult to make—even harder to prove."

"It struck me again this weekend just how much Sobel and Menge looked alike," she said, pulling two prison photos from her desk and handing them to me.

I looked at them. "There's a little resemblance, but they're not twins."

"Those were taken when they first came into the system, but look at these." She handed me two other pictures. "They were taken just a few months ago."

Menge had lost weight. Sobel had beefed up. They had the same haircut and uniform and looked almost identical.

"I just keep thinking this has something to do with it."

I nodded. "You're probably right. Usually are."

Through the window behind Anna, I could see that the rain had stopped and the yard had opened, but raindrops continued to drip off the loops of razor wire into the puddles on the pavement. Two inmates passing by stopped to carry on with one another. Their broad smiles, easy laughter, exaggerated gestures, and crotch-grabbing made them look like they were standing on a street corner somewhere enjoying the good life instead of a prison yard in the middle of nowhere enduring a hard life.

"I found another connection between Martinez and Matos," she said, flipping through her notes. "Not only are they in the same gang, but for about a year now they've been related by marriage. If either of them's involved, my guess is they both are."

I thought about it.

"And they've both killed before, though neither of them're in on murder charges."

"What're they in on?" I asked.

"Martinez on rape and escape—somebody needs to castrate him."

"Daniels is working on it."

"Matos on drug and assault charges."

She studied her notes some more, flipping through several pages.

"I'm convinced Menge wrote Potter up, though any evidence of it is long gone now. I think the colonel shredded it. And rumor has it that Sobel wasn't the only man in PM Menge was doing or being done by."

"Who?"

"Talk is Menge and Pitts were spending a lot of time together in the interview room. Maybe getting tune-ups of a different kind?"

I shook my head. "Not Pitts. Maybe Potter. Milton White said he suspected Potter of having latent tendencies."

"You know how prison rumors are. By the time it made the rounds, it could have easily changed from Potter to Pitts."

I nodded.

She didn't say anything, and seemed ready for me to leave.

"You uncovered a lot in two days," I said.

"You weren't the only one gettin' busy this weekend," she said without really looking at me. "You were just having more fun at it."

CHAPTER TWENTY-NINE

After walking up to the control room and getting copies of all the logs from the night of the murder, I was back in my office poring over them, Gregorian chant drifting out of the small boom box on my desk and filling the room.

I had done some counseling earlier, but had been distracted and ineffective, anxious to go over the logs.

It wasn't true of all prisons, but at PCI every time an employee entered or exited the institution, they were logged in and out by an officer in the control room. The same was true of certain key places on the compound, including the dorms.

I began to compare the "In" and "Out" times of G-dorm with those of the control room, but I didn't get very far.

The logs from G-dorm were sloppy, and I could tell that entries were missing—like when Daniels and I had entered together that night. Technically, the employees themselves were supposed to sign the logs, but many times the officer on duty would just do it for them.

I had seen some poorly kept logs over the years, but those of Pitts and Potter were some of the worst. Still, they had what I needed.

I picked up my phone, called Dr. DeLisa Lopez in Psychology, and asked to see her.

"I've got several more inmates waiting for me," she said with just the hint of an accent, "but if you come down right now, I'll try to work you in."

When I walked into her office a few minutes later, she was making notes inside a file folder on top of the filing cabinet in the right corner behind her desk. I sat down, but didn't say anything.

DeLisa Lopez, the new psych specialist at PCI, made me think of heat—from her dark, sun-baked skin to her slow, sultry movements that reminded me of summer.

She looked up and gave me a quick little smile. "I'll be with you in just a moment. Let me just finish this up."

When she had scribbled the last of her notes, she closed the file folder, dropped it in the open drawer, slammed it shut, and sat down.

"Everyone here makes inmates wait while they talk to staff, usually about nothing, and it's disrespectful. Don't get me wrong, I don't coddle inmates, but being here's their punishment. I'm not here to punish them."

I nodded.

"I'm glad you agree. I've got several more men to see after you who I don't want to keep waiting any longer than I have to, so what can I do for you?"

I decided to be as direct as she was.

"What were you doing in the PM unit on the evening that Justin Menge was murdered?"

"My job," she said, her bearing and tone defiant.

"It's just a question. Not an accusation."

"It was just an answer. Not a defense."

"See anything that might be helpful?"

"Helpful with what?"

"Finding out who killed Justin."

She shook her head. "Sorry."

Though our exchange was direct, even abrupt, we were both still smiling and there was an underlying, if uneasy, playfulness to it.

On a bookshelf to my left, amid textbooks, DC binders, and her collection of miniature Florida lighthouses, Latin-pop dance music twisted out of a boom box like a merengue on speed.

"You seem defensive," I said.

"I'm not," she said.

We fell silent for a moment, the soft music in the background the only sound in the room. She held my gaze, and I really noticed her eyes for the first time. They were very deep, very dark, and rimmed with sparkling gold and copper flecks.

"You're always this abrupt?" I asked.

"You know what kind of environment this is. Maybe I'm a little paranoid. If I come across defensive I'm sorry. I didn't used to be like this. Just since I started working here."

"Why work here?"

"I won't for long," she said. "I was in a situation in Miami where I had to move, so I took the first thing I could find."

I nodded.

"Anything else?" she asked.

"Did you see anyone else while you were down there?"

"Potter, when I went in. That's about it."

"Which inmates did you see?"

"Carlos Matos, Chris Sobel, Milton White."

"And were the cells still unlocked at that time?"

She nodded. "I was in there early and got out early."

"Really?"

"Yeah. Why?"

"The log shows you signed in, but never out."

"I didn't sign out. I'm still down there. Seriously, Potter's an idiot. He wasn't anywhere around when I left, and the doors were unlocked so I didn't have to be buzzed out. Pathetic security. Everyone knows that'll get inmates raped, assaulted, even killed. They just don't care."

"Why didn't you come forward when you heard about Justin

Menge's death? You had to know we'd want to talk to you."

"I figured you'd come and talk to me when you got around to it."

I was pretty sure she was lying, but I didn't know what to do about it, so I decided to leave her alone for now and see what developed.

"Besides," she added, "I don't have anything to contribute."

"Well," I said with a smile, "I can't really argue with that."

CHAPTER THIRTY

When I left DeLisa Lopez's office, I stopped by the PM unit while it was still empty to have another look around the crime scene. The PM inmates would be moved back the following day, and then any investigation of the physical site would be much more difficult—not to mention completely compromised.

Though the quad had been empty for a while now, the smells of sweat, sleep, stale smoke, and blood lingered like bad memories, and the humid, overcast day seemed to have moved inside, its slate clouds diffusing what little light was present. As I walked, my shoes tapped on the bare concrete, echoing through the emptiness.

Beneath the sagging crime-scene tape across his cell door, Menge's blood on the floor seemed to cry out. It wasn't a scream or an angry yell, but a sad and pitiful cry that grieved the interruption and incompleteness of a life cut loose too soon.

I heard footsteps and spun around to see Tom Daniels coming up behind me.

"It's what we all come to in the end," he said. "Little more than spilt blood."

I nodded.

"Came down for one last look around."

"Why're you bringing them back in so soon?" I asked.

"Wanna see what happens. One of 'em's a murderer. Shake 'em all up and see what comes out."

"Maybe more of this," I said, nodding toward the blood-stained floor.

He shrugged. "Maybe, but maybe it'll just be an attempt and we can catch him. Or maybe someone'll start braggin' about it, 'cause they all like to brag about what they do."

I shrugged and shook my head doubtfully. "Any word on the shank?"

"It's definitely got traces of blood on it," he said. "FDLE'll let us know if it matches Menge's—and if there're any prints on it."

"Any word on Sobel?"

He shook his head. "Oh, but get this," he said. "We found his prints in Menge's cell."

"I figured they'd be all over it," I said.

"Just a partial on the door and on the light fixture."

"Really?"

He nodded. "Everything else had been wiped down. I remember thinking when I had to reconnect the light that the murderer must have disabled it for concealment. We've gotta find him."

I thought about it some more. "So Sobel touched the door and the light after everything was wiped clean."

"Or he missed those when he was wiping everything clean."

We looked around some more.

I told him about DeLisa Lopez.

"Think she's involved?"

"She's lying about something."

"Oh, yeah, we found a plastic spoon in Matos's cell. It was still in the lock. He's one of the one's she visited. You gonna follow up with her?"

I nodded.

Neither of us said anything else, and eventually he wandered away.

I climbed the metal stairs to the catwalk and went into Matos's cell. The place had obviously been thoroughly searched and with little regard for his property. I really didn't expect to find anything, and I didn't.

I realized what a waste of time this was and decided to go do something more useful—like look for Merrill or interview other suspects.

When I walked back out onto the catwalk, I saw four Hispanic inmates closing in on Daniels. They were all muscular and heavily tattooed, one of them with a two-foot length of galvanized pipe in his hand.

"We got a little message for you, motherfucker," the one in front said in heavily accented English. "Leave Juan Martinez the fuck alone."

I crept down the steps as quietly as I could and came up behind them.

"You know he did not do what you say he did, so just find another little bitch for your punk ass plans. Understand?"

I recognized the inmate talking as Julio Fernandez, but I didn't know any of the others.

"No," Daniels said. "Could you say it again? Your accent's real heavy and—"

"Oh, we got us a smartass, tough motherfucker here, don't we, fellas?"

The men nodded and voiced their agreement. Tom Daniels was a tough motherfucker.

"*Si,*" one of them said. "Big hairy balls."

"How 'bout we break your fuckin' skull and see if you understand then?" Julio said.

"Just the four of you?" he asked.

I smiled. I had never seen this side of my father-in-law before. Of course, I had never seen him sober in a situation like this before either. He actually seemed to want to fight them. Then it hit me—*of course he does. He's so angry about what happened to*

Sarah he's gonna get himself hurt or killed.

"Four?" Julio asked. "It won't take all four of us, old man. I can kick your ass all by myself."

I glanced over my shoulder into the wicker. I couldn't see any officers, but it was partially blocked by the stairs. Had someone buzzed them in or had the door been unlocked?

"I think you just like to hear yourself talk," Daniels said. "Sounds to me like you're just trying to impress your little bitches."

I couldn't believe what I was hearing. This was a very different Daniels.

I was puzzled at the source of his confidence. Surely it wasn't my presence. Maybe he thought he could back the guy down with his aggression, but the reverse seemed to be happening. Or maybe he thought he really could handle himself. But I wasn't going to take that chance. Susan would never forgive me if I let anything happen to her dad.

When Julio drew the galvanized pipe back to strike Daniels, I grabbed it from behind, snatched it from his hand, and hit him on the side of the head with it.

He went down.

Blood poured out of his right ear, and he shrieked in pain as he raised his hand to it.

You didn't have to hit him with it. You could've just taken it away.

His cry startled me, and I felt nauseous for the pain I had inflicted. I recalled telling Mike Hawkins how we were supposed to turn the other cheek just a few hours before. Maybe that wasn't possible in my current situation, or maybe if I concentrated on just being a chaplain and didn't get involved in investigations, or didn't work in a prison, I could do it. I had to figure it out.

The nausea quickly subsided, the reflection abruptly halted, as the other three inmates surrounded me.

I swung the pipe and they backed up a step. When they did, Tom Daniels kidney-punched the one closest to him and he went down.

Two down. Two to go.

I swung the pipe again, catching one of them at the base of the neck. There was a loud crack like the snap of a branch, and I feared I had broken his neck, but the moment he hit the floor, he was scurrying to his feet again.

Within an instant, Daniels was beside me, and we were backing toward the door as the two still on their feet were moving in on us. They never rushed us, only walked steadily after us. And in another moment, I knew why.

As we continued to back our way out of the quad, I bumped into what seemed to be a new wall.

When I turned around, I could see that the wall was actually a large Hispanic inmate. He smiled broadly, exposing gaping holes where his front teeth should be, and ripped the pipe from my hand.

The other inmates swarmed around us.

"Hello, *Jésus*," the leader said. "Fellas, aren't we glad to see *Jésus?*"

They all indicated they were glad to see *Jésus*.

"I really don't want to be killed by someone named Jesus," I said. "And I certainly can't *hit* someone with that name."

"Shit," Julio said. "When you think about it, it fits—you will go from the hands of *Jésus* into the arms of Jesus."

"You're right," I said to Daniels. "He does love to hear himself talk."

The smile left his face as he drove an uppercut into my abdomen that doubled me over and left me gasping for air.

From that position, searching for the air that had suddenly rushed out of the room, I watched as Tom Daniels, in one fluid motion, kicked *Jésus* in the groin, snatched the pipe from his

191

hand, and hit Julio in the mouth with it.

Blood, spit, and teeth sailed through the air and splattered on the bare cement floor.

Jésus and Julio both went down, though I'm not sure who hit the floor first, nor who was in the most pain, but neither of them made any attempt to get up.

Daniels shook his head. "They just got finished cleaning up this place."

With the shepherd stricken, the sheep scattered. The two close to us were joined by the one who had remained on the floor back where all the fun began, and they rushed out of the quad.

"I just want you to know," I said as Daniels walked over toward me, "that I will always take very good care of your daughter and won't ever do anything to upset her *or* you."

As he helped me up, I said, "You gonna have them locked up?"

He shook his head. "Let's leave them out so they can fuck up some more."

Though I was moving slowly, he matched my pace as we walked out of the quad. When we neared the door, I looked up through the glass to the wicker. There was still no sign of anyone.

"You think someone let them in?" I asked.

He shrugged. "Quad door was unlocked. It's possible that the outside door was too. That's the problem with using these dorms the way they do. It creates bad habits. Hell, the outside doors aren't locked half the time."

He was right. G-dorm had been designed for maximum control over close custody inmates—inmates who didn't leave their cells except for showering and limited exercise—but it was being used like an open bay dorm on one side and PM on the other. On one side, the doors stayed unlocked most of the time, open population inmates coming and going all the time. On the other the cell doors stayed open, but the quad and dorm doors did not—or weren't supposed to. It was easy for errors and accidents to happen, but like most things at PCI, it wouldn't be corrected until a serious incident occurred—and only then if a staff member was involved or an inmate filed a lawsuit.

He added, "Maybe it was buzzed open for an inmate assigned to clean or something and he let the others in."

"Be hard not to notice them in there with us."

"Maybe," he said. "But with the quad closed down right now, maybe they're not looking in it at all."

"So you're not going to pursue it?" I asked.

He shook his head. "Let's just let everything play out. Keep everyone in the mix, see what happens—at least until we know for sure who our guy is."

"I just hope no one gets hurt while we wait. Not everyone can take care of themselves like you."

"I'm going over to have a little talk with Martinez before I go."

"I would ask if you wanted me to go with you," I said, "but you obviously don't need backup."

CHAPTER THIRTY-ONE

Later that afternoon, Susan called from her car to tell me she was on her way to Tallahassee and wanted me to meet her there that evening to have dinner with her parents. I asked her if we were doing this because our last meal together had been so much fun.

She also said she had another surprise for me.

Dinner with her psychopathic parents *and* another surprise. My karmic condition was far worse than I realized.

Though dreading the evening and the potential drama it held, I looked forward to the drive over. I had been wanting some uninterrupted time to think about and process the case in light of the new information we had, and this provided the perfect opportunity.

I took Highway 71 to Blountstown, turned onto 20 to Bristol, then cut over on 212 through Greensboro to I-10, all the while letting thoughts of the case flow through my mind.

How had Menge's body gotten from the floor to the bed? Who had moved it? It seemed a loving act—the careful placement and the partial covering with the blanket. Were the victim and the killer close? Had they been intimate? That would put Sobel in the lead—unless Menge and Potter really had something going on too.

Where was Sobel? How had he gotten out? Who had the juice to make that happen? I let that thought linger a moment, exploring it further.

Was it just a coincidence that Menge was killed the only night Paula came to visit him? Did she have something to do with it? She was certainly benefiting the most—financially anyway. There were other benefits and motives, as well, though. Did she kill Sobel after the memorial service? It was possible.

How had the killer gotten in the cell, killed him, drained the blood, moved the body onto the bed, covered it, and gotten out of the cell without being seen? Was Milton White's theory right or did the killer have an accomplice?

Where was Merrill? I was beginning to get worried. I needed to be going to Pine County instead of Leon.

Thinking of where I was headed made me think of Susan. I loved her and felt genuine hope for us. I knew it wouldn't be easy, but we could have a good marriage—a good family for our baby. Remembering that she was pregnant gave me that drowning sensation again, and I felt trapped, but it quickly passed, replaced by excitement. I wanted to be a dad. I was ready for that.

The case was moving so fast, information flying at us so rapidly, though how much of it was true was difficult to know, and there were so many suspects, so many leads, I couldn't keep up. Did Menge really have enough on Martinez to be a credible threat? Had Martinez killed him because of it?

And what about the shank and the blood-covered CO uniform? Had an officer or staff member committed the crime with a shank to make it look like an inmate or had an inmate gotten hold of a CO shirt somehow to make it look like an officer?

Why hadn't DeLisa Lopez signed out? What was she really doing down there? What was she hiding? Why was she lying?

Where was the video with the tune-up on it? Did it really exist? If it did exist, I had to find it. I had an idea where it might be, but couldn't look for it on my way to Tallahassee. I needed more time. I needed for things to slow down just a little so I could catch up.

It felt good to think about everything, but by the time I reached the Tallahassee–Thomasville exit, I continued to have far more questions than answers. Still, it helped to just ponder some of the questions, and I could feel some subconscious stirrings, so maybe it wouldn't be long before something would bob to the surface as an insight of some sort.

When I arrived at Tom and Sarah Daniels's house, I found the front door ajar.

I was early, and I knew Tom was still at the prison. Alarmed, I rushed in and found Sarah waving a small handgun at a young Hispanic guy in a dark brown uniform.

Though she had the obvious advantage, she was hysterical, her voice frenzied, her movements frantic, and I thought she was actually going to shoot him.

"John," she yelled when she saw me. "Oh, thank God. I'm so glad you're here."

"What is it? What's wrong?"

"He tried to rape me."

I walked past the thin guy with straight, shiny black hair and over to her. "You're all right now. You're safe. Let me have the gun."

She handed me the gun, and I turned toward him. He looked as surprised to see me as I was him.

"You're a priest?" he asked.

"You're with UPS?"

"Yeah. Are you her priest? Can you settle her down? She's really crazy."

"I'll kill you, you bastard," Sarah yelled.

Before this moment, I had never heard her raise her voice or use profanity. Not once in the nearly ten years I had known her. She had always been a meek, quiet little enabler for a husband who abused alcohol but had never abused her—at least not physically.

I stared at her in shock.

Like her daughter, Sarah Daniels had brown hair and eyes. However, unlike Susan, she was petite, a full six inches shorter. Her hair was cut much shorter than Susan's, streaked with gray, and it had a brittle texture I had never noticed before.

"Well, I will," she said defiantly. "The sick fucker tried to rape me."

"I just tried to deliver a package. That's all. I never tried to rape nobody. She pulled the gun on me before I had a chance to even give her the package, let alone try to rape her."

"Where's the package, then, huh?" she screamed, her eyes narrowing as her face contorted into a mask of rage. "Where is it?"

"Right there," he said, nodding toward a small cardboard box near the front door. "It's right there where I dropped it when you pointed the gun at me."

He backed over to the door, carefully picked up the package, and brought it to me.

As I watched the scared young delivery man retrieve the package, I noticed how messy Sarah's house was. In stark contrast to its previous immaculate state, it looked as if a different family had taken up residence.

The package was addressed to Sarah Daniels, and all the information was correct. The return address was an Internet bookstore.

"Did you order a book off the Internet?" I asked.

Sarah was pacing behind me. She stopped abruptly when she heard my question.

"Yeah?"

"May I open it?"

She nodded.

I carefully opened the package while keeping the gun on the fearful delivery man, which wasn't easy. Inside I found two books: *Worse than Murder: Women's Stories of Rape* and *Advanced Self-Defense Techniques for Women.*

"A package. I deliver them. I work the same route every day. If I tried to rape women, I'd get caught. Call my supervisor. She'll tell you. No complaints. No problems. I'm a good worker. I go to school at night at FSU. I make good grades. I'm no criminal. Certainly no rapist."

I nodded.

Tom Daniels ran through the front door. "Everything all right?"

"Oh, Tom," Sarah said, and rushed into his embrace.

"What is it?"

I told him.

He shook his head slowly as he continued to hug his wife. "It's okay. Everything's going to be all right. I'm here. I've got you now."

In his arms, head buried in his chest, she began to sob.

"I'm sorry," Daniels said to the delivery man. "Try to understand. She's been through a lot. You can go now. I'm very sorry. Please don't mention this to anyone. And not just for her sake. Just a hint of this kind of accusation could ruin your life."

"Yes, sir. I won't. I understand." He bowed slightly and backed out of the house, not even stopping to pick up his cap.

In about half an hour, Sarah was back to someone I recognized, and, while she cooked and we waited for Susan to arrive, Tom and I sat on the back patio watching the cool evening breeze blow the leaves off water oak and magnolia trees onto the brittle yellow grass.

The one thing that had not changed about Sarah was her desire to serve. Unable to be still, she had always cooked or cleaned or waited on Tom and Susan. And though she didn't seem to be cleaning very much these days, she was still in perpetual motion. She had never been able to relax, never had any downtime or fun. She just worked until she dropped in the bed beside Tom late at night and quickly fell asleep.

"It's getting worse, isn't it?" I said.

"No better, no worse."

"You've got to get her some help."

He shook his head. "She won't go."

"Don't give her a choice."

"Don't tell me what to do," he said, and for a moment I saw a flash of the old Tom Daniels, the one I recognized the way I did the woman in the kitchen.

I didn't say anything.

I thought about how Daniels used to be—quiet, sullen, continually seething. He rarely came out of "his" room, a spare bedroom with a desk, couch, TV, and hidden bottles of vodka. He spent more time passed out than anything else. When he was out of his room, around family or friends, he was the center and life of the gathering—gregarious, witty, charming, manic. I had always suspected him of being bipolar, his alcohol abuse an attempt at self-medicating.

"Sorry," he said, but it sounded more obligatory than sincere. "She won't leave the house. I was shocked when she wanted to go to Susan's last weekend. That's why I was willing to barge in on you guys."

"She's got to get some help."

"I just can't get her to, and right now I feel like *forcing* her would be the wrong thing to do."

I frowned and shrugged. He had a point. "Mind if I try?"

He shook his head. "Probably help you better understand what I'm dealing with."

I walked into the kitchen and attempted to engage Sarah. After a while of gently trying to broach the subject, I decided that the density of her denial called for a far more direct approach, but no matter what I did, I couldn't get through to her. She was fine. Everything was fine. How was I? She was so happy to see Susan and me together again. Happy, happy, happy. Fine, fine, fine. We were just having ourselves a little utopia here in Daniels Land, and weren't we so blessed, wasn't God so good to us?

As I walked back to the patio, I realized Daniels had been right. I now had a far better understanding of what he was dealing with—and why Susan was acting the way she was.

"You're right," I said.

He shrugged. "It's no consolation."

"How are *you* handling it?" I asked.

He shrugged and gave a small laugh that lacked warmth or humor. "I had channeled all my anger into prosecuting Juan Martinez. When Menge was killed and my case went away . . ."

"How sure are you Martinez did it?"

"Killed Menge?"

"Raped Sarah," I said, the words straining to squeeze out of my constricted throat.

The old anger flashed in his weary eyes. He took a moment to gather himself, then said, "Certain."

I nodded.

"Once she washed away all the evidence I knew it was up to me to make the case," he said. "No one else would even try."

As I sat there in silence, looking at the pain and anger on my father-in-law's face, the occasional sounds of Sarah's food preparations coming from the kitchen, I realized again how much this unimaginable event had become a part of their family's history, identity.

"She picked him out of a photo array I created from inmate head shots, was aware of an identifying mark on his body. That was enough for me. I can't get him for what he did to her anymore, but taking him down for killing Menge would be the next best thing."

"And if it wasn't him?"

"I'll get him on something else. It's my mission in life now. Create a safer world for women like Sarah and for your wife. I hate to even think of him out there in the same world with them. And I know you feel the same way, but it's different for a dad—you wait. You'll see. Nothing in this world matters as much as family, as your children. Nothing."

I thought again about Susan's pregnancy—this time with excitement. I couldn't wait to have a child of my own. While I was thinking about the mother of my children, she slipped in and stood near the door, listening to what her dad was saying.

"Trust me . . . wait 'til you hear your little girl say 'I love you, Daddy.' "

"I love you, Daddy," Susan said, then crossed the room, plopped down on his lap, and hugged him.

In mock strain, his voice barely above a whisper, he said, "She's not so little anymore."

"I am to my husband," she said, jumping out of his lap and onto mine.

In the same voice Tom had used, I said, "I . . . can't . . . feel . . . my . . . legs."

"So, besides failing to be funny," she asked, "how are my two guys?"

We took turns telling her.

"I'm so glad to see you two together like this. Makes my world complete again."

"Well, grandkids would make mine," Daniels said. "How long you two gonna make me wait?"

"Let's talk about it over dinner," she said. "It's ready. Come on. It'll do Mom good."

She was right. Telling Sarah Daniels she was soon going to be a grandmother did her a world of good.

It was temporary, of course, but it was something, and for the moment it was enough.

When the meal was complete, Susan pulled a business card out of her purse, jotted an address on the back of it, and told me to meet her there in half an hour.

"Why don't we just go together?"

"It's a surprise," she said. "And I know how much you like those."

CHAPTER THIRTY-TWO

The capitol of Florida is one of the most beautiful towns in the South. I say *town*, because that's what it is. It's a college town that happens also to house the state capitol. The colleges, FSU, FAMU, TCC, infuse the town with youth and energy—hopeful, idealistic students who have their whole lives in front of them. But it also has a quiet, settled feeling. It has history—it's one of the few capitols in the South that wasn't destroyed during the Civil War. Things that look old in Tallahassee are. And its developers were smart enough to leave as much of nature undisturbed as possible. Massive oak, pine, and magnolia trees line its red clay hills and form canopies above its gently sloping roads.

As I drove through the streets of Tallahassee, brown and rust-colored leaves drifting down on my truck from the canopies above, I realized again how much I loved this town, and I wondered if I'd be back this weekend to use the tickets I had worked so hard to get for the FSU game.

I drove up Apalachee Parkway, turned right at the capitol, and drove down Monroe Street toward Lake Ella Park. At the park, I took a left onto Eighth Avenue, crossed through two intersections, and parked in front of a modest Victorian country cottage that bore the address Susan had written on her business card.

Burning candles glowing brightly in the darkness, their flames flickering in the cool October breeze, lined both sides of the small cement walkway leading to the front door. I followed them.

When I neared the door, which was partially opened, I could hear sultry jazz playing softly inside. I climbed the red brick–lined steps and crossed the threshold to find my Georgia peach waiting for me. In the soft glow of candlelight, the outline of her body cast a subtle silhouette on the hardwood floor.

She wore a peach-colored stretch satin chemise with gold embroidered lace trim, her breasts pressing against the silky cups, pulling the two thin straps taut over her delicate shoulders. She was leaning against the arm of a white sofa, the only piece of furniture in the room, her long, elegant legs curving down to arched feet in beige high heel mules.

She motioned me over to her, and I went.

"God, you look so good in a collar," she said.

"I was thinking I was overdressed."

Without changing her position, she pulled me to her. I dropped to my knees between her long legs and began kissing her toes, working my way up from there.

When I reached her stomach I lingered. Inside, the life that had resulted from our love was forming, growing, becoming, and would soon come forth and we would be a family. As taut as her abdomen was, the skin covering it would soon be stretched, then eventually loose and stretchy, and I couldn't wait.

Next I put my lips around one of her nipples the way our child would, and realized that soon the full round shape it took during arousal would be its normal state.

As beautiful and arousing as she was, I worshiped her body as much for the life it was producing as anything else, and somehow being intimate with the body that was giving life to my child made me feel even closer to her.

"Now I know where the term 'making love' comes from," I

whispered in her ear.

"You're okay with me being pregnant?"

"I'm excited. I was just caught off-guard. I'm so thrilled. I love you so much."

"John?"

"Yeah."

"Let's make love—the world could use more of it."

An hour later, we lay entwined in each other, our sweaty bodies sticking to the hardwood floor that was beginning to turn cold beneath us. Actually, it had been cold the entire time, but we were only now noticing.

"This is my present to you," she said.

"The gift that keeps on giving—and the one I enjoy receiving over and over again."

"Well, of course *that,*" she said. "I'm yours, body and soul. I love you. But I was talking about the house. I rented it for us today—with an option to buy it if we want to. I'm opening a new office here in Tallahassee. Isn't this perfect for us? An intersection where both of our worlds could meet."

I looked around at the small house, which could only be described as a fixer-upper, a smile spreading across my face. It wasn't just that it was right for us, it was that I realized the sacrifice she was making.

"It's perfect."

"We'll be close to my parents."

"We've got to do something for your mom."

"I know," she said. "But Dad's doing well, isn't he? He's an amazing man. Always has been, but since what happened to Mom, he's been extraordinary. We can help them. I know this place'll take a lot of fixing up, but so did we and we're doing *that.*"

"I realize the sacrifice you're making," I began, but she covered my mouth with hers.

"We're family. There's nothing I wouldn't do for you. Nothing."

Later that night I had a dream so vivid, seemingly so real, that it was more like a portent, as if a vision of a future moment I would someday experience with the most profound sense of déjà vu.

The last of the setting sun streaks the blue horizon with neon pink and splatters the emerald green waters of the Gulf with giant orange splotches like scoops of sherbet in an Art Deco bowl.

A fitting finale for a perfect Florida day.

My son, who looks to be around four, though it's hard to tell since in dreams we all seem ageless—runs up from the water's edge, his face red with sun and heat, his hands sticky with wet sand, and asks me to join him for one last swim.

He looks up at me with his mother's brown eyes, open and honest as possible, and smiles his sweetest smile as he begins to beg.

"Please, Daddy," he says. "Please."

"We need to go," I say. "It'll be dark soon. And I'm supposed to take your mom out on a date tonight."

"Please, Daddy," he repeats as if I have not spoken, and now he takes the edge of my swimming trunks in his tiny, sandy hand and tugs.

I look down at him, moved by his openness, purity, and beauty.

He knows he's got me then.

"Yes," he says, releasing my shorts to clench his fist and pull it toward him in a gesture of victory. Then he begins to jump up and down.

I drop the keys and the towels and the bottles of sunscreen wrapped in them, kick off my flip-flops, and pause just a moment to take it all in—him, the sand, the sea, the sun.

"I love you, Dad," he says with the ease and unashamed openness only a safe and secure child can.

"I love you,"

I take his hand in mine, and we walk down to the end of his world as the sun sets and the breeze cools off the day. And we walk right into the ocean from which we came. A wave knocks us down and we stay that way, allowing the foamy water to wash over us.

He shrieks his joy and excitement, sounding like the gulls in the air and on the shore. He plays with intensity and abandon, and for a moment I want to be a child again, but only for a moment, for more than anything in this world, I want to be his dad.

We forget about the world around us, and we lose track of time, and the thick, salty waters of the Gulf roll in on us and then back out to sea.

CHAPTER THIRTY-THREE

The next morning before the yard opened, I asked one of the officers to escort Juan Martinez up to my office so I could talk to him in private. So far, I had left him to Daniels, and I still would. This wasn't about the murder—I probably wouldn't even mention it. This was about what he had done to Sarah Daniels. After so closely witnessing her deteriorated condition, I had to confront him.

While I waited for him to arrive, I tried to pray. As usual, being involved in a murder investigation had caused my spiritual life to suffer—and this time it wasn't good to begin with.

A few minutes later when the escort officer appeared at my door, I motioned him in. He opened the door and Juan Martinez, his hands cuffed in front of him at his waist, walked in and sat down across the desk from me.

"I'll be in the VP," the officer said. "Call me when you're finished with him."

"Thanks."

He then closed the door and walked out, leaving the two of us alone.

I stared at Martinez for a long time.

"I did not do it," he said. "Menge did not have anything on me—"

"But you *did* commit a murder of a different kind. A much slower, more painful one, a violation of the soul as much as the body."

"You sound like Daniels. Talkin' all this shit to me."

"She picked you out of a photo array," I said, not wanting to call her by name. "She was also able to identify your scars and tattoos."

He smiled, his whole demeanor changing suddenly. His expression, posture, and body language defiant, cocky. "You know why he hates me so much? I gave his old lady a taste of a real man, and now he can't satisfy her."

It was nothing short of an admission. He felt untouchable now that Justin was dead. I had such rage for him I could feel a physiological change in myself, the spike in adrenaline already making me jittery.

On unsteady legs I got up and walked over to him. Without saying a word, I took his cuffs off and dropped them on my desk.

"Stand up," I said.

He did.

"What did you say?"

He smiled.

I had the urge to knock the nasty little smile right off his face.

I went with the urge—a right hook to the head. I could feel teeth cut into the flesh of my fist.

His head whipped away from the punch and snapped back, but he didn't go down. He steadied himself against the wall behind him and glared at me. The smile was gone, but he made no move to hit me back like I had hoped he would.

"You scared?" he asked, as he wiped blood and spit from his mouth.

"Of what?"

He slung a long string of blood-laced saliva onto the floor. "I'll do the same to his daughter."

I hit him again.

And again.

And again.

Three quick punches that bounced his head off the wall behind him and landed him on the floor. Tears streamed down his face as blood dripped from his nose.

It took him a minute, but he climbed back to his feet and grimaced, then he gave me an obnoxious smile, a sickening red film of blood covering his teeth.

"You hit pretty good for a priest," he said. " 'Course, never been hit by a priest before."

That jab hurt far more than a physical one would have—even coming from him. A stab of guilt and shame sliced through me.

I had just unleashed all my anger and frustration onto another human being, something I had refrained from doing for a very long time now, but in my current condition my normal restraints weren't in place. I had just stepped over the line between justice and vengeance, losing not only my religion, but my credibility—if not as an investigator, certainly as a minister.

Sure, I could use what he had done to Sarah to justify my actions, his admission of guilt, his implied threat against my wife, but the truth was those were all excuses—and had nothing to do with why I had done what I had.

I had hurt the man who had hurt Sarah, who had threatened to hurt Susan, yet I felt worse than I did before he came into my office. And it wasn't Martinez I was worried about. He deserved far worse, and Daniels would make sure he got it. It was me, the state I was in, the way in which I was regressing.

I realized that he would not hit me back. He was demonstrating his superiority over me, both morally and physically, by his enormous control, and it was amazing the power it seemed to give him.

I drew back my fist, and he flinched, the smile contorting, his mouth twisting it into a gaping wound.

I didn't hit him. Instead, I leaned in close to his bloody face. "Know this. I wish you ill."

He didn't say anything, just squirmed uncomfortably.

"You'll never leave this institution. Not in this lifetime. You'll never hurt another woman again. Not as long as you live. Not ever."

He tried his best but was unable to smile at that.

CHAPTER THIRTY-FOUR

"I can't do it," Max Williams said. He was an earnest, young black man with kind eyes.

"What?"

"Be a Christian," he said. "Not in this place."

Obviously, neither can I, I thought as images of Juan's blood-smeared smile flashed in my mind. It was later in the day, and I still felt enormous guilt for what I had done to Martinez, and anger and frustration over how he had responded.

"But you could somewhere else?" I asked.

His eyes narrowed in thought, then he nodded slowly. "I think so."

Max Williams, as far as I could tell, was a good kid whose only crime was having brothers and cousins who were not. He had been with them when they were arrested, and taking the fall with them hadn't given him the cynical worldview you'd expect. Using the time he was doing wisely, he was the best bible student I had—probably the best inmate who attended chapel. He was devout without being judgmental, spiritual without being overly religious.

"Tell me why that is," I said.

"I'm not talkin' about the way most of these cons—or even most people outside—practice it. I'm talkin' about the real deal."

"Which is?"

"What you're always tellin' us. First and foremost compassion. Fighting injustice. Loving God and loving our neighbors. But how can I when my neighbor's a predator who doesn't understand love?"

As I listened to him, I realized how little I lived out my faith—anywhere, but especially here. He was right. It was far more difficult in this environment. It wasn't just that I was a part-time chaplain and part-time investigator. It was that I was, at best, only true to my faith part of the time. I was not fit to be this man's chaplain, and if I had more integrity, I'd resign.

For quite a while now, my religion was one of compassion and justice—the attempt to feel what other people are feeling, helping them through it, and watching out for the weak and marginalized, attempting to protect the powerless from the powerful. But lately I had been losing sight of my message and my mission, falling into old patterns and thought processes I had believed were no longer part of who I was.

"How can I turn the other cheek when it's gonna get me killed?" he asked.

I didn't answer.

"How can I fight against injustice when I'll suffer the retaliation of an untouchable officer with all the power?"

I nodded my understanding, but still didn't say anything.

"How do *you* do it?" he asked.

I was speechless. I thought about how I had neglected my chaplaincy duties, how I had blood on my hands from the violence that deep down I enjoyed.

"I don't," I said.

He looked confused and distressed. "*What?* Sure you do."

"No I don't. Not even half the time. And I don't have it half as hard as you."

He was silent a long time.

I was sure what I had done to Juan Martinez had already made the rounds on the compound. Pain and incomprehension filled Max as he glanced back in the direction of the dorms. Now, the same distress joined his look of dawning comprehension.

"So it's true?" he asked. "Was I right? It can't be done in here?"

"It *can* be done. I just don't do it."

"But you tell *us* to . . . you—how can you tell us to do things you don't?"

"I shouldn't."

He was silent again, a perplexed look on his face, his eyes misting. "We need somebody to show us how to do it, not just tell us."

"I know," I said, mist in my own eyes.

"Who do we look to?"

"Only one obvious answer."

"But he wasn't in prison," he said.

"Sure he was. To humanity, to poverty, to tyranny. And he was imprisoned—arrested, tried, sentenced, and executed. It just all happened very quickly."

He thought about it for a minute. "So you're saying a Roman soldier and a correctional officer aren't that much different? So it can be done?"

I nodded. "When we're willing."

"Willing?"

"To risk it all. Everything. Being willing to suffer and/or die."

He looked puzzled.

"There're a lot of wolves in here. If you live like a lamb . . ."

"You get eaten," he said.

I shrugged. "Sometimes. Sometimes not. But you've got to be willing to . . ."

"I'm not willing to do that yet."

"I guess neither of us are," I said. "Maybe we will be one day—if we continue to grow . . . find the courage to live out our convictions."

He nodded, then fell silent, and when he walked out a few minutes later without saying another word, I realized I alone was responsible for the look of disillusionment on his face.

Whether it was a spiritual impression or something surfacing from my subconscious I wasn't sure, but I had a thought that I couldn't help but believe was one of the keys to solving the case. It happened as I was praying in the sanctuary, and it was a grace—a surprising, unexpected, undeserved blessing—considering the state I was in and what I had just done. Of course, that's what grace is—an unconditional gift.

Later in the afternoon I was supposed to teach a bible class on the parables of Jesus, but as I walked around the sanctuary, my mind kept coming back to a parable told to Jesus's great, great, great grandfather. It concerned the love triangle between Israel's greatest king, David, his loyal servant, Uriah, and the woman they both loved, Uriah's wife, Bathsheba.

As I thought about the familiar story, pulse quickening, mind racing, I felt that some aspect of it held the solution to Justin Menge's murder. Like most things spiritual, I didn't know how or why I thought it. It was vague and ambiguous, but I knew that in time, like a developing photograph, it would come into focus.

Turning it over and over in my mind I went through the story line by line.

In the spring, at the time when kings go to war, David stayed behind, sending his men, including Uriah, under the leadership of Joab to fight the Ammonites.

One night, while walking on his roof, David saw Bathsheba bathing, and, even though he was told she was the wife of Uriah the Hittite, he sent for her. She came to him, and they slept together, which was nothing short of rape on his part since she couldn't refuse the king even if she wanted to—though nothing in the story suggests she did.

When David discovers that she's pregnant with his child, he sends to the front lines for Uriah, hoping that he'll believe he got his wife pregnant while on leave. But Uriah, loyal to the king and faithful to his fellow soldiers, refuses to even go into his house while the other men are in danger on the battlefield.

Finally, David dispatches Uriah back to the battle with a letter instructing Joab to put him on the front line where the fighting is fiercest, which he does. Uriah dies, David marries Bathsheba, and after losing their first child, they go on to have Solomon, who not only becomes the wisest of all men, but a direct antecedent of Jesus of Nazareth.

What was it about this story that revealed Justin's killer or killers? What aspect of it was relevant? If Justin Menge was the Uriah character, then who was David? And who was Bathsheba?

At the moment, I couldn't see what the story had to do with the case, but I knew eventually I would. I just needed to meditate on it and remain open, which I committed to do.

CHAPTER THIRTY-FIVE

"I love you," I said to Anna.

We were seated on the top of a picnic table at the state park during our lunch hour. All around us, oak and magnolia leaves and pine needles drifted toward the ground in the cool October breeze.

We were the only two people in the park.

She had packed a lunch for us, but neither of us had eaten. There were things we needed to say to one another, and it was obvious that both of us could think of little else.

"But?" she said.

"But?"

"Yeah," she said. "That sounded like an I-love-you-*but*."

"It wasn't. It was just an I love you, *Anna.*"

She smiled.

"For as long as I can remember you've been *the* woman in my life," I said. "The woman by whom all other women are judged. The woman whose company I most enjoy. The woman I most want."

"Now comes the 'but,' " she said.

My half-frown and raised eyebrows expression told her she wasn't wrong.

"You know, you could just stop right there, and this would be a perfect day."

I nodded.

"But you can't, which is why *I* love you. Well, one of the

many reasons. But I love your integrity most of all. Well, maybe not most of all, but it's up there."

I smiled at her.

"I admit it. I'm stalling." She took a deep breath and let it out, her elegant shoulders rising and falling. "Actually, I've got a couple of things to tell you first. I may not be able to after I hear what comes after your 'but.' "

I nodded.

"First," she said. "DeLisa Lopez is rumored to be having a relationship with Carlos Matos."

I looked off at the small pine needle–covered hill in the distance and thought about it.

"She came up here because she had a bad breakup with a boyfriend who started stalking her. He's an ex-offender, and though they were never caught, everyone I talked to believes their relationship started when he was still inside. I bet she was down there that night seeing Matos and is trying to keep it a secret."

I nodded. "Thanks."

"The other significant thing I uncovered was that Potter has a history of violence against gays."

That came as no surprise.

"One of his victims said he kissed him before he beat him up."

I shook my head.

"Several of the assaults were at gay bars. Potter claimed he went in mistakenly and went crazy when he was hit on."

"Funny how he keeps making that same mistake over and over again, isn't it?"

"What if he was attracted to Menge? And either because he doesn't want to be, or he's jealous, or because Justin turned him down, he kills him."

"Entirely possible," I said.

"And maybe Chris ran because he knew he was next."

I nodded. "That's as likely as any other scenario we have," I said. "Good work. You gather great info, make good deductions—you should be a detective."

"I just do it to spend time with you."

I didn't say anything for a moment, and we sat there in silence, the weight of her admission hanging in the small space between us. If I told her I had returned to Pottersville or even considered a job at the prison for the same reason, it would only make what I had to do that much more difficult.

After a while, I said, "Anything else on Sobel?"

She shook her head. "Think we'll ever see him again?"

"Depends."

"On what?"

"Who killed Menge."

She thought about it and nodded.

"Okay, I'm ready. Back to the 'but.' Let's have it. But?"

"But," I said and paused for a moment.

You can do this, I told myself. *Think of your son, of what he deserves, of what his mother deserves, of what you owe her.*

Of course, I didn't know if Susan would have a boy or a girl, but since my dream, all I could picture was the boy from the beach.

"I find myself married again," I continued. "And if I'm going to stay married, I've got to give my marriage my very best effort."

She nodded her agreement.

"Thing is . . . my heart still belongs to you. Well, Jesus and you, but Susan can live with being second to Jesus. She just can't tolerate being third to you."

She smiled, but the sadness that had rested on her face remained.

It broke my heart, and I wondered if perhaps the message I

was supposed to receive from the David, Uriah, and Bathsheba story was for my personal life and not the case.

In the silence, the soft sound of the gentle wind easing through the yellowing and brittle grass echoed through my head.

"I'm sorry," I said. "I'm just lost here. I don't know what to do. I don't even know what I'm saying."

"Yes, you do," she said. "You're right. It hurts like hell, but it's right. I understand what you're saying."

"The thing is," I said, "I don't know how to do it. It's not just that you're in my heart, but that my heart is yours. How can I feel this way? I love Susan. I really do. And I think we stand a chance at . . . at a good marriage."

"And I'm in the way."

"No," I said. "Not in the way. It's nothing you're doing. It's me. It's my . . ."

She shook her head. "It's us. We share something that transcends marriage and time and reason."

"Merrill said the same thing."

"He's right. I believe that. I believe that somehow, someday we'll be together. I feel like it's one of those things that's meant to be, that *will* be. That's why I can stand by and let you become the husband of another woman. Because in the depth of my heart I know that you'll only be hers in this life, but in another you'll be mine."

In every, I thought. "But what if this is the only life we get?"

"You're the theologian. Something you need to tell me? Seriously, this is just the beginning, isn't it?"

I shrugged. "I think so, but there's no way to know."

"Are we willing to gamble that we'll have another shot at being together?"

I didn't say anything. I wasn't sure I could.

"What were you going to say to me today?"

She knew me all too well—knew that I had yet to say what I

had come to say.

In one of the two small ponds down the gentle slope before us, an egret with a bright bill moved in such a way that he appeared to be tiptoeing through the reeds at the edge.

"What?"

Should I tell her about Susan's pregnancy? Would it lessen her pain? Part of the reason I'm doing this is so my child won't suffer through a divorce the way I had.

The breeze picked up and swept yellow and rust-colored leaves across the surface of the water before us and gently waved the Spanish moss in the cypress trees above us.

"You brought me out here to tell me something today," she said. "Just tell me what you were going to."

"Just that if I'm going to do this, to really be with Susan, to be a family, I've got to, well, not be around you for a while. It hurts too much. It was bad enough when I thought only you were married. That was torture. This is worse."

"Yeah," she said, tears brimming now. "It is. I had no idea what I had been putting you through."

I gave her a helpless expression but didn't say anything.

She'll understand if you just tell her that you and Susan are going to have a baby. It won't hurt her as badly. Just tell her. But it makes everything seem so final.

"Go ahead and finish what you were going to say," she said, her voice breaking, then gaining strength and turning hard. "I've got to go."

"Just that Susan's pregnant," I said, "and that if I don't come around you as much, it isn't because I don't want to."

CHAPTER THIRTY-SIX

Rows and rows of pine trees stood where once had grown tobacco and before that cotton. They abruptly stopped and opened up into a five-hundred acre farm enclosed by a freshly painted white wooden fence. At the center of the fence that ran along the highway, a gated entrance of cypress and wrought iron with a sign above it reading THE H. H. CORRAL guarded a blacktop driveway lined on each side with royal palms.

When I turned into the drive, the gate opened. I was expected.

It was late Tuesday afternoon. Merrill had been missing for two days, and on one, not even Dad and his deputies had been able to turn up anything.

I had come to Pine County to look for myself.

Beyond the palms, herds of Black Angus and Holsteins searched the cold ground for something to eat though there were several bails of hay and feed troughs filled with grain in a portable corral at the center of each field.

At the end of the private drive, in a large pecan grove, beyond a red brick driveway and parking area, sat an enormous Mediterranean home with mahogany balustrades, cypress beams, arches with keystone surrounds, and a variegated barrel tile roof. It was the nicest house I had seen in the Panhandle—maybe in the Southeast. It was the home of Howard Hawkins and judging by it, the sheriff in Pine County did a whole lot better than the sheriff of Potter County.

As I got out of my truck and walked toward the door, pecan

shells crunching beneath my feet, a middle-aged man with silver hair and red cheeks pulled up in a golf cart. He was a big man, over six feet and about fifty pounds overweight, but he hid it well with good posture and nice clothes.

"You must be John," he said, extending his hand to me. "Howard Hawkins. Hop in. I've got to go open the feed gates. You can ride with me. When we get back, we'll have cocktails and dinner with my family."

He was charming, confident, and personable, nothing like the redneck right-wing simpleton I had expected. I liked him immediately.

"Thank you," I said and climbed into the cart.

He drove the cart faster than was safe, faster than I thought possible, weaving in and out of trees and bushes and crushing pecans, pine cones, and leaves under the small tires.

"I met your dad a couple of years ago," he said. "He's been the sheriff of Potter for—how long?—twenty years?"

"Longer," I said.

"He's a hell of a sheriff. Hell of a sheriff. Good man, too. I've heard the same about you."

He brought the golf cart to a stop in front of the feeding corral I had seen on my way in and hopped out quickly. The moment we pulled up, the cows gathered around. Now that he had opened the gate, they began to pour in, rushing the grain, ignoring the hay.

The herd was one of the best in the area, their bodies and the coats that covered them thick and healthy. They were gentle, too, and Hawkins was gentle with them, patting and talking to them as they filed by, calling them by name.

"They're beautiful," I said. "And so gentle."

"I've raised every one of them since they were born. They're like my children. Speaking of children . . . should I be worried about my son? I hear an inmate was killed in his dorm."

"Everyone in prison's at risk, but so far I don't see that your son's in any real danger. In fact, the other inmates may be in danger from him."

He smiled and nodded appreciatively. "That's my boy."

When he looked at me and I wasn't smiling, he said, "You don't suspect him, do you?"

I shrugged. "His name keeps coming up. He's one of only a handful who *could've* done it, and the murder weapon was found in his cell."

"Well, that's because he's being set up," he said, sitting back down behind the wheel. "I'm glad you came to see me. I can see we've got a lot to talk about. But let's save it until we're back at the house, sitting down over drinks. Who knows? Maybe you can get me drunk, and I'll do a lot of confessing to you."

His smile was broad, his eyes wide, his expression charming. He had the southern politician thing down. Anti-Christ or not, this man could get votes and win elections.

We sped through the pasture and into another one across the drive, dodging cows and trees and tractors as we did. Two times we actually came off the ground as we bounced over bumps and ditches.

While he was opening the gates, I said, "This whole place yours?"

He nodded. "Over six hundred acres. Beautiful, isn't it? I think when the good Lord comes back he may actually touch down right here."

"Are there oil rigs on some part of the property I haven't seen yet?"

He smiled again. He did that a lot. Each time he did, the fine smile lines in his face went from wind-chapped red to bloodless white and you could see just how deep they were.

"You haven't heard my story? Well, I'll have to tell it to you over drinks. I try to do everything I can over drinks."

"I *used* to," I said, and smiled right back at him.

CHAPTER THIRTY-SEVEN

We had drinks on an interior courtyard that overlooked the heated swimming pool. I knew it was heated because as we were being seated, Sharon Hawkins, Howard's daughter-in-law and Mike's wife, jumped out of the pool and apologized to Howard for being in it when he had a guest. He told her it was all right, but there was something that passed between them that let me know it wasn't.

The courtyard was surrounded on three sides by the house, tall archways leading to French doors beneath a second-story balcony supported by cypress beams. As it grew dark, small atmospheric lights began popping on in various places to set just the right mood, and I had to keep reminding myself this was a private residence and not an exclusive resort.

"I own most of Pine County," he said. "Well, most of it that hasn't been developed. The rows of pine that fill this beautiful parcel of north Florida all belong to me, and since paper is the primary industry in these parts, I'm a very wealthy man. My great-grandparents first owned it. They grew cotton on it. After the slaves were freed, my grandparents grew tobacco and supported sharecroppers. My parents planted it in pines and now I'm reaping the benefit of their foresight."

"It's quite an inheritance. So why be sheriff?"

"I've got a vision. I'm building a community here. You could say that Pine County is the closest thing to the Kingdom of God on earth there is. Do you know what our homicide rate was last year?"

I shook my head.

"Zero."

One of your citizens has been murdered now.

"We have no crime to speak of. I mean a few small things from people passing through or some of the lower-class day workers, but it's only petty stuff and they're swiftly and severely punished. We have the best schools in the state. Highest SAT scores. You know how many resource officers we assign to our schools?"

I shook my head.

"None. Our kids don't carry guns to school. They don't do drugs. They respect their teachers and their peers."

"I'm surprised more people aren't pouring in here," I said, though I was really wondering what would make someone like Justin Menge move to such a beige and banal place.

"Oh, they'd like to. Believe me. But we've worked too hard to let people who have no idea what we're all about come in and destroy it. We've paid a price to have safe streets and schools. To have happy children who want to contribute to society, to give something back like me, not live on welfare checks or get rich quick by selling their souls."

"How can you keep them out?"

"Told you, I own nearly all of the undeveloped land. And I'm not selling." He paused for a moment to light a long, thick cigar. He twirled it around in his mouth several times, then puffed vigorously as he held his gold lighter to the other end. "Oh, we let in the occasional family. If we need a doctor or a dentist, but we vet the hell out 'em first."

He walked over behind the wet bar and fixed himself another rum and Coke and me another Cherry Coke. "I distrust a man who doesn't drink. You sure you won't join me?"

I nodded.

He shook his head. "I know I have a lot of critics," he said. "But what man or woman doing something different doesn't? I'm sure you have critics."

"A few," I said with a smile.

"Jesus certainly did," he said. "Anyway, what person wouldn't want to live in a safe place with good schools and a real sense of community?"

I didn't answer. I assumed it was rhetorical.

"Exactly. Like Jesus or the founders of this country, I take the criticism gladly and am honored to be in such good company."

"But Jesus's vision of the inclusive Kingdom of God was inclusion, filled with drunks, prostitutes, the poor. The Kingdom is built on compassion, not righteousness—and it's filled with 'whosoever will.' "

"Maybe so. But I haven't figured out how to get everyone in *and* maintain what we have. Maybe we're not supposed to until the kingdom finally *does* come. I'm just trying to take good care of my family and the good people of this great county. If I do that, then I sleep good at night. It's not that I wouldn't like to save the world. I just lost that kind of idealism long ago."

I didn't respond.

"Come on. Let's eat. Then we can talk about Mike."

We walked through a foyer with a serpentine staircase crafted of stone, oak, mahogany, and wrought iron. Hanging on the wall behind it were four antique Indian tribal screens with carved teak frames.

In the Old World kitchen beneath a chandelier of burning candles, we found the Hawkins family: Sharon, Mike's wife; Julie, Kevin's wife; Charlotte, Howard's wife; and Julie's two preschoolers, Sam and Sandy.

"Kevin's still on patrol," Charlotte explained. "He's sorry he can't join us."

"See," Howard said. "For everything we enjoy, there's a sacrifice to be made. Kids today don't understand that."

"They do in Pine County," Sharon said, and I thought I detected a hint of sarcasm in her voice.

"True."

Beneath the flicker of the candles, we ate a wonderful southwestern meal and enjoyed lively conversation about everyone's day. It was something out of Norman Rockwell. Everyone seemed relaxed and genuinely respectful and loving of one another—except for Sharon.

"How's my Mike?" Charlotte asked.

"The chaplain here thinks he may've been involved in the murder," Howard said.

She shook her head. "Not Mike. He's not even supposed to be in there. He's innocent. He's not violent. And this isn't just a mother talking. Ask anyone."

"You know who the victim was?" I asked, glancing over at Sam and Sandy.

"Yes," Charlotte said in a strained voice. "We know, but Mike wouldn't've done that. They all had a chance to do that when that man was sitting in *our* jail. And they could've easily covered it up then."

Sharon made a scoffing sound that made me think they *had* done something to Justin Menge in their jail. And it probably wasn't the first time either.

"Our lives are open books, John," Howard said. "We're politicians. We live in a glass house. Feel free to take as close a look as you want to at us. We're clean. We're rich and a lot of jealous people start rumors, but being wealthy isn't a crime."

After dessert, Charlotte and Sharon started clearing off the table while Julie took Sam and Sandy upstairs for a bath.

"You ought to consider moving out here with us," Hawkins said. "There's a couple of really nice places available and we've been looking for a new pastor for our chapel. I think you'd really like it. Especially if you and Susan are thinking about having kids."

An alarm sounded inside me when he used Susan's name. I hadn't mentioned her to him. I hadn't even told him I was married.

"I'll think about it. I had a friend who came out here last weekend looking around. Did you happen to see him? Merrill Monroe. He's a rather large African-American in his mid-thirties."

Sharon dropped a plate in the kitchen and it shattered against the tile floor, echoing through the large, open room.

"No," Hawkins said. "I sure didn't."

"He's missing now. This was the last place he was known to be."

"Was he looking at property?" he asked, his calm demeanor never wavering. "I'd give the local real estate agent a call."

"No, just looking."

"Well, we'll keep our eyes open for him. I'll tell my deputies."

"I appreciate it. Thanks for the hospitality—the good company and the delicious meal. You have a lovely family and such a nice place out here beneath the pecan trees."

"You come and visit anytime. I'll walk you to the door."

At the door, he stepped out onto the porch with me and pulled the door shut behind him. "Remember what you said in there about my family and my place? About how special they are?"

"Yeah."

"Well, they are. I'd do anything to protect them. Anything. There's nothing I wouldn't do to keep what's mine. Nothing."

CHAPTER THIRTY-EIGHT

"Juan did not kill Justin Menge," Carlos Matos said. "I swear it on the soul of my children." He crossed himself, then continued. "We were together the whole day. Even after we were back in the cells, we were talking back and forth the entire time. And I lied about him cutting me. I was trying to get him in trouble at the time. I was cut by someone else on another matter, but that has all been taken care of now."

It was the following afternoon, a Wednesday—one week since Justin Menge had been murdered. I'd joined Carlos Matos in the waiting area of the medical department where he was required to sit until the doctor could see him. We were the only two people in the large room. The officer assigned to watch it was leaning out the partially opened door smoking.

I held a file folder with logs from the night of the murder and was on my way to confront DeLisa Lopez when I ran into Matos.

"You lied?" I asked.

"*Sí*. I am very sorry, Father."

"Or did Martinez get to you again and you're lying now?"

"No, *señor*. I swear."

"Or were you lying then *and* now? I'm beginning to think I can't trust you."

"I am telling the truth. Juan did not kill Justin."

"He could've had it done," I said, suppressing a yawn.

After leaving the Hawkins's, I had driven around Pine County looking for Merrill for much of the night and had felt my sleep deficit all day.

"He did not have a reason."

"Menge was going to testify against him," I said.

"No, he was not, and everyone knew it. Juan was not afraid of that. They did not have anything on him. Nothing. You think Juan told Menge something—confessed some crime to him. Why?"

I shrugged.

"Well, he didn't. He would not. Why would he?"

"Then why was Menge going to testify against him?"

"I already told you, *señor*," he said. "The inspector's trying to set him up."

"Fortner?"

The medical officer might as well have been smoking in the waiting room for all the good leaning out the open door was doing. Every gust of the cool October wind blew his smoke directly at us. I coughed, attempted to breathe shallowly, and began to fan myself with the file folder I was holding.

"No," he said, shaking his head as if the thought defied all logic. "He could not do something like that. It was the big inspector. What is his name? Daniels? He has been screwing with Juan since he has been here."

"Why?"

He hesitated, looking at me as if wanting to tell me but thinking better of it.

As I looked at him—at his thick, shiny black hair and dull black eyes, and the way his blue inmate uniform strained to hold in his thick body—I wondered what DeLisa Lopez was thinking. Could such a beautiful woman really be involved with such an average man?

"Tell me," I said. "It may be the only way to save your friend from a murder charge."

He leaned in close, looked around, then whispered, "Daniels thinks Juan raped his wife."

"Daniels's wife or Juan's?"

"Juan does not have a wife," he said. "Daniels's."

"Did he?"

"He did not, but the inspector thinks that he did."

A large black nurse, whose pants swished together as she moved, walked into the room and over to the vending machines in the corner closet. The soft hum of the machines grew louder as she opened the door and went inside. It took her a while, but she finally coaxed a diet Dr Pepper and two Snickers out of the machines.

"Menge was not going to testify against Juan. He did not know anything. Even if there was something to know, Menge did not know it. He and Juan never even spoke."

I nodded.

The officer glanced back in our direction, blowing smoke out of his nose as he did. I waved to him, signaling everything was fine, but he didn't acknowledge it.

"Was Ms. Lopez in your cell around the time of the murder?"

Eyes growing wide, jaw dropping, he was stunned into silence.

He started to say something, but stopped.

The officer opened the front door all the way and Anna walked inside, waving the cloud of smoke away with her hand as she did. As she walked over to the door leading to psychology and classification, she gave me a polite nod and strained smile.

"If you can give her an alibi, you should," I said, "otherwise she could get charged with murder."

"She was not."

"I already know she was in the PM unit that night," I said, holding up the file folder, "and I know you were one of the men she was there to see."

"*Sí*. She came by earlier, but this was way before Menge got killed."

"You two having an affair?"

"She would not . . ." he began, shaking his head as he trailed off.

"Don't be so hard on yourself," I said with a smile.

"No, I mean . . ."

I knew what he meant, but as he explained it, I wondered if he and DeLisa could fit in the roles of David and Bathsheba. If they were having an affair, they might. What if Menge caught them and was going to report it in his attempt to get out early to be with Sobel? They could've killed him to cover it up.

I felt like a real bastard for what I was about to say next, but I figured his reaction would tell me more than his words ever would. Besides, I was angry at myself for what I had done to Anna, hurting inside, and felt like spreading some of it around.

"Listen," I said, "you're not going to get her in trouble. We've already got her for sex with inmates. Evidently, she's carrying on with several in the institution. I just want to know if you can provide her with an alibi during the time Menge was murdered."

The muscles in his neck and arms tensed, his jaw flexed, his black eyes burned.

Very slowly and deliberately he said, "She was down there that night, but she was not with me. If she needs an alibi, I am not the one to give it to her."

"So she could've killed him?" I asked.

"Sounds to me like she could do anything," he said, still seething, his knuckles cracking from how tightly he was clenching his fists.

When Matos was taken into medical, I walked out of the waiting room and down the long corridor toward DeLisa Lopez's office. On the way, I passed Anna in the hall. We both smiled and spoke, but it was strained and awkward, and I wasn't prepared for how much more angry and empty it made me feel.

My heart hurt, and I felt disconnected, adrift.

I turned and called after her.

When she slowly walked back toward me, I said, "Are you okay?"

She nodded without really looking at me. "Any word from Merrill yet?"

I shook my head. "I think Howard Hawkins is involved."

"I'm worried about him."

"Me, too."

"Please let me know when you find out anything."

"Sure."

She nodded, her full lips twisting as she frowned, and began to walk away.

"Hey," I said. "We don't have to ignore each other."

She turned around slowly, her head down. "I can't do this," she said, lifting her deep brown eyes, wounded and sad, up to meet mine.

"I'm sorry," I said. "I never meant—"

"I've put in for a transfer."

"*What?*" I asked, loss and longing gripping my heart.

"Central Office. There's a position open and they think I can just lateral in. I won't even have to interview."

"But—"

"It'd make it easier," she said. "I need a change anyway."

"Anna, I never meant—"

"I'll miss you," she said, lifting her hand and touching my cheek, before turning and walking away.

For a long moment I didn't move. I couldn't. I just stood there, the scent of her perfume swirling around me.

When I was able, I walked over to DeLisa Lopez's office door and looked inside. Through the narrow pane of glass I could see that she was intently engaged in counseling an inmate. I watched for a moment before walking away. She was obviously a caring and compassionate counselor.

As I waited, I opened the file folder I was carrying and pulled out the copies I had made of the control room logs from the night of the murder and looked through them again.

Before, when I had studied the logs, I had concentrated on the ones from G-dorm, but my subconscious must have registered something wrong in the control room logs that my conscious mind, concentrating on G-dorm, missed.

I found where DeLisa Lopez had been logged in that morning. It was just a few minutes after me. As I followed the list down, I saw the comings and goings of the staff and visitors of the institution.

Anna and Merrill were logged in just a few minutes after Lopez, Fortner a few minutes after that. In the early afternoon, Tom Daniels was logged in and Merrill was logged out as his shift came to an end. I saw where I was logged out at the normal time and then back in for the PM unit Catholic Mass that night.

I ran my finger down the page, examining every entry for the entire day and the following morning. I found where Daniels and I had been logged out in the early morning hours after we had secured and processed the crime scene. And then I saw where staff members began to be logged in the next morning. However, what I didn't see was where DeLisa Lopez had been logged out.

It wasn't there.

She had come into the institution early Wednesday morning and not left it again until the end of her shift on Thursday evening. She had spent thirty-two long hours inside the institution.

It could go unnoticed easily enough. I wouldn't have found it had I not been trying to identify the woman who was seen in G-dorm the evening of the murder. There was no other reason to look at the logs. Well over a hundred people entered and exited the institution every day, arriving when one set of officers were in the control room, leaving when there was another. Unless someone was really studying the logs, looking for discrepancies, like I was now, no one would ever know—and, even if someone asked, the person could claim that the control room officer simply failed to log him or her out. I thought about how many times I had worked late, catching up or covering a special program, and how surprised the control room was to see me when I walked through the gate because they had no idea I was still inside the institution.

The how was easy. What I needed to know was the why. Why, on the night of the murder, had DeLisa Lopez never left the institution.

That's what I was about to go in and ask her when the officer in the waiting room opened the door and told me I had an emergency telephone call. Rushing down the hall and through the door, I picked up the phone. It was Sharon Hawkins, and in a surprisingly flat, matter-of-fact voice she told me Merrill was in Howard Hawkins's jail and would not survive the night.

CHAPTER THIRTY-NINE

The temperature was falling with the descent of the sun, and the heater in my old Chevy S-10 wasn't working, but that wasn't why Sharon Hawkins was shaking.

"Why're you doing this?" I asked.

"I can't take it anymore," she said. "I'm leaving. They'll hunt me down and kill me, but I don't care. It might be different if I had children, but . . ."

"We won't let that happen. You can come with me tonight. Merrill and I will look out for you."

"For the rest of my life?"

"For as long as it takes."

"I believed in his vision," she said. "Howard's. It makes sense, you know? Can't save the world. We've got to take care of our families no matter what. That's what God wants us to do. But he's a dictator. He's building a kingdom and he's the king. I can't do it anymore—living in his prison, watching him steal and kill and abuse, and all in the name of God, family, and community."

Sharon Hawkins sat rigid in the seat, her right arm outstretched, French-manicured acrylic fingernails drumming on the door. Her hair was a blonde dye job that should've been better considering how much money the Hawkins family had. Her makeup was too heavy, thick globs of mascara sticking her eyelashes together. Yet for all her attempts at cosmetic improvement, she was still a very plain-looking woman.

"He didn't start off being a monster," she said, still looking out the window at the darkness. "In the beginning, back when I first met them, he was different. His vision seemed pure, but as his power grew, he became a monster." She turned suddenly and looked at me. "He's killed four people that I know of. Maybe more. *Probably* more. Your friend may already be dead."

"I doubt it."

She laughed again. Her laugh was devoid of humor, full of futility. "What're you planning to do?"

"Find out what they're holding him on, and—"

She looked at me in astonishment. "What they're *holding* him on? They're not holding him on anything. *Jesus.* You don't get it. This isn't a regular jail. Things aren't done in a regular way here. He hasn't been charged with anything. He hasn't *done* anything. He hasn't been arrested. He's been abducted."

I had encountered men like Hawkins before, though not many as extreme—people, usually men, who, in their small realm, had unlimited power and no accountability—people who had lost all touch with reality. All it takes is a lot of wealth or charisma, a little madness, and a total lack of responsibility, and in time you have a monster. The Howard Hawkins of the world, and there are many, are the Saddam Husseins, the David Koreshes, and the Bin Ladens at the local level, whose low profile enables them to remain beneath the radar, inflict damage for decades until they finally self-destruct or draw outside attention to themselves. Otherwise, they're never apprehended. And men like Howard are most often to be found in the small rural areas where their authority goes unquestioned, their power unchallenged, where decent country folks are not equipped to deal with them. I may not understand what Hawkins does or why, but I can't imagine any of it will come as a surprise.

"They're not even keeping him in the jail," she said. "They've got him in the dungeon."

"The *dungeon?*"

"That's what they call it. It's an underground room that was part of the old jail. It has a cell where they keep all the unofficial prisoners. No one's ever gotten out of it."

"Until now."

She gave me that same futile laugh I was already weary of hearing.

"Why is he doing this?"

"Why do men like Howard do most of the things they do? If you do whatever the hell you like long enough, you begin to think you're invincible. Plus he thinks God is on his side, that he's some special visionary. I can tell you his reasons aren't based on any logic most people would understand."

I thought about how nice it'd be to have Merrill in on what had gone from an information-gathering and bail-posting mission to a jailbreak. I could call Dad or Jake, but I didn't want this to become official yet. We needed to keep everyone in play until we could find out who killed Justin and why, and amass enough evidence to put him away. Still, if the Hawkins clan were as lawless as Sharon suggested, I would need backup. As a compromise, I left a message on Daniels's voicemail to get backup and come get me out of the Pine County Jail if he didn't hear from me again within an hour.

"Any suggestions on the best way to get Merrill out?"

"Wait 'til seven. Kevin'll be on duty by himself. I could distract him."

"How will you do that?"

"Fuck him," she said in a dispassionate monotone.

"That won't be—"

"Do it all the time. Since Mike's been in prison, Kevin sneaks into my room at least twice a week and does what he wants to me."

"By force?" I asked.

"He doesn't exactly rape me, but I can't say no."

"Tell you what, just pretend, and I'll take care of the rest."

She shrugged. "Whatever. Just get your friend and get the fuck out of this county."

"I will, but you're going with us."

To that, she responded with her signature laugh again. It said things were foreordained, resistance was futile, that people like us were merely pawns of the powerful.

"He sat there and lied to you," she said. "And you'd never have known it. He's amazing. The nicest man in the world—on the surface. Only the surface. He told you he hadn't seen your friend while at that very moment he was being tortured in the basement of his jail."

"I didn't believe him."

"I'm not saying you believed him, just that he's a good liar. And acting like Mike couldn't have possibly killed that other inmate when that's what they sent him there to do. He should've gotten an Academy Award for that one."

"Run that by me again. Who sent Mike in to do what?"

"Howard. When Mike was arrested, Howard got him sent to PCI so he could keep an eye on Justin Menge. He was inside anyway, so why not?"

"What's Mike in on?" I asked.

She shook her head. "He's a bad drunk. Wouldn't be a problem if he'd just stay in Pine County where daddy can fix everything, but he's got to hotdog all over the place. He's in on three different third-degree felonies. He got his third DUI, driving with a suspended license for the third time, and resisting an officer with violence all at the same time."

"And Howard couldn't help him?"

"Happened in Bay County. Nothing he could do."

"But he got him moved to PCI once he was inside? That wouldn't be easy."

She shrugged. "It's what he claims. Howard's crazy, but most people don't realize it. He's still got a few friends in power here and there, and he's got enough money to turn the wheels— that's what he calls it."

I thought about it. I guessed it was possible, and whether it was or not, the fact still remained that Mike and Justin wound up in the same PM quad in the same prison.

"Justin didn't touch Kevin's kids. He put him at PCI so he could kill Justin Menge if it came to that, and soon he'll be out, coming back to us, to me, to my bed."

"Why not just kill him when he was in custody here?" I asked.

"They couldn't without drawing a lot of attention from the outside world. He was getting too famous."

"So you're saying they actually sent Mike to PCI so he could kill Justin?"

She nodded. "If he had to. They were pretty sure he wasn't going to do anything, but they wanted to make sure."

"That's a little extreme, isn't it?"

"Not to extremists. Remember, they don't think like you and me."

"Why wait until now? He's been in there with him for a while. Why the delay?"

"He was scared. Told his dad someone threatened him— someone he was truly afraid of."

"Any idea who?" I asked.

She looked up and pursed her lips as she thought about it. Finally, she shook her head. "I'm not positive, but something like Charles or Chuck or—"

"Chris? Was it Chris Sobel?"

She nodded. "Yeah, I'm pretty sure that was his name. Who is he?"

"The victim's boyfriend."

Her eyebrows arched and she cut her eyes over toward me.

"They were in prison together?"

"They met there."

We were quiet a moment, the flat, straight road stretching out before us, its yellow lines seeming to race to meet the beam of my headlights.

"You willing to testify to all this?" I asked.

"I won't live long enough to testify to that or anything else, but I'm willing. I'd love to see Howard's kingdom crumble."

"We just might be able to make a case after all."

"Make a *case?*" she asked in shock. "Haven't you been listening? We're not going to make it through the night."

CHAPTER FORTY

Sharon Hawkins had large, natural breasts. They sagged down against her rib cage, flattening out on top as they did.

I knew this because she had them out showing her brother-in-law when I snuck up behind him and slipped a snub-nosed .38 behind his ear.

"Now you've been fucked," Sharon said with a smile. "How does it feel?"

"What?" he said. He turned around toward me slowly. "What the fuck?"

"You're about to find out," I said. "Take me to the dungeon."

"Dungeon? What? What dungeon? What the hell're you talkin' about? Dungeon."

As Sharon put on her bra and shirt in no particular hurry, I reached down and removed Kevin's gun from its holster. He didn't move to stop me, but I could see in his eyes he thought about it. When I had taken his gun, I slipped it and mine into my coat pockets.

His eyes widened.

"One more time," I said. "And I mean *only* one more time. Take me to the dungeon."

He laughed. "What dungeon? You been listening to this crazy whore?"

I thought about what Martinez had done to Sarah, what the Hawkins men had done to Sharon, and of all the violence men commit against women all the time, and it made me so angry, so full of rage, so fearful for Susan and Anna I didn't know what to do.

I snapped out a hard right jab that popped him right on the nose, and his head jerked back. He yelped and covered his face with his hands, tears filling his eyes.

"You're a fuckin' *preacher* for God's sake," he said, his voice wet and nasally.

"Sometimes," I said. "And sometimes I'm just a guy looking for his friend."

"You better tell him, Kevin," Sharon said.

"Shut up, bitch."

I popped him again. This time an uppercut that tagged the bottom of his chin. His head snapped back like before, but this time there was choking.

My hand and wrist hurt, and I could feel my knuckles beginning to swell.

"Okay, okay. I'll show you the damn dungeon, but there's nobody down there. You're making the biggest mistake of your life. Both of you." He glared at Sharon. "Your life is *so* over, bitch."

I slapped Kevin hard across the face with my open hand. He grabbed his cheek and stared at me in shock.

"I'm not crazy about that word," I said.

Sharon laughed, this time with real delight. "So he bitch-slapped you. Get it?"

Kevin shook his head at her. "You're a dead woman."

"You think that scares me anymore? You stupid little bastard, you don't get it, do you? My life was over the moment I became a Hawkins."

"I'm gonna fuck you one last time before I kill you, and it's gonna hurt."

I slapped him hard across the face with my open hand again,

and he whipped his head around toward me, eyes blazing with anger.

"Nobody's talking to me. I feel left out. Don't ever threaten her again."

"He couldn't hurt me," Sharon said, looking at Kevin. "His dick's too little."

"It's probably hard to tell tonight," I said, "but I'm basically committed to nonviolence, but if you'd like to slap him, I'd love to let you."

She smiled, took a step toward him, reared back, and slapped him so hard his head whipped to the side.

He made a move toward her, and I stepped between them.

"You don't even have your gun out," he said.

"Then now'd be the time to try something."

I could see the flicker of thought in his moist eyes, but it quickly died. "The time'll come. We'll—"

"You should take some initiative. Do something on your own. Like you said, I don't have the gun out."

"Yeah," he said like a sullen child, "but you've got it where you can get it."

"Take me to Merrill."

"All this over a nigger," he said, shaking his head.

I drove a hard body punch to his lower abdomen. He fell to his knees, doubling over as he did. On the ground, he attempted to find some air, but there was none to be had.

"I *really* don't like that word."

When he could take a breath, he threw up, his body lurching forward in violent heaves. Eventually, he led us to the back of the jail, through a door, into a storage closet, through another door, and down a rusting spiral staircase.

The dungeon lived up to its name. It was dark and smelled of human suffering. From an unseen corner hidden in the shadows I could hear the constant, mind-numbing sound of water dripping from an open pipe.

Emerging from ancient and jagged concrete, black and rusted bars formed a small cell along the back wall. Inside, Merrill was standing, his large hands gripping the bars. His face was swollen and disfigured. His upper lip was bloody and busted, his right eye swollen shut.

So much violence. I'm sick of it, of being around it, of being part of it, of being it.

"I's just thinkin' this jail needed a chaplain," Merrill said with a smile, which with the condition of his face looked like a fun house mirror reflection.

"Not to perform Last Rites I hope?"

"Well, hell, yeah, soon as I get my hands on that rat motherfucker in front of you."

"Unlock the cell."

He took out his keys, his hands jittering so badly they jingled, then took a step toward the cell door before stopping and shaking his head. "I can't."

"Open the door, bitch," Merrill yelled at him. "Don't make me more pissed than I already am."

Kevin Hawkins bowed his head and handed the keys to me. When I had unlocked the cell door, Merrill limped over to him, and in a voice so low I had to strain to hear it, said, "Live with the certain knowledge that your days are numbered."

The entire time Merrill talked, Hawkins never lifted his head.

Sharon laughed, but it was free of the futility it previously held. Instead, it was filled with a very real hope.

"Told you we'd take care of you," I said.

"Well, you shouldn't have," Howard Hawkins's voice boomed from behind us.

I reached for the .38 in my jacket pocket, but he jammed a shell in the chamber of his shotgun before I could even touch the handle.

Chapter Forty-One

"Well, now," Hawkins said. "I's afraid of this."

"Let's do them tonight, Daddy," Kevin said as he dug the guns out of my jacket pockets. "Have that big nigger in the ground by mornin'."

"Sounds like Junior's scared," Merrill said.

"Not without reason," I said.

"True."

"By God but I hate a sassy nigger," Kevin said.

"He really just say that?" I asked.

"You thinkin' what I'm thinking?" Merrill asked.

"That he's inbred or suicidal?"

"Both," he said, spinning around.

Grabbing Kevin's gun, he pointed it at his head, and used his body for a shield.

"Unless you want to see how small your boy's brain really is," he said to Hawkins, "drop it."

Without protest, Hawkins eased the shotgun down onto the wet cement floor. When he was upright again, he held up his hands.

"We won't give you any trouble. Go ahead and leave. Just do two things. Leave the girl and don't ever come back to Pine County."

A wide, distorted smile spread over Merrill's face. "If she wants to, hell, even if she don't, Mrs. Hawkins is comin' with us. And as for Pine County, hell, I been thinkin' about buyin' a place next to yours."

"You're—" Hawkins began.

"Holdin' all the cards," Merrill said. "So shut the fuck up. And just pray that cancer kills your ass before I do."

"Cancer?" Sharon asked in shock.

"You can't believe what all these dumb motherfuckers say in front of a dead man. Only I ain't dead. I like Lazarus come back from the grave. Shouldn't count a nigga out before you kill his ass. You and Junior in the cell. Now. I ain't got all damn day. I've got to get home and get some rest and think about how many different ways I'm gonna fuck with y'all."

They quickly moved into the cell.

"Don't kill them," Tom Daniels said, descending the stairs. "Let's wait until we can arrest them and get them inside one of our prisons."

"Welcome to the party," Merrill said to him. "You a little late."

"Well, my son here gave me my invitation a little late."

Just before Sharon and I had walked in, I'd left a message on his voicemail letting him know where we were and what we were doing—just in case it didn't go according to plan.

"It's a good thing I came," Daniels continued. "I've got two other deputies cuffed to each other inside a cell upstairs."

Merrill shrugged. "All you did was save their lives. Whatta you want, a cookie?"

"No need to thank me. But my daughter'd never forgive me if I let something happen to her new husband. By the way, she thinks you're helping them move this weekend." He looked over at me. "I figured out how Hawkins did it. Potter helped him. I think we've got a solid case." He nodded over toward the cell. "Now it looks like we'll have the whole family inside."

"That's good," I said. "They don't like to be separated. Now they can recreate their little city set on a hill experiment inside.

See if it *really* works."

Merrill looked over at me, his swollen face a lopsided question mark.

"You've got a lot of catching up to do."

"Good thing I learns fast for a sassy nigger."

CHAPTER FORTY-TWO

The morning sunlight dancing on the gentle ripples of the Apalachicola River refracted into sparkles so intense they could only be looked at a moment at a time. Merrill and I were seated by the river's edge in a couple of wobbly, uncomfortable wooden chairs. Merrill didn't seem to mind—not about the chairs or the blinding reflection or much of anything. He just seemed happy to see daylight, happy, like his ancestors before him, to be a free man of color.

"They say when they first came to Africa to get slaves they got African tribes known for their docility," he said, as if giving voice to a stray thought. "Said they'd make good slaves and not cause any trouble."

"Yeah?"

"I ain't from that tribe."

I nodded.

"I'm from the give-me-freedom-or-give-me-death-motherfucker tribe."

A large limb with three turtles floated by on the other side of the river. When it bumped the base of a cypress tree, two of the turtles fell into the water. The day was so quiet, the water so calm. I heard the two small *ker-plunks* from where I sat.

"Those motherfuckers beat the hell out of me," he said. "They'd wake me up in the middle of the night—hell, it may've been the middle of the day, I couldn't tell—just to take turns punching me. I ain't as pretty as I used to be. And they did things to me. Not sexual things, but belittling shit."

"Yeah?"

"I'm gonna kill 'em."

I didn't say anything. I understood how he felt, and his need to give voice to it, but I hoped that eventually, after he had healed, he'd reconsider his wish for retribution. The line between vengeance and justice is often a fine one, but there is a line. Merrill would have to figure out his own lines for himself. All I could do was be his friend, help him however I could.

The line in my own life, the one I seemed to be tripping over so often lately, was between compassion and justice, and like Merrill, I had to figure a few things out.

"I wanna hunt 'em down and take 'em out," he said, still staring at the river.

"Won't have to. Eventually, they'll come after Sharon."

"Maybe."

"They will."

"They come after us and we take them out, it's self-defense," he said. "We go after them it's . . ."

"Something else," I said. "It's a fine line, but . . ."

"Situation like this it's all somebody like you got."

"And you," I said.

He looked at me again, and I could tell he was considering what I had said.

"I need to tell you something."

"Okay."

"But first I've got to tell you something else."

I nodded.

"I'm a better man because of you."

My eyes stung, and I had to blink several times. He had never said anything like that before, and, though I doubted it were true, and thought it much more likely just the opposite was the case, it meant more to me than he would ever know.

"You like nobody I've ever known—or known about," he said.

"Thanks. And ditto."

"You got all these lines and codes—like the shit we was just talking about," he said. "You got faith—and not just in God, but in yourself and me, and fuck all if I understand it, but in humanity. You got this way of making people want to be better, but you never seem to judge us when we're not."

"You must've really thought you were going to die in that dungeon."

"Don't laugh this off," he said. "Hear what I've got to say."

I nodded. "I'm sorry," I said. "That was—"

"You do this balancing act thing between like mercy and righteousness," he continued, "and you're always thinking, always examining, always questioning—yourself and everything else. Thing is, that's who you are. You slip too far to one side or the other then you're not you."

I nodded again. He didn't have to say anything else. He had noticed the change in me, too, the hardness, the anger and violence that were much closer to the surface now, the rage that more quickly rushed out.

"I know you can handle yourself. You plenty tough. But to be tough—when you have to—and still have compassion, that's an art. That's *your* art."

We were quiet for a moment.

"I'm struggling," I said.

"I know."

"I'm not sure what to do."

"You'll figure it out. This is temporary. Just don't forget who you are."

"Thanks for reminding me."

We were quiet again, this time for a while.

"Maybe they got sense enough to stay in Pine County, and

this won't involve you. They realize there's no way for them to win out here, that even if they get us, your dad or Daniels would square it, then none of this need involve you."

"I'm involved, and I'm gonna stay involved. No matter what. Besides, I don't think they think like that. Being in touch with reality don't seem to be hallmarks of the Hawkins'. Normal rules don't apply."

"Normal laws of nature do. If I cut they ass, do they not bleed?"

"Literate bastard, aren't you?"

"Some kind of bastard," he said with a lopsided smile. "Sharon says Hawkins really think he's untouchable, invulnerable. Whole life's taught him to think that way."

I nodded.

We were quiet a long moment, and I knew healing was beginning to take place in both of us.

"I know what it's like to be an inmate now," he said.

I didn't say anything, just thought about the paradigm shift he must be experiencing—like the doctor who's diagnosed with the type of disease he specializes in.

"I'll be a different CO now," he said.

I nodded.

A few minutes later, Tom Daniels arrived with what looked to be breakfast. He handed us each a paper cup of coffee and began to pass out glazed doughnuts. When I took the lid off my coffee, the steam rising from the cup warmed my nose, and I realized how cool the morning was. October in Florida is usually like the end of summer in most places, but not this year.

"So how we gonna take down the Hawkins clan?" Daniels asked.

He had not called FDLE or taken any other action against them last night, feeling it best to complete our investigation first, knowing he would no longer be in charge—maybe not even involved. All we had on them at the moment was what they had done to Merrill, and they could fabricate evidence and an arrest report too easily, explain his wounds away by saying he had resisted arrest, even charge me and Daniels with breaking him out of jail. That would all get very complicated very fast. We didn't just want them on false arrest and imprisonment, which would be difficult to prove anyway, so we hadn't notified any authorities—and if they were as corrupt as we thought them to be, they wouldn't either.

"We were just discussing that very thing," Merrill said.

"And?"

"Think we got it covered," he said.

The doughnuts were soft and warm and sticky on my fingers and I had eaten three before I realized it. Merrill had eaten more.

Daniels shook his head. "We'll get back to that in a minute. For now, let's talk about taking Mike Hawkins down. He is our bad guy, right?"

"Oh, he's a bad guy," I said. "Comes from a long line of them, but it doesn't mean he killed Menge."

"But Sharon told you that's what he was put there to do."

"And I don't doubt that, but it doesn't mean he did it. She said Chris was protecting Justin, that Mike was too scared of him to do anything."

"Well, I think he did," he said.

"Then arrest him."

"Can't. Don't have enough on him yet. It's why I didn't do anything to Hawkins last night."

"I thought that so I could kill them," Merrill said.

"No, but if you'd've let them kill *you*, then we could've taken them down."

"My bad, but nobody told me the plan."

"I'm hoping they'll fuck up in an even bigger way this time

and we can get them all—including Mike."

"Not possible to fuck up any bigger than fuckin' with me."

I remembered something Paula Menge had told me earlier, and must have made a noise, because Daniels said, "What?"

"Paula Menge told me that she hired a PI to investigate Hawkins. She thinks he took off with half of her retainer, but—"

"Probably didn't make it out of the dungeon."

"Least not alive," Merrill said. "He wasn't in there when I was."

"I'll look into it," Daniels said.

"You should probably talk to Sharon too."

"I will."

We were all quiet a moment, each of us still. We were weary and wounded, but had promises to keep and many miles to go.

"So how do we make the case?" Daniels asked.

"Against Hawkins?" I asked. "I thought you were thinking Sobel with Pitts's help. Or maybe Martinez. You giving up on him?"

"I don't think he did it now. I wanted it to be him, but we've got to go were the evidence leads."

"Matos is convinced you've been trying to set Martinez up."

"Wonder what he'll say when I arrest Hawkins?"

"If that's the way it turns out, what will you do about Martinez?"

He looked into the distance.

I followed his gaze. Across the river, Spanish moss on the branches of cypress trees rising out of the water along the banks waved like clean sheets on a clothesline in the morning breeze.

When he looked at me, his eyes were every bit as sad and vulnerable as I had expected of a man who had long since realized he was impotent to protect his wife from the evils of this world.

"I'm not sure. Gotta do something."

I felt like a voyeur, sickened and guilty for seeing something so private, as if my knowing was part of an ongoing violation of him and his family. "I'm sorry."

"Thanks, but right now I'm more concerned about the Hawkins boys. Where's Sharon?"

"Merrill's mom's."

"Mom'll put holes in 'em if they come callin'," Merrill said. "And I'll stay over there at night 'til this thing's over."

Daniels nodded. "We've got him at the right place at the right time. We've seen firsthand how his family operates. We know they sent him in there to do the deed. And we've got him with the murder weapon."

Merrill said, "When this happen?"

"While you were away," he said. "We found it in his cell. Now, we've just got to find his accomplice."

"Who found the shank in his cell?"

"Pitts."

"There's your accomplice."

"Why do you say that?"

"I searched his cell. There was no weapon in it."

Out on the river, a silver pontoon boat sped by, a small fiberglass boat tied to the back bouncing in its wake. On board, a quartet of middle-aged men in jeans, flannel shirts, and baseball caps gave us an obligatory wave.

"You think he planted it?" Daniels asked.

"Somebody did."

"So we're no closer to knowing with certainty who did the deed?"

I shrugged. "We're getting closer all the time, just don't know how yet. Every scrap of information helps. Better to know too much than too little. Eventually we'll get the piece that makes all the others fall into place."

"You're right, I'm just ready to be done with this one."

"Well, we're not there yet," I said, then told them about discovering that DeLisa Lopez was in the institution for over thirty-two hours the day of and following the murder.

Small waves caused by the pontoon boat's wake rippled the smooth surface of the water and slapped at the base of the cypress trees and sandy banks.

"And we've still got to strongly consider Potter, Pitts, Sobel, Martinez, and Paula Menge."

"You tell him about the uniform we found?" Daniels asked.

We nodded.

"Y'all ever find the tune-up video?" Merrill asked.

"I think I've got a good idea where it might be," I said.

"Think?" he said. "Why haven't you gotten it?"

"Been too busy savin' your black ass."

"Well, now you done that, let's go get the motherfucker."

CHAPTER FORTY-THREE

The PCI inmate library was larger and had more books than the Potter County Public Library, the Pottersville High School library, and the Pottersville Elementary School library put together. With use-or-lose funds appropriated each year by the state, the librarian and her assistant flung purchase orders like seeds in the wind, producing an annual harvest of computers, audiovisual equipment, CDs, DVDs, and, of course, books.

In addition to fiction and nonfiction, hardcovers and paperbacks, the inmates were required by law to have access to a full law library, which had its own room in the back of the building. With all of this, plus specially trained inmate law clerks and orderlies, the library of PCI was one of the highest traffic areas on the compound.

When Merrill, Daniels, and I entered, the library was filled to capacity, and there were inmates waiting at the center gate for their turn to come up.

Passing the magazines and periodicals, we continued through rows of shelving lined with every genre of fiction, the most popular of which were the romance, western, and mystery. Inmates browsing for a book they hadn't already read several times tried to eye Merrill and Daniels without being noticed, many of them grabbing the closest title to them and heading toward the door.

Clerks in the law library looked up from helping inmates file appeals to see what we were doing. The young bookish-looking assistant with glasses on his nose, phone to his ear, and feet on his desk didn't even notice.

When we finally stopped at the video counter in the back, a collective sigh of relief seemed to be released from the inmates behind us, while the two orderlies working the video counter had the opposite reaction. Behind them, lining several high shelves, were nonviolent feature films and educational videos on nearly every subject imaginable. Above them, on a DVD/VCR mounted to the wall, a mystery show I had seen on PBS played silently, and scattered all around us were inmates with headphones who seemed to be only half watching it.

"How's it goin'?" I asked.

The orderly closest to me, still eyeing Merrill and Daniels warily, gave me a nod and a grunt.

"You got a National Geographic video about gorillas?" I asked.

"We did," he said, "but it's missin'."

"Any idea what happened to it?"

"None."

"Let me see the case."

He glanced back at the wall behind him and, too quickly, said, "It's missin', too."

"What is that?" I said, pointing to the case I had just asked for.

"That's somethin' else."

"Let me see."

When he hesitated, Merrill growled, "Bitch, give him the damn case."

He turned, using his body to block our vision, but I could hear him slide a disc out of the case and drop it to the floor.

When he turned back around, he handed me the empty case I had asked for.

"Now let me see the disc that was in it."

"There wasn't one," he said, sliding his foot back to better conceal it.

"Hand him the disc 'fore I jump over this counter and shove your ass into that TV up there," Merrill said.

I pointed down at the disc on the floor behind his foot.

He looked at it as if seeing it for the first time.

"Must've slipped out when I picked up the case."

"Must've."

When he handed me the disc, I took it and started walking away.

"What're you doin'?" he asked.

"Borrowing it," I said.

"It's just a blank disc," he said.

"*Oh*, I hope it is," Merrill said. " 'Cause if it is, I'm gonna come back and kick your lyin' ass all over this place."

"Why'd you try to hide it?" I asked. "Justin Menge ask you to protect it for him?"

"I don't know what you talkin' 'bout. Got nothin' to do with no disc. Like I say, shit look blank to me."

I walked out of the library, now far less crowded than when we came in, Merrill and Daniels following me. We crossed over the asphalt road that led from the front to the center gates, and entered the chapel.

When we were in my office, I inserted the disc and we all sat down to watch it.

Glancing around my office, I realized again how impersonal it was. Unlike every other office I had ever had, this one didn't really feel like mine. The shelves were filled with theology texts—mostly reference books I used when studying. The walls were covered with art, the desk with objects, but none of them revealed much about my personality or tastes. There were no pictures of family or friends—nothing an inmate could use to manipulate or intimidate me—nothing very meaningful with one exception.

On the wall directly across from my desk was a framed color crayon picture of Jesus colored for me by Nicole Caldwell. It was a memorial of sorts to her. She had been murdered in this very office while waiting for her televangelist father to finish his service in the chapel. Perhaps the reason I didn't feel completely comfortable in this office had less to do with how impersonal a prison office had to be than the way in which it was haunted for me.

When the first image came on the screen it was of the cement floor of the PM quad in G-dorm. The lighting was bad, and the shots, jerky and largely out of focus, were worse. In the background, Pitts could be heard outside the back door in the exercise area yelling at Jaqueel Jefferson.

The camera angle was suddenly raised and there was a fast zoom to the shower cell where Justin Menge was cuffed to the door, Billy Joe Potter standing behind him.

"I thought Pitts was the fool caught in this Rodney King shit."

"What he told me."

"Why would Pitts say it's him?"

"Maybe he thought it was. Maybe they both went at him."

At first just the bars were in focus, then the bars softened as the deep distress lines on Justin's contorted face sharpened.

Suddenly, his face was slammed into the cell bars as Potter delivered a powerful blow to his kidneys. He let out a yelp and a string of blood-laced spit splattered on the bars.

I winced.

Several more blows, similar, but more severe, followed.

Rage disfigured Potter's face into something I didn't recognize, more of his humanity leaving each time he committed another act of violence.

I grew nauseated, the donuts and coffee in my stomach

threatening to come up, as I saw some part of myself in Potter's angry face and glazed eyes.

"Goddam," Merrill exclaimed. "It was just a matter of time before he killed Menge. I didn't think Potter had it in him."

"Something Menge said or did or wouldn't do set him off."

I thought about Justin's art, about the sensitive soul inside the body being savagely beaten, and my eyes stung.

What's wrong with us? How can we do such things to each other? How could I have ever done that to another human being?

When the disc was finished, Daniels stood up. "Why would Jefferson tell you he recorded Pitts instead of Potter?"

"Maybe Potter paid him. It's probably not a coincidence that he left for outside court the day after the murder."

"Well, I'm glad I didn't stop the investigation and arrest Hawkins. This fucker just moved to the top of my list."

Merrill and I didn't say anything.

"Am I wrong? Doesn't he move to the top of our list?"

"Beatin' and cuttin' two different things," Merrill said.

"Yeah. Cuttin's easier."

They looked at me. "Whatta you think?" Daniels asked.

"Long list no matter who's at the top."

"You're right. It really could be any of them. They all had a reason to do it."

I nodded. "We've got to figure out which one of them crossed the line between wanting him dead and killing him."

As Daniels and I talked, Merrill seemed distant and preoccupied, and I wondered if he was reliving his time in the dungeon or planning his retaliation.

"Let's go through them again," Daniels said, "starting with the sister."

"She inherited most of what Menge couldn't take with him."

"All of it—as long as Sobel's out of the picture," Daniels added.

"And it just so happens that he's murdered on her first visit in four years, but if it were her, she had to have a partner."

"Before he escaped, I'd've said it was probably Sobel," Daniels said.

"Could still be."

"Him escaping could've been part of the plan all along."

"She drugs him, Sobel kills him, and they both inherit."

"Don't count a nigga out just 'cause his ass didn't make Candid Camera," Merrill said.

"Ike Turner?" I asked.

Merrill smiled.

"Who?" Daniels asked.

"Pitts."

"He expected to be on the disc. He's already told us about all the tune-ups he gives."

"And he don't just hit inmates," Merrill said.

"He came down and walked around to all the cells after the service started when he was supposed to be in the officers' station. We were down there. There was no reason for him to do it."

Daniels nodded. "But what about Martinez or Matos? We can't leave them out."

"Martinez certainly has the motive. If Chris was going to testify."

"He was," Daniels said.

"Matos could've helped Martinez or killed him for his own reasons. Did Chris mention anything about a staff member having an affair with an inmate?"

Daniels shook his head. "Not that I remember, but with all that was going on, I probably wouldn't've given it the proper attention."

I nodded.

"We leaving out anybody?"

"The holy man," Merrill said.

"Father James," I said.

Daniels shook his head and let out a heavy sigh. "You know what this is? This is one of those cases that never gets cleared. The kind that haunts you the rest of your life."

"Can you imagine the reasonable doubt a defense attorney could create with this list of suspects?"

CHAPTER FORTY-FOUR

Late afternoon.

Alone in my office.

Phone.

"I'm sending over the book you asked for," Dr. Diaz said.

Still bothered by several nagging questions about murder and how it was committed, I had asked Dr. Diaz, the prison physician, if I could borrow a book on blood a couple of days ago. He told me he had just what I was looking for at home and he'd bring it in the next day.

"Sorry I'm late getting it to you," he said. "It took me longer than I thought to find it."

While he was talking, an inmate orderly in a white uniform appeared at my door, and I motioned him in. He handed me the book, I nodded my thanks, and he left.

"Let me know if you have any questions after you read it," he was saying.

"I will. Thanks."

The book was oversized and heavy with pages marked by sticky notes and passages highlighted in bright pink and yellow. The margins were filled with notes difficult to decipher. It took a while, but I finally found the section I needed and began to read, imagining Justin's cell floor as I did.

After reading the relevant page several times, I wrote the following on my notepad:

Blood usually clots in about five to fifteen minutes after exiting the body and will initially be dark maroon, gelatin-like, and sticky to the touch. Over a couple of hours it will separate into a dark maroon-blackish clot surrounded by a pale yellow serum. This is due to some contraction of the clotted blood and a "squeezing out" of the serum, which is not involved in the clotting process.

Blood on a floor will usually dry to a crusty brownish state over a few hours to 3 or 4 days, depending upon the actual temperature, humidity level, and the degree of ventilation. Warmer, drier, and breezy conditions will dry it faster. Blood on clothing is likely to dry much faster—the clothing serving as a wick and spreading the blood out over a larger area. This leads to faster drying. If the clothing is placed inside a container or is wadded, it will take much longer to dry than if it is spread out on the floor or draped over a chair or other object. I thought back to the night of the murder, trying to remember the color and consistency of the blood in the cell. I remembered seeing the dark maroon and blackish clot, the yellowish serum surrounding it, but it was still wet and tacky too. Instead of answering my questions, this gave me more. How does the state of the body and the blood confirm or contradict what we know and what does it tell us about who may have done it?

It just didn't add up, but I couldn't quite figure out why.

My phone rang, and I snatched it up, resentful of the interruption, though the truth was I was more frustrated with my inability to make sense of how the crime was committed than anything else.

"Chaplain Jordan," I said, still preoccupied by my thoughts.

"Chaplain, it's Chris," he said. "Chris Sobel."

"Where are you?"

"I'm scared. In real trouble. I wanted you to know I didn't kill Justin. I loved him. I miss him so much."

"Where are you? Let me come get you."

267

"And bring me back there? You want me dead?"

"Who wants to kill you?"

"Whoever killed Justin."

"And who's that?"

"It wasn't me. I swear."

"They found a set of your prints on his door," I said.

"I was in and out of his cell a thousand times."

"That's why the fact that they only found one bothers me so much."

"I didn't kill him."

"Your prints were on his light."

"I swear. I didn't do it."

"Why'd you run away?" I asked.

"I'm scared."

"Yet you went to Justin's memorial service."

"I had to. I love him. He's all I think about. I want whoever killed him found and punished. He was a very special person. Best man I've ever known. You know he was innocent. He could never harm a child. Justin was my soul mate. We were going to build a life together."

His voice broke and he began to cry.

"I'm sorry."

"I still can't believe it."

I was tempted to respect his grief, but I knew I couldn't. Too much was at stake. And at the moment, like nearly every other one during a homicide investigation, being a chaplain had to take a back seat to being an investigator.

"So you and Justin were exclusive?"

"Yeah. Of course."

"He wasn't involved with Officer Pitts or Potter?"

"*What?* No. Who said that?"

"More than one inmate."

"Of course they did, what else they got to do? Pitts used to beat his ass. He never fucked it."

He had talked to me longer than I thought he would already. Any moment he could hang up the phone, and there was nothing I could do about it. So why hold back?

"Why was Mike Hawkins afraid of you?"

"What? You don't think a faggot can be a badass?"

"You know me better than that."

"There's more to me than meets the eye. I have special skill sets. That's all I'll say."

"Do you have a relationship with Ms. Lopez?"

"No. Why?"

"Was she down there the night Justin was killed?"

"Yeah."

"Was she in your cell?"

"At one point, yeah."

"How long?"

"Not very long. I'm not sure exactly."

"Give me an estimate. Was it before Mass?"

"Yeah."

"There's a witness who says she went into your cell and didn't come out before the murder happened."

It was a lie. There was no such witness.

"I've got to go, Chaplain. I just wanted you to know I didn't do it. And I'm sorry I had to run out on you, but please find Justin's killer."

"I will," I said. "Even if it's you."

CHAPTER FORTY-FIVE

I'd driven less than a mile away from the prison when I realized I was being followed. The dark blue LTD had slipped out of the PCI employee parking lot behind me, and with very little traffic on the isolated prison road, had nowhere to hide.

The truth was they didn't mind being spotted. I could tell. Even on an empty road like this, a good tail could take a lot longer to spot.

I'm supposed to know I'm being followed. It's a message.

The dark car had even darker windows—in the front, too, and all I could tell for sure about the men following me was that there were two of them. I suspected it was two federal agents who called themselves Smith and Wesson. I had dealt with them before, but I wasn't sure which federal agency they worked for. This, of course, was how they wanted it.

I continued driving along, obeying the speed limit, keeping an eye out for children, the offspring of my coworkers, who lived in house trailers near the prison, and thinking about how best to handle the situation.

My old S-10 couldn't outrun them, not even when it was new. Weapons weren't allowed on prison property, not even when they were secured safely in a locked vehicle, so I didn't have one—unless you counted the Barry Manilow cassette the previous owner had left in the glove compartment. I found the tape while cleaning it shortly after I bought it. I had left it in there to be ironic, but now it just might come in handy.

Not only were prisons built in rural areas, they were placed in isolated locations. The road I was on wound around for three miles back to the main highway that led into town. On either side of me whispering pines waved in the wind, their green and rust-colored needles falling to the ground like dirty snowflakes.

Occasionally, I passed a trailer or a small house, many of which had school-age children playing in the yard, waiting for working parents to come home again.

After I had passed the residential area, I sped up, and when I reached a large curve in the road I was several car links in front of them.

I quickly turned onto a small two-trail logging road and raced down it.

They drove by, but soon realized what I had done, backed up, and pulled onto the road.

Near the dead end, I pulled off onto an even smaller trail, the bushes and branches scratching the thin layer of paint that was left on my truck.

When they reached the dead end, I backed down onto the logging road again, trapping them. Before they knew what was happening, I was out of my truck, Barry Manilow tape in hand.

I approached the car carefully and tapped on the driver's window with the cassette.

When the dark window came down, and I could see that it was indeed Smith and Wesson, I held out the tape and said, "Don't make me use this."

Smith and Wesson—which they swore were their actual names and that they were paired because of them—had always been vague about what they wanted and secretive about who they really were. I found them cartoonish and difficult to take seriously—so I didn't.

"Huh?" Smith, the short round-faced white man in the driver's seat said.

Wesson, the tall, lean black man in the passenger seat, opened his suit coat, revealing his holstered .45, and said, "Don't make *me* use *this.*"

"That might kill, but this," I shook the cassette, "this provides hours of torture."

"What is it?" Wesson asked. "*You* doing kareoke?"

"Barry Manilow," I said flatly.

Looking at his partner he said, "Do what he says."

"What?" Smith asked in confusion.

"Seriously," he said. "I had a girlfriend use that shit on me one time."

"What happened?"

"Lost my erection."

"Listen to it enough," I said, "and you never get it back."

"We need to talk to you, funny man," Smith said.

"Yeah, I've been wanting to catch up."

They both got out of the car, Wesson walking around to join me and Smith on the driver's side. As if committed to perpetuating stereotypes, they each had on dark suits and dark shades. They were clean shaven and had closely cropped hair.

All around us, in the bright afternoon sun and soft breeze, the woods danced and sang. The trees swayed, their green and orange tops waving to the powder blue sky. The hum of honey bees drifted over from nearby hives while the small birds flitting about whistled and cawed.

"You don't look surprised to see us?"

"If you're here because you lost Sobel, I'm not."

"How'd you know about—"

"Dead federal judge issues an order letting him out for the memorial service of his inmate lover. Had to involve people like you."

"Told you," Wesson said to Smith, then to me, "He doesn't give you enough credit."

Though not exactly a good cop–bad cop routine, Wesson was always far more friendly than his counterpart.

"Which one of you played the part of his brother?" I asked.

"Could hardly be me," Wesson said.

"Why use a dead judge?"

Smith said, "Whatta we look like? The fuckin' information bureau?"

"That was an unfortunate mix-up," Wesson said, then shrugged. "These things happen. We were in a hurry and our guy fucked up. Usually he's real good about signing the names of judges who actually have a pulse."

"Sobel part of a witness protection program?"

Wesson shrugged, but his face seemed to confirm it.

"Why have him in a PM unit in a state prison in the first place?"

"Just recently agreed to testify and enter the program," he said.

"*After* Menge was murdered?"

They paused for a moment, then Wesson nodded.

"It didn't cross your mind he might be the murderer?"

"Got nothing to do with us. We don't work with choir boys. Him being a killer's part of the reason he can help us."

"So you two got him out to testify and put him in the program?"

They nodded.

"Then lost him?"

They nodded again.

"How?"

"It's not important."

"What's he testifying about?"

"Kidnapping, drug trafficking, and homicide," Wesson said.

I wasn't sure I believed their answers, such as they were, but there wasn't much I could do about it, and who knows, maybe a little of it was actually true. Given my vocation I had to allow for the possibility of miracles.

"Involving who?"

"It's not relevant."

"You won't tell me much of anything, but you want me to help you find him?"

"We understand you're friends with his, ah, lover's sister," Smith said. "We figure he'll try and contact her."

"He called me this afternoon," I said.

"What?" Smith said, standing straighter.

"Why?" Wesson asked.

"Don't act surprised," I said. "No way it's a coincidence that shortly after he reaches out, you do, too."

Wesson smiled.

"What'd he say?" Smith asked.

"You don't know?"

"We're not listening in," he said. "Other agents do that. We're what you call field agents. What did he say?"

"He said he wanted me to know he didn't do it, but I think he wanted to know what I knew."

"What'd you tell him?" Smith asked.

"Only what he could decipher from the questions I asked."

"Well, we've got to find him," Wesson said, "so if he contacts you again we'll be listening in. Try to find out where he is, what he's doing, what he wants."

"Could he be our killer?"

"Oh yeah," Wesson said. "He's had a lot of practice at it. You don't get tapped to testify and offered immunity for shit you overhear in Sunday School."

CHAPTER FORTY-SIX

"You let me shoot his ass, we save a lot of time," Merrill said.

"That's true of a lot of situations," I said.

It was Friday night. We were sitting in Merrill's new car—a black BMW with gold trim and rims—in downtown Panama City, parked across the street from a gay bar at the end of Harrison Avenue. Billy Joe Potter had gone in about half an hour ago, and though at least a decade late to even be retro, he was dressed for disco. We were waiting for him to come out. Merrill, still angry from his time in the dungeon, was in an especially mean mood, and I knew any confrontation we would have with Potter would be, among other things, highly entertaining.

"You not gonna let me shoot him, what we gonna do?"

"Watch and await developments."

"You need a brotha with some time on his hands, you gonna take that approach. I've got some white supremacist dungeon masters need loosin' from they motherfuckin' mortal coils."

"You just don't want to be this close to a gay bar," I said.

He smiled, and with much of his swelling down, he looked more like himself again. "Don't you just wanna hit 'em?"

"Who?" I asked. "People like Potter or homosexuals?"

"Gays. I want to shoot people like Potter."

"Absolutely not."

Downtown was dead. Obviously not a nocturnal creature, the revitalized area that had so much life coursing through its arteries during the day was a lifeless shell at night. With no event at the Marina Civic center, only the occasional car passed by on its way to the assisted living towers where an elderly person was returned to their half-life by younger people anxious to get back to their full ones. Beyond the towers, the well-lit marina was mostly motionless, with the exception of the random homeless person, duffle bag draped over a shoulder, or a stray kid on a bicycle, fishing pole resting on his handlebars.

"Don't the thought of it just make you sick?"

I shook my head.

I was familiar with how Merrill felt—witnessed it in the majority of heterosexual males I knew. Good men, who wouldn't ever utter a racist or sexist word, but didn't give a second thought to their homophobia. I was familiar with it, but disappointed by it—especially from Merrill, who as an African-American man in a small Southern town knew all too well the hate and prejudice of ignorance and unfounded fear.

"It used to," he said. "Back in school. Why the change?"

"Wasn't just one thing. Growing up. Gay friends. Working with AIDS patients when I first moved to Atlanta—which was about the same time I stopped taking the bible literally."

"Well, my ass ain't that enlightened yet."

It was obvious he was feeling better and wanted to enjoy himself. I went with it.

"Your ass ain't a lot of things—including bigoted. You're not gonna hit someone for being different from you."

"Unless they ass provoke mine."

"Like locking you in a dungeon. Not for looking on you with desire."

He smiled again. "Hell, I can't be goin' around hittin' *everybody.*"

"True."

We were quiet a moment, then I told him about Sobel's call and what Smith and Wesson said about him.

"Why you think Sobel called?" he asked.

"Find out what I know. No other reason for him to call really. He's free. I think he really wanted me to know he didn't do it."

"So you wouldn't quit looking for who did?"

"And where I wouldn't think badly of him."

He nodded and thought about it for a moment. "If he's not the killer, and if he really did have . . . you know, feelings for Menge, and the feds are right about him, then he probably try to take out whoever *did* kill Menge."

After a while, the door of the bar opened and Potter and a smaller man stumbled out and began walking up Harrison toward McKenzie Park.

"How we gonna handle this?" he asked.

"Civilly."

"I'm nothing if not civil."

We got out quietly and followed them, going behind the bar and entering the park from the opposite side. The park was deserted, its benches and gazebos empty, the sound of its fountains the only noise.

Spotlights on the ground lit the bottoms of enormous oaks, but they were insufficient for the job, giving the trees a foggy look and leaving much of the rest of the park in darkness.

Potter and his companion walked around for a while and then stopped in a particularly dark corner beneath a giant oak tree. In a moment, the little man dropped to his knees in front of Potter and began to unzip his jeans. As he did, Potter glanced around the park. For several moments the little guy did his best with his hand and mouth, but got very little in the way of response from Potter. Eventually, Potter drew back and hit the little guy hard in the face. The little guy fell to the ground and Potter jumped on top of him and began hitting him repeatedly.

We ran up behind them, and with a running uppercut, Merrill knocked Potter off the smaller man and onto the ground a few feet away.

"That's no way to treat a lady," Merrill said.

When Potter sat up, he straightened and dusted off his shirt before anything else, including rubbing his jaw. He was wearing tight black jeans and a pullover black shirt with long sleeves and a zipper down the middle.

"A zipper?" Merrill asked. "What? You ain't had time to do any shopping in the last few decades? When did these last go out of style? Early seventies? This shit ain't dated, it's carbon-dated. I thought you guys were spiffy dressers?"

"Spiffy?" I asked him.

He shrugged. "I ain't all that experienced with civility."

"Actually," I said, "they've come back in since then and gone out *again.*"

Helping the other man to his feet, I said, "You okay?"

He had a red welt on his left cheek and he was crying, but I didn't see any blood. As soon as Potter had jumped him, he had held up his arms in a defensive posture that had blocked most of the blows. Potter wasn't just inept, he was weak—his bulk that of fat, not muscle—and the few punches that actually got through didn't seem to do any real damage.

He nodded. "What's going on?" Turning to Potter, who was still on the ground, "Why did you do that?"

Potter didn't say anything.

"He hates homosexuals," I said.

"Oh, you're one of *those* kind? Just accept who you are and get on with your life."

"Who the fuck do you think—" Potter began, rising to his feet.

Merrill stepped forward and backhanded him back down to the ground.

"I just want you to know, I didn't hit you because you're gay. Now, tell me the truth or I'll turn your ass out and everybody at

PCI will make you their little bitch."

Potter looked down, but didn't say anything.

"Got it?" Merrill asked.

Shoulders shaking, tremors running the length of his body, Potter began to cry.

"Ah, shit, man, don't do that."

I found myself studying Merrill again. I did it often. He was one of the few people on the planet who consistently surprised me. He integrated so many personas, all of which he could slip into with the ease of a veteran actor doing a one-man show.

I started to say something, but froze as Potter reached behind his black zipper shirt and came out with a gun. Getting to his feet, he said, "Now tell me who's the little bitch?"

"Still you," Merrill said.

Stepping toward Merrill and pressing the gun into his forehead, he said, "Say goodnight, bitch."

"Goodnight, bitch," Merrill said, and bitch-slapped Potter so hard his body whipped around with his head.

In the split second I was waiting to see if Potter was going to shoot, I realized he no longer had the gun.

"Gay or not, I just can't let some chubby cheek redneck motherfucker point a gun at me and not bitch-slap his fat ass."

"And him wearing a zipper shirt," I said.

"Now, bitch, tell me why you killed Menge. Was it because he wouldn't go down on you or because he would or because they videoed you working out your sexual frustration on him?"

Potter didn't say anything.

"You don't have to say anything," Merrill said. "We seen the movie you starred in."

Potter's eyes grew wide and he started to say something, but stopped himself.

"May I go now?" the little guy asked me.

"What's your name?" I asked.

"Why?"

"Because I'm tired of thinking of you as Little Guy, and I may need a statement from you."

"For the police? No way. You don't stay in the closet by being in the paper."

I thought about it. There was no way we could make a case without him, but there was also no way I was going to be responsible for outing him.

"You can go. Just be more careful."

"And," Merrill added, "a little more selective about who you blow in an empty park at night."

CHAPTER FORTY-SEVEN

On Saturday, after cramming most of my stuff and a fraction of Susan's into our new home, Merrill, Sharon Hawkins, Susan, and I went to the FSU–North Carolina State football game at Doak Campbell Stadium.

The stadium was packed, the crowd wild, a garnet and gold sea of pure adrenaline-powered energy. Several times throughout the game I got caught up in the moment, in the thrill of the drive, in the suspense of the outcome, and forgot about crime and criminals, murder and death, of blood flowing from mortal wounds.

Though it was an evening game, the sun was still up through the first quarter, and I could see the top of the capitol just above the stadium wall to my right. As the darkness grew and huge moths, like fireflies, began to dart around, the temperature dropped and all I could see of the capitol was the red flashing light on its roof.

At first Sharon didn't seem to know how to act. She sat stiffly and flinched as the fans around her yelled at the players, the refs, the coaches, and each other, but by the middle of the second quarter she was one of the rowdy crowd.

"I've never been to a game before. This is wild. I love it. Thanks for bringing me."

Though her mouth was right at my ear, she had to yell because of the roar of the crowd and the announcer's booming voice, who, though he had the most powerful PA system in the

South, still felt it necessary to shout.

"You're welcome."

"My life's been way too sheltered," she said.

"Think of all the possibilities."

She smiled, but I could tell she wasn't thinking about them. She was still convinced that all this was just a pleasant dream in the middle of a horrible life that resembled a nightmare.

It was an exciting game, though FSU lost by three points. Merrill and Susan didn't talk much and she grew icy toward him when he talked about Anna, which was often. Just hearing her name made her absence from my life all the more obvious, emphasizing how much I missed her.

Near the end of the fourth quarter, Sharon saw one of the Pine County commissioners. Her enjoyment of the game came to an abrupt end, and by the time we reached Wings and Rings she was shaking, her unfocused eyes gazing into the distance.

"They'll come after me," she said. Her words were quiet, but confident, spoken with the certainty of fate.

We were all silent a moment. Susan's eyes were wide, full of fear and understanding.

"One can only hope," Merrill said.

"You're safe," I said.

She gave me her laugh of futility, and I realized it was the first time I had heard it since we left Pine County.

"You are," Merrill said. "This'll be over soon."

All around us, the beer flowed like water from a natural spring and I felt myself wanting to dive in, while buffalo chicken wings and onion rings were downed by Seminole-clad college students who were as uproarious in defeat as in victory. We sat in a booth at the very back, but we still had to yell to hear each other over the music and the crowd.

"Are *you* in danger?" Susan asked me.

Merrill smiled. "His parish full of thugs, rapists, murderers.

He in danger every time he pass through the front gate."

There had always been tension between Susan and Merrill, but lately it had intensified—probably because they were seeing so much more of each other.

Ignoring Merrill, Susan kept her eyes on me, her face taking on the pallor of morning sickness. She started to say something but stopped.

"And I'm only making it worse," Sharon said. "Y'all shouldn't've taken me into your lives. Somebody's gonna get hurt. Maybe killed."

"No *maybe* about it," Merrill said.

I didn't say anything. I knew that the kind of man Merrill was wouldn't let him not respond to what Hawkins had done to him. I also knew he knew how I felt about vengeance and the need for true justice and compassion, and I respected him too much to tell him again.

"You're right. They won't stop until they kill us."

"I kill them first," Merrill said, "they got no choice but to stop." He looked over at me. "When they come after us—which make it self-defense."

"You can't be serious," Susan said to Merrill, then turned to me. "He's not serious, is he? I mean, you're in the business of punishing murderers. You can't just kill someone."

"I'm in the business of keeping inmates captive against their will," he said. "But that's got nothing to do with this."

She looked at me. "You can't just let him kill someone."

"I look like I could stop him?"

"You could try. You could talk to him."

"Merrill knows how I feel, and I understand how he does."

"What about right and wrong? What about the law?"

"Two different things," Merrill said.

Susan studied Merrill for a long moment, then looked back over at me as if I were a stranger.

In the midst of everything, I made a mental note to call my sponsor.

"What would you do if it were you?" she asked me.

"Protect myself and my loved ones as best I could, but it's not me, and it's too easy for people to say what they'd do when they've never been put in a remotely similar situation. I don't think you understand the kind of people we're dealing with—that we deal with every day."

"But you don't have to be like them to deal with them, do you?"

Sharon looked at Susan with surprise. "These guys are *nothing* like Howard and Mike."

She thought about it. "Look at what Dad's doing. He's working hard to keep Martinez in prison, and he's not breaking the law or worse—take it into his own hands—to do it."

A couple of tables away, a heated argument over a decision Bobby Bowden had made in the fourth quarter turned into a shouting match, and a pitcher of beer was turned over, splattering the jeans of those who sat nearby as it hit the floor.

"And what Dad or he would do," Susan said, not even using Merrill's name, "is not what I'd expect from you. I thought you were different."

"He is," Merrill said.

She didn't say anything.

"You know he is. He the reason I'm not over in Pine County right now with a big stick. One thing you can count on, he in something, he's gonna figure out the right way to be in it."

"Like helping his friend," Sharon said. "Protecting me—and *you.*"

"I don't need you two to explain my husband to me."

Sharon said, "If I just take off, who knows, maybe they'll never find me."

"You can go wherever you want to," Merrill said, "soon as

they not a threat to you."

"Well, *I've* got to go," Susan said. "Right now."

She made a move to slide out of the booth. I got up and let her out.

"Later," Merrill said.

"Stay with Merrill," I said to Sharon. "Don't run off. This won't take much longer."

Susan didn't wait on me and when I reached the car, she was already inside.

"Why'd you get so upset?" I asked.

She shook her head.

"Please tell me."

"I don't know . . . I just got so scared. And then I got so angry that he thinks he knows you better than I do."

"I was just trying to be honest with you," I said. "I do believe in compassion, but . . ."

"Are you becoming like the criminals you work with?"

"I'm trying not to, but . . . I don't know. All I can do is try to figure it out as I go along. I don't have a manual. I know there's a time for mercy, there *is,* but there's also a time for justice."

"In this life?"

"Yeah," I said. "Why else would your dad and I do what we do? I still believe one day God will somehow make every crooked place straight, but for now, she's left it up to us. I've always equated justice with fighting for the powerless, the disenfranchised, and though Merrill is anything but weak, there's something about what the Hawkins did to him that reminds me of the white supremacy of the Old South, of lynchings, and the corruptness of absolute power."

She nodded. "I can see why you would see it that way, but you have some blinders on when it comes to Merrill."

I thought about it for a moment. "I'm sure I do."

"Just tell me you're not like him. Tell me you couldn't murder someone. Tell me prison hasn't changed you that much."

"You know what I'm like."

"I *thought* I did."

"You've known me a long time, you think I could commit premeditated murder?"

She shook her head.

Susan's car was cold, the breath coming from her rigid body forming small clouds as she talked.

"But you're just going to let him kill those people—or get killed trying to?"

"I don't *let* Merrill do anything."

"I don't hear you trying to talk him out of it."

She was right. I hadn't been.

"Do you not care if he kills them?"

I thought about it. I wasn't sure I did—at least not in self-defense, but was that really what it was? Was it really all that different? What had happened to me? At one time I had been convinced that I was supposed to extend compassion to everyone regardless of their response. I believed it my duty to minister mercy—whether or not it was received. Now I seemed to be picking and choosing who was worthy. Were power-hungry sociopaths like Hawkins exempt?

"Think about what you preach," she continued. "What you stand for. Your message is one of compassion."

"And justice."

"You can't think if he kills them justice is served. You can't be this big a hypocrite."

I let out a harsh, involuntary laugh. "Don't be so sure."

Chapter Forty-Eight

I met my sponsor at a coffee shop in Panama City the next morning.

His name was Dennis, but everybody called him Den. He was a retired cop from New York with a lot of time in the program and a decade completely clean. He was tough, direct, and always available—though I seldom called him.

"Been so long I heard from you, I figured you for dead."

I loved the way he talked, not only his accent and the speed his words shot out, but his speech patterns. Just hearing his voice made me feel better.

I told him some of what was going on, but more of how I was handling it, the thoughts and feelings I was having, and some of the things I had done.

"You drinking?" he asked.

I shook my head.

He studied me for a long moment.

"Going to meetings?"

"Not regularly."

"You've never gone regularly. You goin' at all?"

"Not lately, no."

He nodded to himself as if I had confirmed his suspicions.

Meetings had never been a big part of my recovery process. I went sporadically at best, but it had never been a big issue between us. As long as I wasn't drinking he was okay with it.

"Self-reliant bastard, aren't you? Works for you, though."

"Some of the time."

"Most of the time. How close you to drinking?"

I shook my head. "Nowhere close."

"Why I don't press the meetings. Still, be better you go."

I nodded.

Our coffee came, and we went through the ritual of preparing and drinking it. As a general rule no one drank more coffee or smoked more cigarettes than recovering alcoholics—yet another way in which I was a misfit.

"So you're not drinking?"

"Acting out in other ways."

"Rage and what not?"

I nodded.

Den was a large man with big fleshy paws and an enormous balding head. As if to make up for the hair missing on the top of his head, he wore the sides and back too long, and I loved that about him.

As usual, he had on a short-sleeved Hawaiian-style shirt unbuttoned and open, a wife beater visible beneath, gray chest hair bursting out of the top of it.

"This is not so much about sobriety as serenity," I said. "I feel so hollow. My thinking's all messed up."

"And your spiritual life's for shit."

"Exactly," I said, and I realized that just talking to him was helping.

"This case won't go on forever."

"There'll always be another, and I wasn't doing so good before it started."

"It possible you expectin' too much from yourself?"

I gave him a wry smile. "That's usually not a problem."

"I know better. You got a lot of shit on you right now and you're still not drinking. Start there. That's no small thing. Second, so what you smack around a rapist? So the fuck what?"

"It's not just that. I'm slipping. I can feel myself sliding back into somewhere I don't want to be."

He nodded. "I understand that, and I realize you got to get your head right. I'm just sayin' lighten up on yourself a little. So you ain't a fuckin' saint, so the fuck what? Who the fuck is? You're a cop."

"I'm a chaplain."

"You're both. So you're actin' more like a cop at the moment. You'll be doin' that other shit again soon enough. I'm not sayin' you aren't fuckin' up. I'm sure you got shit you got to get straight—especially in your head. I'm just tryin' to put all this shit in perspective for you."

I nodded. "You have. Thank you."

"How long it been you taken some time off?" he asked.

"I went to the FSU game this weekend."

"I ain't talkin' 'bout a Saturday. You're supposed to take those off. When's the last vacation you had?"

I shrugged.

"Maybe rage's not the only thing you subbing for booze."

I nodded. He was right. My approach to my work had become compulsive.

"I want you to go on retreat."

"Okay."

"Don't sit there tell me okay, you don't mean it," he said.

I smiled again.

"I set it up, you're goin'."

"As soon as the case is over."

"Don't fuck with me."

"I'm serious."

"I'll set it up. Go ahead and pack a bag now. Soon as you clear the case you're on your way."

CHAPTER FORTY-NINE

DeLisa Lopez was scared.

Her face was pale, her eyes bloodshot, and it was obvious she had not been sleeping or eating. She had not missed work the last few days because she was sick. She wore loose clothes that hung off her and a big, open coat, in which she tried to hide.

When I had stopped by her apartment after work earlier in the afternoon, she cracked the door just as far as the chain would allow and peered out at me warily. After convincing her to let me in and seeing her condition, I talked her into letting me take her to Rudy's for something to eat.

On the drive over, I had confronted her, and she had confessed.

She'd been having an affair with Matos and had been in his cell the night of the murder.

She'd done it before.

Ordinarily, the cell doors in the PM quad remained open, so it wasn't much of a problem for her to sneak in and out, but with a lockdown in place, she had been trapped inside. When Matos left the cell, he disabled the lock, so all she had to do was find a time to sneak out, which she did in the early morning hours when there was only one crime scene tech left in Menge's cell. Prepared to explain her presence if caught by saying she had been called in because the control room sergeant had mistakenly thought she was Menge's psych specialist, she slipped out of the quad, through the center gate, in the back door of the medical building, and into her office where she had spent the night.

Carla, Rudy's teenage daughter, took her order at the booth in the back while I called Susan. Reaching her voicemail, I asked her to meet me at Rudy's or call me as soon as she could.

When Carla came back behind the counter, she said, "She's a mess."

She said it with compassion and without judgment, as if commenting on her clothing, which I knew she'd get to sooner or later.

"And that outfit . . . you get her out of bed?"

I nodded.

"Still trying to save the world?" she asked, her tone more biting than playful, and I knew why.

"Man's gotta have a goal."

"What's the new wife think about these goals of yours? She know that the world you seem to be saving is predominantly female?"

I didn't think that was true, but I said, "Gotta start somewhere."

Prior to patching things up with Susan, I had spent most nights at Rudy's—reading in a booth in the back while Carla, who Rudy required to keep the place open all night, got some sleep. For the past few months I hadn't been around much, and since Susan had moved to Tallahassee it had only gotten worse.

"Sorry I haven't been around as much lately."

Carla shrugged and made an expression that either said it didn't matter or it was to be expected.

Back at the booth, I found DeLisa huddled in the big coat she wore, staring out the window nervously as if expecting someone unpleasant to drive up.

When I sat down, she whipped her head around toward me.

"You okay?"

She shook her head. "No, I'm not."

I nodded, encouraging her to continue.

"I'm scared."

"Of what? Is it related to work? To Menge's death?"

"I can't talk about it," she said, shaking her head.

As usual, Rudy's was cold, the condensation covering the plate-glass windows looking like a frozen sheet of ice beginning to thaw. It was empty, which was also usual. Rudy's was more a lunch place for the workforce of Pottersville than a place you take the family for an evening meal.

"You need to," I said. "With someone. Do you have anybody you can—"

She shook her head.

"Then why not me?"

She shrugged.

"You were close to Justin, weren't you?"

She nodded. "I saw him on a regular basis—not that he needed therapy. He didn't. He just was committed to becoming the best person he could be. He liked counseling."

I nodded.

"I liked him, but I *loved* his art. He was so gifted. I was in awe."

"He really was," I agreed.

"Is this just between us? No matter what I say?"

"Unless you say you killed him."

"I didn't. But I used to break the rules sometimes. Sneak in pens or paints for him. Not often, but—one time all his materials were taken away and he crushed up M&M's and used them for paint. It was amazing. It really was, but he didn't need to waste time on M&M prints when he could be working on a masterpiece."

"I agree."

She started to say something else, but stopped as Carla arrived at our table with coffee, waffles, and bacon.

"Why do you keep it so cold in here?" DeLisa asked.

"Keeps me awake," Carla explained. "And makes me sleep lighter when I do sleep. I'm here alone a lot at night."

I avoided her eyes. What could I say? I started to apologize again, but she walked off before I could. When she was gone, DeLisa took small sips of her coffee with jittery hands, spilling some of it on her saucer as she did.

I waited to see if she was going to pray over our food. When she didn't, I said a quick one to myself without bowing my head or closing my eyes.

"Oh, that's good coffee," she said, then set it down and began to eat like a starving person just pulled off the streets and given her first real meal in weeks.

My waffle was sweet and sprinkled with pecans, the bacon lean and crisp. I saturated both in syrup and ate in a manner not dissimilar to DeLisa's—though I hadn't missed any meals. I lifted my fork to Carla and nodded toward her when she looked over our way.

"Glad you like it."

When I saw that DeLisa was nearly finished, I asked Carla to throw on a little more for us, which she promptly did.

Though Rudy's was a southern fried restaurant, it looked more like an Omelet House or Waffle Shoppe, which it had been at one time. The grill ran along the back wall and was visible over the counter in front of it, and I watched Carla as she worked. Her life was more difficult than any teenager's should be, but you'd never know it to watch her.

"God, I feel so much better just from having eaten," she said.

"You haven't eaten lately?"

"I haven't left the house. Not much of a cook, so I don't keep a lot of food there."

"Who're you so scared of?"

"Chris Sobel," she said.

"Why?"

"Justin had decided *not* to testify against Martinez. He told me the day he was murdered."

I nodded.

"It was all fabricated anyway. Martinez hadn't told him anything. They'd never even spoken. He was doing it to get out early to be with Chris."

"What does that have to do with you being afraid of Chris?"

The small bell above the door jingled and she spun around to see who it was. When she saw that it was a young couple, she turned back toward me. It was Michael and Shebrica Pitts. If DeLisa recognized him, she gave no indication. When Pitts saw me, he grabbed his wife by the arm and ushered her back toward the door.

"I'll be right back."

I jumped up and ran over to them.

"You weren't on the disc," I said. "Potter was."

"You gonna do this here?" he asked.

"Why would you say it was you?"

He didn't say anything.

"Because that fat bastard paid him to," Shebrica said.

"Shut up."

With one hand he pushed the door open. With the other, he grabbed Shebrica's arm again and pulled her out of it.

"I ain't lettin' you go to prison for that cracker," she said to him, then to me, "He didn't beat anybody and he didn't kill anybody. Billy Joe paid him a bunch of money to say he beat that boy."

When she was through the door, the hydraulic hinge pulled it shut. I let them go. I didn't doubt that Potter had paid Pitts to say he was on the disc, but that didn't mean he hadn't administered several tune-ups of his own.

The moment I sat back down at the table, DeLisa began to tell her story.

"Chris Sobel is a very dangerous man. He was in on some drug charge, but he's a killer. He just didn't get caught for it."

"How do you know?"

"Justin told me."

The bell sounded again and an elderly couple entered slowly and ambled down to a booth on the opposite end where Carla had coffee waiting for them by the time they reached it. They both smiled at her adoringly, and the old man patted her hair gently with a shaking, disfigured hand.

"Even if Justin was right about him, how is he a threat to you?"

"Because I know."

As she talked, her eyes searched mine, and I could tell she was looking for acceptance, but expecting judgment.

"What do you know?"

When Carla brought our second round of food, she set it down quickly without speaking and hurried away.

"Justin was going to testify that Juan Martinez had confessed to him that he had killed a man in Pensacola. He knew enough details—including how it was done and where the body was hidden—to convince a jury and put Martinez away for the rest of his life."

Tears formed in her eyes and she stopped talking as her chin began to quiver. She was no longer interested in the food, and neither was I.

"But Juan didn't do it. Chris did. It's how Justin had all the details. They knew how much Inspector Daniels wanted Martinez so they made a deal. Setting up Juan would help Chris *and* Justin. Enable them to be together."

The small bell above the door jingled again, and she jerked her head back to see who it was. It was just the wind. This seemed to disturb her more than if it had been someone, as if she feared an apparition had entered, and when she turned back to face me she looked ghostly herself.

That's it! David and Uriah. Justin was murdered for the same reason Uriah had been—to cover up another crime. It's been there in front of me all the time.

I finally had the one piece of information that put all the others into place, and the picture they formed was shocking and disturbing—and I hoped I was wrong.

"But Justin decided not to testify," I said.

She nodded.

"Do you know why?"

"He just couldn't go through with it. Knew it'd eat away at him. I think he began having second thoughts about Chris, too."

"And when he decided not to testify . . ."

"He was killed. I think Chris did it, and since I know, I think he'll come after me."

CHAPTER FIFTY

"I figured I'd find you here," Pete Fortner said.

He had entered Rudy's a few moments before holding a file folder, and motioned me over to the opposite side of the diner. We were now standing near the last booth, as far away from everyone else in the restaurant as we could get.

"You found me," I said. "Pete Fortner. Ace detective."

He let out an unpleasant sound that could have been a sarcastic laugh.

His bushy mustache needed trimming, the shadow of his beard on his face was dark, and behind his glasses his eyes looked hollow and weary.

"How are you?" he asked.

"I've been better," I said. "How about you?"

"Daniels has completely shut me out of this thing," he said. "Had me running all over the place. Even got me sitting in his chair in Central Office answering the damn telephone while he's over here."

I shook my head. "Sorry."

"How's it going?"

"May finally be getting somewhere."

"You got any idea where he is now?"

"Who?"

"The inspector."

"Home, I guess," I said.

He held up the folder. "This came for him today. Tox report."

297

"May I?" I asked, taking the file without waiting for his response.

He nodded. "I'd rather give it to you than him anyway."

I studied the contents of the folder.

"He was drugged up pretty good, wasn't he?"

I nodded. "He sure was. The killer made it easy on himself. Gave him barbiturates to make him sleepy and easy to control and heparin, which according to this is an anti-coagulant."

"Blood thinner?"

I nodded. "Made him easy to manage and thinned his blood, then put him face down on his cell floor, slit his throat, and just let him bleed out."

Pete shook his head. "Sick son of a bitch."

"Maybe. Definitely smart son of a bitch. He knew just what he was doing."

A few minutes later, while Carla was clearing the dishes from the table and I was trying Susan again, Merrill walked in, Sharon Hawkins following closely behind him. After I left a second message for Susan, I joined them at the table.

Susan should have been here by now—or called. I wasn't worried yet, but I was getting there.

When I returned to the table, Merrill nodded at DeLisa. "Counselor here say she just gave you a clue."

I nodded, then told him about the tox results Pete had dropped off.

"You got it?"

"I think so. Need to talk to Paula Menge to be sure."

"Well, give her a call and let's get this shit over with."

Sitting across from each other, Sharon and DeLisa seemed to be looking into an emotional mirror, each reflecting the other's fear. As I looked at them, realizing that two different men were the cause of their terror, I wondered how many women lived in fear, a heavy sense of dread and detachment distancing them from everything else because of the men they had allowed into their lives.

Merrill reached across the table and handed me his cell before I could ask for it. I punched in Paula's number and waited. As I did, I noticed something taking place between Sharon and DeLisa I didn't quite understand. They seemed to be measuring each other, figuring on whether the other was friend or foe. It would seem there were some instincts not even fear could suspend.

It took Paula several rings to answer the phone, and her voice sounded soft and sleepy.

"I wake you?"

"Chaplain Jordan?"

"Yeah."

"I must've dozed off. Too much wine. I'm glad you called. I could've drowned. I'm in the tub."

"How're you holding up?" I asked.

"Good days and bad," she said, as if she had said it a thousand times.

"If it's okay, I need to ask you one more question."

"Sure. Fire away."

"Are you sure Justin ate during your visit?"

"Positive. Told you. He ate a ton of junk out of those vending machines."

Her words made my heart sink and my temples throb.

"I bet I fed ten dollars into those machines. I think it was because we were so nervous, but we ate and drank a lot—especially Justin. He must've really developed an appetite in there. Before, you couldn't get him to eat, but that night I couldn't get him to stop."

"Thanks."

"Why does it matter?"

"I've got to go right now, but I'll tell you soon. I promise."

Merrill unzipped his black leather jacket and turned the collar down. DeLisa's eyes widened at how big his neck was.

Ending the call with Paula, I punched in Susan's number again and got her voicemail. Without leaving another message, I called her office and found that she had left at the normal time. I then punched in Sarah Daniels's number, worried, but still hopeful.

"Oh, John, thank *God. Where* are you?"

"What's wrong?"

"Get back to the prison right away. Tom called and told me goodbye. He sounded so bad. I think he's being held hostage. He was making an arrest. Please. You've got to help him. Please."

"Tell me exactly what he said."

Susan pulled into Rudy's parking lot, and relief began to join the dread inside me.

"He said he was finally able to get the man who . . . attacked me, but ran into trouble when he went to arrest him. I think somebody had already killed him."

"I'm on my way."

I ended the call as Susan was coming through the door. I looked over at Merrill.

"See if Pete'll keep an eye on them," I said, nodding toward Sharon, DeLisa, and Carla.

He headed toward Pete's table as I went to meet Susan.

"What's wrong?" Susan asked.

"I need to talk to you and I don't have a lot of time."

"Okay."

"Come over here."

I led her over to an empty area in the back.

"What is it?"

"It's gonna be hard to hear. I wish I didn't have to tell you—

wish I had more time, but I want you to know before I do anything."

"God, you sound so ominous."

"You know I love you," I said. "Everything's going to—"

"Quit with all the buildup. Just tell me."

"I just want you to know—"

"I mean it, John, just tell me."

"I love you. I'm here for you. We can get through this together."

"Tell me now or I'm walkin' away."

"I'm pretty sure your dad killed Justin Menge," I said.

CHAPTER FIFTY-ONE

"What?" she asked in shock. "No."

"I'm sorry, but he did. Justin decided not to testify and—"

"He was with *you* when it happened," she said, her voice soft, pained.

"He was with me when we discovered what had happened, not *when* it happened. It had happened a while before that. That's why the changes in the body and the blood never matched the time of death. Of course, the blood thinner your dad gave him kept the blood from clotting all the way so that helped it look like the time of death was more recent than it was, but it was still obvious that something was wrong with it. I kept wondering why he didn't seem concerned about time of death, why it didn't bother him that the body and the blood contradicted what we thought we saw, why he kept saying that *we* established time of death, not the autopsy.

"When I first saw your dad he had already killed Justin—he even let it slip that he had just seen him, but caught himself and said it was Sobel. My guess is the syringes he used to drug him, the shank he used to kill him, and the CO uniform he wore over his clothes to keep the blood off him were in his satchel. He said he left his notebook in PM—that was his excuse to return to the quad with me—but he never got it when we got down there, never mentioned it again."

She shook her head, refusing to hear what I was saying, refusing to allow for even the possibility it could be true.

"I'm sorry," I said, "but it's true. He went into his cell, caught him off guard, overpowered him, filled him with drugs, then laid him on the floor, and slit his throat so that nearly all of the blood drained onto the floor under his body."

"John, I've heard y'all talk about this so much I know exactly what happened. You two were standing there when Menge walked back to his cell. You saw him go in. Dad never left your side. He couldn't've—"

"That wasn't Menge. It was Chris Sobel. He'd gone to meet with Paula so Justin could stay behind and meet with your dad in secrecy. It's why Paula said Justin seemed so different. It wasn't Justin. It was Chris Sobel."

"There's no way. You'll never make me believe it—never."

"I wish I couldn't prove it, but I can."

"How?"

"By Justin's stomach contents," I said, deciding to share with her everything I now knew in hopes of convincing her. "The autopsy shows his stomach was empty. The ME said he hadn't eaten anything since lunch, but the person visiting with Paula ate several items from the vending machine in the visiting park. That was Chris Sobel, not Justin. Justin was already dead by then. It was Chris we saw walk into the quad, not Justin—Pitts even said that's who he buzzed in at first."

She took a step back from me.

Across the diner, Merrill looked to be finishing up with Pete. As Merrill spoke, Pete continued to eat.

"You forget how well I know this case," she said. "Sobel's prints were in Menge's cell. He went to Mass late, didn't have shoes on, *and* he escaped. Why would he escape if he was innocent?"

"I'm so sorry—and I wish I had more time—but I need you to trust me."

"No."

"I'm sorry, but I've got to get to the prison. Either your dad's in trouble or he just killed Juan Martinez."

"And of course you'd rather believe he killed someone than—"

"No. Please. Listen to me."

"Why're you doin' this?" she asked. "If you don't want to be with me just say. Don't—"

"If you want to ride to the prison with us, I can take you through it step by step."

She nodded, Merrill walked up, and without saying anything, the three of us made our way toward my truck.

In the dark parking lot, Susan said, "Start with motive. What possible motive could he have? Why would Dad kill his star witness?"

Merrill's eyes widened, and he looked at me. I nodded, and he shook his head.

"Justin had decided *not* to testify against Martinez and instead *to* testify against your dad."

"So Dad *killed* him? Do you know how many times witnesses have decided not to testify over the years?"

"You're right," I said, trying to make my voice as soothing as possible. "But this is the first one that could hurt him."

"What? How?"

We reached the truck and quickly climbed in.

"This was a crime to cover up another crime," I said, *which is why I kept thinking about what David did to Uriah.* "Menge could testify against your dad for manufacturing evidence and suborning perjury. And I think he was going to. In an attempt to take revenge on Martinez, your dad committed crimes that wouldn't just cost him his job, but his freedom. He was trying to help and protect your mother. He wasn't about to let Justin take him away from her. He did this to cover up his previous crimes."

I pulled out onto the empty, rural highway and began racing

toward the institution.

"He wouldn't do that," she said. "He wouldn't risk prison."

"He was already at risk—exposed because of what he'd done. I think he saw this as his best chance to escape it. He had a good plan, he executed it well, and he'd be the one investigating it. He even asked me to help him—something he had never done before—so he could keep me close, keep an eye on me. The odds were in his favor. He controlled the investigation, kept other agencies out, kept us from getting information from the lab."

"Sobel's the one whose plan's working. He's got you believing he didn't do it and Dad did."

I thought about how strong Susan's denial was. It seemed impenetrable, and I knew it came from years and years of living in a dysfunctional family where everyone pretended everything was okay and denied that Daddy had a drinking problem.

"He *does* look good for it," I said, "because when he came back into the quad pretending to be Menge, he had to go into Menge's cell. He stepped into the dark cell, unable to see because your dad had disabled the light earlier when he had killed Justin. It's why Father McFadden couldn't see inside, said it was darker than the other cells. It's also why Sobel's prints were on the light. He had to hook it back up. And when he did, what he saw made him cry out. That's who we heard. He's a killer, but we're talking about someone he loved. I'm sure he was shocked, but he pulled it together very quickly and knew what he had to do to keep from being implicated right then and there."

Squeezed between Merrill and me in the seat, she looked up at me, tears filling her big brown eyes, and I could tell that what I was saying was beginning to chip away at her defensiveness.

"Chris and Justin had swapped uniforms and IDs. Chris ripped his name label off the shirt Justin was wearing. That's why Chris was missing one. It was also why there was a square patch with very little blood on it on the shirt Justin had on. The blood was on the label. He then moved the body of his lover onto the bed and covered him up—that's how his body was in one place and his blood in another. It actually helped your dad be truer to what the flyer said—except lividity was already set and couldn't change. And since death occurred before we thought it did, the blood was already changing colors, the serum separating by the time we entered the cell. Chris got blood on the uniform he was wearing—Justin's—so he took it off, wadded it up, and left it in the corner. There was blood on his boots, too. He took them off and put them under Justin's bed. He then put on Justin's only remaining clean uniform, ripped the tag off, and swapped IDs with him—which is why Menge's didn't have any blood on it, but I guarantee there are traces of Justin's blood on Sobel's even though he washed it off. For a while he waited, then he called out Menge's cell number and went to Mass. When Potter sent him back to get shoes, he came back to Mass wearing tennis shoes, not boots—and he hadn't been buzzed into his cell because it was already unlocked— rigged so he could slip into it after trading uniforms with Justin when he got back from his visit with Paula."

I paused for a moment from building the case against her dad clue by clue, but she didn't say anything, just looked at me with a mixture of anger and disbelief.

Beside her, Merrill remained silent as well.

"Your dad's also the one who planted the murder weapon in Hawkins's cell. His mistake was doing it *after* Merrill had searched it. We knew it had to be planted, but it couldn't have been done by an inmate. They were locked in another quad by then. All of this fits the evidence. Otherwise, we have a murder being committed in a locked cell in which no one went into or came out of."

She shook her head, tears streaming down her cheeks now. "What are you gonna do?"

She looked so vulnerable, so completely helpless, which, along with the fact that she was pregnant, made her pain all the more unbearable for me, and I wanted to take it away. I wanted to comfort her, but there was nothing I could do.

"I'll give your dad a chance to prove me wrong."

"And if he can't?"

"I'm sure a jury will show compassion because of what happened to your mother."

Merrill nodded, but still didn't say anything.

"So if he can't prove to you he didn't do it, you're gonna turn him in?"

"Susan, he killed an innocent man."

"To protect Mom. Do you have any idea what they've been through? He's all she's got. She needs him."

"He should've just taken the hit for suborning perjury. With Menge's testimony he would've lost his job, but served very little jail time. I'm sure he didn't want what happened to your mom to become public knowledge, and he thought he wouldn't have any problem killing Justin and setting up one of the other PM inmates for it. I think he was trying to leave it as an unsolved—which is why he went to such lengths to make it seem like an impossible crime and not frame any one person— which was brilliant. At one time or another, he said he was convinced that nearly all our suspects had done it—including DeLisa Lopez."

Merrill's phone started ringing.

"Whatever he did," she said, "he did for her. He's all she's got. If she loses him . . ."

"She'll still have us."

"*Us?*" she asked.

"Yes."

"You really think I could be with someone who could do this to us after all we've been through? You think I could just be your wife, have your baby, and pretend you didn't destroy what's left of my mom and dad?"

"What're you saying?"

Before she could answer, Merrill said, "Juan Martinez has been shanked. He's dead."

I nodded.

"They think Hawkins did it."

I shook my head.

"Say he then attacked Daniels."

"Is he okay?" Susan said.

"Hawkins got the worst of it. Your dad's just a little bruised and scratched up."

"We've got to stop him," I said. "He's out of control. He took Martinez out—setting up Hawkins for it."

She shook her head. "Who are you?"

"May wanna turn around," Merrill said, "they on the way to Bay Medical."

I slowed the truck, pulled off the highway, made a U-turn, and sped back in the direction of the hospital.

CHAPTER FIFTY-TWO

Susan sat rigid and speechless between us, the only sounds she made were occasional sniffles.

"How long you think it'll be 'fore Sobel go after him?" Merrill asked.

"He may not have known before, but I can't imagine he hasn't figured it out by now. Probably just be waiting for the right opportunity."

"Like when Daniels is alone and vulnerable," Merrill said, "laid up in the hospital?"

We rode along in silence for a few moments, until Susan finally turned to me.

"Please, John. He was doing it for Mom. Please think about what she's been through—what *he's* been through, what this has done to him. Wouldn't you do the same for me?"

Martinez's bloody smile flashed in my mind.

"I'm not exactly sure what all I'd do to a man who did to you what Martinez did to your mom, but your dad didn't do it to Martinez."

"He made a mistake. He did a terrible thing, but don't destroy his life over it. Where's your compassion? Is it just for inmates?"

I should have known this would be her reaction. As the child of an alcoholic with years of a sick sense of loyalty, a total commitment to the family myth, she would be unable to do anything that felt like betrayal. In a dysfunctional family, the family itself is everything—guarding its secrets, maintaining its facades are all that matters.

During our reconciliation it seemed as if she had broken out, removed herself far enough from the family to be free of its powerful undertow, but had I been paying attention lately, I would have seen that was not the case. She had become aware, but awareness and action are two different things. She'd been on her way to working through it, but something happened to prevent her parole from parental purgatory. It had to be what happened to her mom. What Susan was experiencing now, had been experiencing the past several months, was one of the many effects of the crimes committed not only by Juan Martinez, but by her dad too.

"I can't just ignore what he's done—for his sake as much as anyone's. I want to help him. If he had killed Martinez . . . and I think he probably has now . . . but we're talking about Justin. I can't just pretend it didn't happen."

"Not even for me?"

"I'm sorry. Don't you see it's for his own good?"

The empty road was flat and straight, stretching out for as far as I could see, and I was grateful for what I usually found boring since I felt numb, unable to concentrate on driving.

"Not for our child?" Susan asked.

Merrill looked over at me but didn't say anything.

"For our family?" she continued. "Because I can't be with you if you do this. I can't be your wife or have your child if you could do what you're about to do to *my* family—to *me*."

When my parents divorced, I swore I would never do the same thing to my kids. Never. No matter what. It was one of the reasons why Susan's news that she was pregnant hit me so hard. From the moment I heard it I knew I was out of options.

"Don't say that," I said. "Try to understand what I have to do. We've worked too hard, come too far. And we've always wanted a child of our own."

"I just can't. I'm sorry. I know myself. There's no way."

"Maybe in time?"

"No," she said, shaking her head, "if you do this, I won't get over it. Not now. Not ever. I can't. I couldn't. Please, for me, for the sake of *our* family, don't do this."

I had seen Susan like this before. Once she truly made up her mind, she would never relent. She didn't get like this often, but when she did, I always knew she was not making vain threats.

"You're asking him to do something he can't," Merrill said.

"There's a world of difference between self-defense—even retaliation—and murdering an innocent man just to cover up a crime," I said. "You've got to see that."

"Can't you understand the way our family—*your* family has been violated? Can't you understand the desire for revenge?"

"Of course. He shouldn't've killed Martinez, but I understand. And if that's all he'd done—"

"You don't know he killed—"

"I'm pretty sure."

I looked over at Susan again, searching her face for any sign of love, any sign of understanding. There was none. She regarded me with the contempt reserved for the worst of all crimes—betrayal. And I was guilty. What could I say to her, how could I explain?

"I'm sorry," I said.

"John, if you turn him in, I'll leave you. I'll have to—and I won't have your baby either. I can't. I just . . . won't be able to. I mean it. If you could do this to him—to them, to *me*, then I'll . . ."

Tears stung my tired eyes, and my head began to throb. The full weight of what I was doing, of what I still had to do resting heavily on me.

I couldn't move. Couldn't breathe. Just kept driving.

I figured she'd be hurt, even angry, but not at me. I never dreamed she'd act like this.

"You sure about this?" Merrill asked Susan. "He's got to do this. You know you forcin' him in a corner he can't get out of."

She considered Merrill for a long moment but didn't say anything to him.

"He's given up so much for you, for your marriage."

I thought of how I had hurt Anna, how sad she looked the last time I saw her, how she was no longer part of my life.

She dropped her head and began to cry.

"Please don't do this. I love you. We can have a good life. We can get through this."

"What if *I* turn him in?" Merrill asked.

She shook her head. She was resolute. Her decision was final. I would always be guilty of betrayal.

We fell silent a moment. Eventually, my phone rang.

I didn't feel like answering it, didn't want to talk to anyone, but I knew I had to.

"This bastard's dead unless you can convince me he didn't do it."

It was Chris Sobel.

"What?" I asked, stalling. "Who? Who is this?"

"You know who. And you know who this is. Convince me he didn't do it, that he didn't murder Justin just to save his own ass, or your wife will be down to one parent."

"Chris, listen to me . . ."

Merrill and Susan turned toward me. They knew what it meant.

"He's not going to get away with it. We're on our way to get him right now."

"Then you'll see him die."

"Don't do it. Don't let him—"

The connection was broken. Chris was gone. Daniels was a dead man.

No one said anything, and we rode the rest of the way in silence.

As we pulled up to the entrance of Bay Medical Center, Merrill and I looked for Sobel, but didn't see him.

"In or out?" Merrill asked.

"Out. Find Daniels, make sure he's safe and stay with him. I'll meet you inside."

When we pulled up to the front door, Merrill jumped out and ran toward the main entrance.

"Stay down," I said to Susan.

"I want to be with him," she said, sounding like a little girl fearful for her daddy.

As she started to get out, I grabbed her, desperate to protect her, to make one last attempt.

"The fact that he sent the flyer to me and how well it was planned let's you know it was premeditated—a cold-blooded act of murder. We've got to turn him in—for his sake."

Before Merrill could get inside, Daniels walked out. I could tell by the way he greeted Merrill and waved to us, he had no idea we knew.

Susan jerked her arm out of my hand, jumped out of the truck, and ran toward him.

As Merrill tried to usher them toward my truck, I looked around for any sign of Sobel.

When they neared the truck, Susan grabbed her dad by the arm and pulled him away from Merrill. As Merrill tried to grab her, she snatched her arm away and swung at him. As she did, his chest exploded and he collapsed onto the asphalt.

A split second later I heard the distant clap of Sobel's rifle.

CHAPTER FIFTY-THREE

I dove on top of Merrill.

Susan screamed. Daniels grabbed her wrist and pulled her back into the hospital.

Beneath me, Merrill moaned. Blood was everywhere, on his clothes, on the blacktop, still pouring from his chest, and now all over me.

I waited, but there were no other shots.

With all the strength I could gather, I hoisted Merrill into the truck, slammed the door behind him, and ran around to the other side, crouching as if that could keep me safe from a bullet.

Back in the driver's seat, I popped the emergency brake and punched the gas pedal, my back tires screeching as we sped away.

Rounding the corner of the building, bouncing over sidewalks and cement parking lot curbs, I raced to the emergency room entrance.

Horn honking, we slid to a stop. I jumped out, ran around the truck, and opened the passenger door.

By the time I had Merrill out of the truck, two nurses and a young guy in pale green surgical scrubs were there with a gurney.

"Gunshot wound," I shouted. "Just happened."

After I helped get Merrill onboard, they quickly pushed him in, yelling various orders to the others waiting inside, one of them remembering to tell me I'd have to hang around because the police would want to talk to me.

I spun around, searching the parking lot for Sobel. I didn't see anything, but had to stop looking in order to move my truck for an incoming ambulance.

I parked illegally next to the curb further down and ran back through the emergency room and around to the lobby to look for Susan and Daniels. There was every chance Sobel would try again once he realized he'd shot the wrong man. As I ran through the halls, everyone I passed stopped and stared in shock at the blood on my clothes.

I found Susan in the lobby alone. She was crying as she strained to see through the plate-glass window. She startled as she heard me running toward her and spun around in a defensive posture. When she saw the blood on my shirt, her eyes grew wide and she ran over to me.

"Are you—what happened?"

"It's Merrill's. Where's your dad?"

"Out there," she said, jerking her head toward the door. "He went after him. Please go help him, John. Don't let him get killed. Please. Don't let anything happen to him."

"Call Dad and tell him what's happened. Find a security guard and stay with him."

I then stepped on the mat that opened the automatic doors and ran through them.

CHAPTER FIFTY-FOUR

Attempting to keep my gaze wide and unfocused, I scanned the area slowly looking for movement. Things were far more still and quiet than I had expected. There were no police or hospital personnel where Merrill had been shot, and only now could the sound of sirens be heard in the distance. The rifle had not been loud. Perhaps most people who heard it didn't know what they were hearing. It probably wasn't until Merrill reached the emergency room that anyone called the police.

As I searched for any sign of Sobel or Daniels, I began with the staff parking lot to my left, panning slowly to the visitors' lot directly in front of me, and finally toward the emergency room and doctors' parking to my right. It was then that I saw him.

Limping along, gun drawn, Tom Daniels moved down Bonita Avenue toward 98 in the direction of GlenCove Nursing Pavilion and the First Methodist Church in pursuit of someone I couldn't see.

I took off after him, noticing for the first time I wasn't armed.

Running across grass, jumping over hedges, and winding through parked cars, I reached the spot where I had seen Daniels just moments before. He was gone.

I scanned the area again.

Nothing.

Continuing in the direction he had been headed when I saw him, I ran toward the quiet, mostly empty 98.

I didn't get very far.

I actually ran past them, realized what I had seen, and had to come back.

Down a slope in an overgrown vacant lot near a drainage ditch, Tom Daniels was on the ground, Chris Sobel standing over him holding a gun to his head.

I walked slowly toward them, the tall weeds depositing small seeds and moisture onto my pants as I did.

Daniels was seated on the ground, leaning against the base of a small oak tree, a welt on his left cheek, blood trickling from his right nostril, his right eye swollen nearly shut.

As I neared them, I tripped over an empty beer bottle in a paper bag half hidden in the tall grass, accidentally kicking it forward. It almost cost Daniels his life.

Without taking his eyes off Daniels, Chris said, "Don't come any closer, Chaplain."

He seemed calm and in control. I wondered if he felt as though he had nothing left to lose and killing Daniels the only thing left to gain. If so, he was even more dangerous than usual.

"Okay," I said, and continued slowly easing toward them.

"I didn't mean to shoot Monroe. I actually liked him. It was this murdering motherfucker I was trying to hit."

Murder leads to murder, violence to more violence, a downward spiral, a widening gyre.

"I know," I said.

"You know what he did?"

"You visit Paula in Justin's place?"

He nodded. "Not so this piece of shit could kill him."

His shaved head gleamed in the faint light of a street lamp, its stubble looking like the five o'clock shadow on a weary man's face. It was amazing how different it made him look. No wonder Paula didn't realize he was the man she had thought was her brother the night of the murder.

"I came back to the quad, went into his cell to exchange

uniforms and IDs with him, and . . . I got his blood on the uniform I was wearing—*his* uniform—there was so much blood. I loved him so much and he was—and there was all that blood. I couldn't just leave him like that. I put him on the bed and covered him up."

He jammed the barrel of the small .38 harder into Daniels's head and pulled back the hammer.

He closed his eyes, squeezing them hard against the horror, tears streaming out as he did. On 98, the occasional traffic produced an intermittent breezy noise that sounded like shifting wind in an open field. The sirens in the distance drew closer.

I nodded toward Daniels. "He was having Justin accuse Martinez of one of your crimes?" I asked.

On the ground, Daniels was motionless. He didn't shake his head or give protest to anything we were saying, just sat there staring into the distance.

"We had a deal. . . . He was gonna get out when I did. We were going to leave everything behind and be happy. He would paint. I would take care of him."

"But Justin decided not to testify against Martinez."

"He just couldn't do it. He was too honest, too good, too pure to lie—even against a fuckin' rapist like Juan. He tells this piece of shit he's not going to do it. This bastard tells him he understands. Just meet with him secretly one more time to give him a chance to convince him. If he's still not comfortable, he won't bother him again. All the while he's planning to murder him. And I helped him by meeting with Justin's sister, but I had no idea."

"I know."

"He wanted to see his sister so badly, but I told him, if we're careful and we pull this off, he'll be able to see her all the time."

I nodded.

For a moment, no one said anything, and I could see that

Chris was reliving something in his mind. He still held the gun on Daniels, hadn't even shifted his weight, but his distant stare and faraway expression let me know he was somewhere else— probably with Justin.

"Justin had changed his mind about me, too, though. Hearing the details of what I'd done to that dealer in Pensacola was just too much for him. We weren't going to be together, but he was going to wait until I got out to turn this cocksucker in. He knew it would probably come out that I had been the one who had committed the crime, not Juan. But he'd have to do it soon, because once I was out, he'd be much more vulnerable."

We were all silent a moment, and things seemed to slow down, as if the world around us was creeping by at quarter speed.

"How could you do it?" Chris asked. His tears were dripping down on Daniels. "To Justin? Sweet, innocent Justin."

"He was going to take me away from my family," Daniels said. He was answering Chris's questions, but he was looking at me. "Take me away from Sarah when she needed me most. Sweet, innocent Justin my ass. All he was doing was looking out for himself. He didn't care what Martinez had done, that he would get out and do it again. He didn't care about my wife or what I was trying to do to save her. All he cared about was Justin. Didn't even care about you, did he?"

I eased toward them some more.

"Chaplain, I asked you not to come any closer. I'm gonna kill him for what he did. I don't want to kill you, but I will if I have to. This'll all be over in a minute. Please, just back away."

I thought about how easy it would be to just back away and allow him to avenge the death of his lover. I thought about how much Daniels deserved it, how easy it would be to pick up Sobel later, how less complicated and costly it would be for me, how easier my future would be if I'd just let it play out.

319

"I can't."

"But he deserves it."

"I know."

"Don't really see any way you can stop me."

In my most reasonable, reassuring voice, I said, "Can't we just talk about—"

Judging I was close enough, I dove for him, tackling him to the ground. As I hit him, his gun went off, putting a round into Daniels's right arm. As we hit the ground, my head struck something hard—a root or a rock or an anvil—and I felt dazed.

With just a fraction of my faculties, I began to wrestle Chris for his gun. We both had a hand on it, but neither could get it away from the other—until he grabbed a handful of my hair, picked up my head, and slammed it down on whatever it had hit before.

I could feel the world start to fade, blackness closing in on me quickly like an aperture, and I made one last effort to get the gun away from him. Instead of trying to get the gun, I merely tried to make him lose it—and it worked. I slammed his gun hand down on the ground as hard as I could, punching him in the stomach as I did, and he let go of the gun.

Just as he did, Tom Daniels stepped into view and shot him, a single small caliber round in the back of the head. He was dead instantly, and, as I lost consciousness, I figured I was about to be too.

CHAPTER FIFTY-FIVE

I spent a lot of time over the next week wondering what I could have done differently, how I could have solved the case sooner and prevented more bloodshed.

At nearly every turn in this case I had gone for justice instead of mercy. I had achieved neither.

On Halloween, just a week after we had moved back in together, I received divorce papers from Susan—signed this time in bright red ink. It looked like blood from the wounds of our relationship—fatal wounds this time.

I had called her several times. She had not returned any of my messages, and the one time she actually answered the phone, she hung up on me. I had moved my stuff out of her house when she wasn't home, so I hadn't seen her since the morning her dad had killed Chris Sobel.

I'd picked up the divorce papers when I checked the mail during my lunch break, and when I returned to the prison that afternoon, I went down to Anna's office to show them to her. We hadn't spoken in a while, and I hoped divorce papers from Susan would provide the excuse I'd been looking for.

I tapped on the door and walked in as I normally did.

The only thing in the office was the state-issued furniture—a desk, matching bookcase, and three chairs.

Gone were the angels.

Gone was the angel.

The only thing of Anna that lingered was the faint hint of her perfume, which in time would fade and be gone, too.

I sat down at her desk and spread the divorce papers out in front of me and began to think about all that might have been.

I breathed deeply through my nose, trying to take in as much of her as I could, running my hands along the desktop where hers had rested so often. I sank back into the chair where she had sat day after day of our incarceration together. And I knew doin' time would never be the same again.

I don't know how long I had been there when DeLisa Lopez came in and sat down across from me.

"Not the same around here without her, is it?" she said.

"No, it isn't."

"I was looking forward to getting to know her."

I nodded.

We sat in silence for a moment as time crawled past like prison time always does. Prison time is the slowest time there is, but when Anna was here it had always gone far too fast to suit me. Now I would be doin' time like everyone else.

"How are you?" she asked.

"Been better."

"Anything I can do?"

I shook my head.

Our voices seemed small and lost in the empty office, their sound bouncing off the bare walls and tile floor with nothing to absorb them. Nothing warm, nothing personal. Now there were only cold, hard surfaces.

"Carlos has been transferred to another institution," she said, "and no one has come to reprimand me, to fire me."

"And they won't."

"You had him moved rather than report me?"

I nodded.

"Thank you."

"I know how easily people in helping professions can cross

the line. Usually a result of compassion or neediness."

"Or a combination of the two."

"If it happens again, I'll have to report you."

"It won't," she said. "You won't have to."

"You're a bright, beautiful woman, and there are a lot of free guys out there to choose from."

She glanced down at the papers on the desk in front of me. "You one of them?"

I shook my head. "Haven't been for a very long time. Probably won't ever be."

"Shame," she said, stood up, and walked out of the room.

Chapter Fifty-Six

As usual, when I stopped by Merrill's hospital room I found Sharon Hawkins beside his bed. As far as I knew, she hadn't left him much since he came out of surgery.

He was sleeping. She was flipping through the pages of a magazine. She turned the pages quickly and forcefully, scanning up and down, but not reading—the same thing over and over again: flip, scan, repeat. She seemed bored and restless.

"I'll be here for a while if you want to get out," I said.

"You won't leave until I get back?"

"I won't."

She stood, stretched, and grabbed her purse. "I'm not with him because I'm rebelling against what I came from or he makes me feel secure or I don't have anywhere else to go or anyone else to be with."

"I think far more of you both to think that."

She smiled. "Of course you get it. You know how amazing he is."

When she left, my mind went back to the same dark place it always did.

A few minutes later, Merrill opened his eyes, looked at me, shook his head slightly, and said, "It's the gay divorcée."

"I came hoping to meet a nurse."

"Think most of them the other kind of gay."

I nodded and we fell silent for a while.

When serious or reflective, Merrill was a man of few words.

Often when we were alone, few words passed between us. We had been friends so long, so much went without saying, that just to be together did more for me than being with any other person in the world—with one exception. In fact, as I thought about it, Merrill and I shared something that words were inadequate to describe, and talking about it lessened it somehow.

"Daniels been indicted yet?"

I shook my head. "Doesn't look like he's going to be. He set up Sobel pretty good. Escaping, shooting you and Daniels makes him look even more guilty. It looks as if Daniels shot him in self-defense. The DA doesn't think he can make a case. So, 'while Tom Daniels remains under a cloud of suspicion he is not being charged with any crimes at this time.' They suspect Sobel every bit as much or more than Daniels."

Merrill nodded. "He was right about the case. Crime's too complicated for most juries."

I nodded.

"Too many other criminals around to create reasonable doubt."

"He's no longer with the department. Resigned, citing his wife's health problems."

"You gonna do anything about it?"

"Did all I could."

"Well, his ass didn't get away with it. Karma a bitch."

I shrugged.

"You tell the sister?"

I nodded.

"Think she might do anything?"

I shook my head.

"Susan still hangin' up on you?"

I shook my head.

Creases formed on his forehead as his eyebrows shot up.

"I've stopped calling."

He smiled, and we fell silent again.

In a little while, he said, "What about the baby?"

"Talked to an attorney. Said no court had ever ruled in favor of a man trying to prevent a woman from aborting his child."

"Always a first time. Set a precedent and shit."

I smiled.

We both fell silent again.

"How are you feeling?" I asked.

"Not," he said, and held up the little button that controlled his pain meds.

"I haven't heard Sharon's little futile laugh lately."

"I'm good for her."

"And vice versa?" I asked.

He nodded and smiled.

"You talk to Anna lately?"

I shook my head.

"I have."

I raised my eyebrows, trying not to beg him for information.

"She loves her new job."

I nodded, trying, but unable to catch my breath.

"Better hours, no commute, no criminals, big ass paycheck."

"She deserves it. I'm happy for her."

"You look it. Got that hit-in-the-gut happy look."

"It's genuine."

"It's the best career move she could've made. Plus, she'll be able to finish her degree sooner."

I nodded.

"Which is why everybody scratchin' they heads over her puttin' in for a transfer back to PCI."

He laughed as my face lit up.

"It's illogical, but most babes' motives got more to do with they hearts than they heads."

"Thank God for that," I said, and tried to stop grinning. "Thank you, God, for that."

ABOUT THE AUTHOR

Michael Lister, a novelist, essayist, and playwright, is the author of the acclaimed "Blood" series featuring prison chaplain John Jordan (*Power in the Blood, Blood of the Lamb, Flesh and Blood, The Body and the Blood, Blood Sacrifice, Blood Money,* and *Rivers to Blood*), and a second series featuring 1940s Panama City PI Jimmy "Soldier" Riley (*The Big Goodbye*). He is also the author of two stand-alone novels, *Double Exposure,* a literary thriller set in the north Florida river swamps of the Apalachicola River Basin, and *Thunder Beach,* a mystery/thriller set during the annual biker rally on Panama City Beach. His website is www.MichaelLister.com.